SELECTED STORIES

SELECTED
STORIES

Anton Chekhov

WORDSWORTH CLASSICS

This edition published 1996 by
Wordsworth Editions Limited
Cumberland House, Crib Street
Ware, Hertfordshire SG12 9ET

ISBN 1 85326 288 9

Typeset by Antony Gray
Printed and bound in Great Britain by
Mackays of Chatham plc, Chatham, Kent

INTRODUCTION

As a medical student in Moscow in the 1880s, the young Anton Chekhov began writing humorous short stories for magazines. These were immediately popular and by 1888 he had already been recognised in Russia as an eminent young writer, his stories appearing regularly in the leading literary journals of St Petersburg and Moscow. His influence on European literature has been immense. In England almost all his works began to appear in translation from as early as 1903. Writers such as Shaw, Virginia Woolf, H. E. Bates, Elizabeth Bowen, Somerset Maugham and, particularly, Katherine Mansfield, who was possibly the greatest exponent of his method, have all expressed their admiration of his supreme artistry.

Chekhov's originality lies in his unique combination of tragedy, comedy and pathos, and above all in his peculiar technique which relies on the sensitivity and intelligence of his readers. Chekhov's stories, like his plays, are essentially concerned with the incommunicable, and have been criticised by the uninitiated for their lack of action. Chekhov presented people as he saw them, often engaged in seemingly irrelevant or trivial incidents that are actually laden with underlying implications. The requirements of the magazine market had taught him to be succinct, and he never says more than is necessary, supplying only the most scant outlines. The structure of Chekhov's stories has been compared to that of lace, whose beauty depends as much on what is left out as on what is put in. His method demands that the reader fills in details for himself. The climax or major events are often untold, happening in the reader's imagination, with the effect that Chekhov's characters continue to exist beyond the confines of the story.

This selection of his tales, published originally in England in 1918 as *Stories of Russian Life*, contains some of Chekhov's earliest published works. 'Death of an Official' and 'Lean and Fat' were both written in 1883, and though essentially comic pieces recounted with cool detachment, they both, particularly 'Death of an Official', expose defects of the pre-Revolutionary regime in Russia which encouraged the most obsequious servility and consequent absence of self-respect with its hierarchical systems. Typically, Chekhov expresses no moral judgement himself, leaving this to his readers.

Stories such as 'Children' and 'Little Jack' illustrate Chekhov's extraordinary ability to inhabit his characters, and to move smoothly from the consciousness of one to another. He will adopt the rhythms and vocabulary of a particular character's speech in his narrative so that it becomes difficult to distinguish an authorial voice, and to detect where Chekhov's sympathies lie. In 'The Malefactor', and indeed many other stories, Chekhov shows an issue from two entirely different perspectives, using a gentle irony which is comic and yet sheds serious doubt on the validity of an absolute established morality. 'The Head Gardener's Tale' also questions conventional systems of justice, and seems in its concern with 'the beneficent influence of faith in mankind' to reflect the author's own attitude.

Compassion pervades these tales which repeatedly illuminate unfulfilled lives. 'Dreams', 'The Trousseau' and 'Not Wanted' reveal the sad disparity between men's grand dreams and the mean reality of existence. Chekhov makes no apology for humanity, treating his characters without sentimentality and equally without cynicism or condemnation. His view is fundamentally tragic, for he is well aware of the intolerable forces we all confront, yet his delight in farcical situations and in the incongruities of human behaviour tempers this. Chekhov's charity and warm humour seem to be all-embracing, and even his most unlikely heroes are treated with melancholy tenderness.

Chekhov's influence cannot be overestimated. His power to evoke atmosphere, seen in the story 'Master Night', is masterly. With his singular gift for distillation, he created a new art-form out of the very brief sketch, though 'In the Ravine' and other longer stories of this collection show that he is no less capable when writing at greater length. The self-effacing charm of Chekhov's personality is reflected in his simple, clear style which has ensured the enduring popularity of these tales where the most ordinary individuals become figures of universal relevance. Chekhov is truly the grand-master of the short story.

Born in 1860 in the small town of Taganrog on the Sea of Azov, Anton Pavlovich Chekhov was the son of a grocer whose own father had been a serf. When Chekhov was sixteen, his father, who was heavily in debt, took the rest

CONTENTS

of the family to Moscow, leaving him behind to finish his schooling. Chekhov obtained a scholarship to study medicine at the University of Moscow, and began to write stories, articles and anecdotes for comic journals to help support the family. His literary reputation grew slowly, and by the time he qualified as a doctor in 1884, his work was appearing regularly in the leading literary journals of St Petersburg and Moscow. In 1886 his first book, *Motley Stories*, was published, and he met the newspaper owner Alexei Suvorin, who invited him to contribute to the magazine *New Time*. Another collection of tales, *In the Twilight*, won him the Pushkin Prize in 1888. That same year he published the long story, *The Steppe*, to much acclaim, and his first play, *Ivanov*. During the next decade Chekhov maintained his prolific production of short stories, but the first staging of his celebrated play *The Seagull* at the State Theatre of St Petersburg in 1896 was a disastrous flop due to the director's failure to understand Chekhov's intentions. Chekhov was dogged by ill-health and in 1898 he was forced to move to Yalta, where he wrote his great plays, *Uncle Vanya* (1900), *The Three Sisters* (1901) and *The Cherry Orchard* (1904). In 1898 *The Seagull* had been successfully revived by the Moscow Art Theatre and subsequent productions of Chekhov's later plays established that theatre's reputation. In 1901 Chekhov married the Art Theatre actress, Olga Knipper. He died of tuberculosis in July 1904, just six months after the premiere of *The Cherry Orchard*, which had opened on his forty-fourth birthday. He is considered one of the greatest and most influential figures of Russian literature and drama.

FURTHER READING

H. E. Bates, *The Modern Short Story*, 1941

J. Middleton Murry, *Aspects of Literature*

Harvey Pitcher (trans.) in collaboration with James Forsyth,
Chuckle with Chekhov: A Selection of Comic Stories, 1975

Avrahm Yarmolinsky (ed.) with an introduction by the editor,
The Portable Chekhov, New York 1947

Marian Fell (trans.), *Russian Silhouettes: More stories of Russian Life*,
London 1915

Overseasoned

ON ARRIVING at Deadville Station, Gleb Smirnoff, the surveyor, found that the farm to which his business called him still lay some thirty or forty miles farther on. If the driver should be sober and the horses could stand up, the distance would be less than thirty miles; with a fuddled driver and old skates for horses, it might amount to fifty.

'Will you tell me, please, where I can get some post-horses?' asked the surveyor of the station-master.

'What? Post-horses? You won't find even a stray dog within a hundred miles of here, let alone post-horses! Where do you want to go?'

'To Devkino, General Hohotoff's farm.'

'Well,' yawned the station-master, 'go round behind the station; there are some peasants there that sometimes take passengers.'

The surveyor sighed and betook himself wearily to the back of the station. There, after a long search and much disputing and agitating, he at last secured a huge, lusty peasant, surly, pock-marked, wearing a ragged coat of grey cloth and straw shoes.

'What a devil of a wagon you have!' grumbled the surveyor, climbing in. 'I can't tell which is the front and which is the back.'

'Can't you? The horse's tail is in front and where your honour sits is the back.'

The pony was young but gaunt, with sprawling legs and ragged ears. When the driver stood up and beat it with his rope whip, it only shook its head; when he rated it soundly and beat it a second time the wagon groaned and shuddered as if in a fever; at the third stroke the wagon rocked, and at the fourth, moved slowly away.

'Will it be like this all the way?' asked the surveyor, violently shaken and wondering at the ability of Russian drivers for combining the gentle crawl of a tortoise with the most soul-racking bumping.

'We'll get there,' the driver soothed him. 'The little mare is young and spry. Only let her once get started and there is no stopping her. Get up, you devil!'

They left the station at dusk. To the right stretched a cold, dark plain so boundless and vast that if you crossed it no doubt you would come to the Other End of Nowhere. The cold autumn sunset burnt out slowly where the edge of it melted into the sky. To the left, in the fading light, some little mounds rose up that might have been either trees or last year's haystacks. The surveyor could not see what lay ahead, for here the whole landscape was blotted out by the broad, clumsy back of the driver. The air was still, but frosty and cold.

'What desolation!' thought the surveyor, trying to cover his ears with his coat collar; 'not a hut nor a house! If we were beset and robbed here not a soul would know it, not if we were to fire cannons. And that driver isn't trustworthy. What a devil of a back he has! It is as much as a man's life is worth even to touch a child of nature like that with his forefinger! He has an ill-looking snout, like a wild animal. Look here, friend,' asked the surveyor, 'what's your name?'

'My name? Klim.'

'Well, Klim, how is it about here? Not dangerous? No one plays any pranks, do they?'

'Oh, Lord preserve us, no! Who would there be to play pranks?'

'That's right. But, in any case, I have three revolvers here' – the surveyor lied – 'and, you know, it's a bad plan to joke with a revolver. One revolver is a match for ten robbers.'

Night fell. Suddenly the wagon creaked, groaned, trembled, and turned to the left, as if against its will.

'Where is he taking me now?' thought the surveyor. 'He was going straight ahead, and now he has suddenly turned to the left. I am afraid the scoundrel is carrying me off to some lonely thicket – and – and – things have been known to happen. Listen!' he said to the driver, 'so you say there is no danger here? Well, that's a pity. I love a good fight with robbers. I am small and sickly to look at, but I have the strength of an ox. Three robbers attacked me once, and what do you think? I shook one of them so that – well, it killed him. The other two I had sent to hard labour in Siberia. I can't think where all my strength comes from. I could take a big rascal like you in one hand – and – and – skin him!'

Klim looked round at the surveyor, blinked all over his face, and dealt his pony a blow.

'Yes, my friend,' continued the surveyor, 'Heaven help the robber that falls into my hands! Not only would he be left without arms or legs, but he would have to answer for his crimes in court, where all the judges and lawyers are friends of mine. I am a government official, and a very important one. When I am travelling like this the government knows it and keeps an eye on me to see that no one does me any harm. There are policemen and police captains hidden in the bushes all along the road. Stop! Stop!' yelled the surveyor suddenly. 'Where are you going? Where are you taking me to?'

'Can't you see? Into the wood.'

'So he is,' thought the surveyor. 'I was frightened, I mustn't show my feelings; he has already seen that I am afraid of him. What makes him look around at me so often? He must be meditating something. At first we barely moved, and now we are flying. Listen, Klim, why do you hurry your horse so?'

'I am not hurrying her; she is running away of her own accord. When once she begins running away, nothing will stop her. She is sorry herself that her legs are made that way.'

'That's a lie, my friend, I can see it's a lie. I advise you not to go so fast. Hold your horse in, do you hear? Hold him in!'

'Why?'

'Because – because – I have four friends following me from the station. I want them to catch up. They promised to catch me up in this wood. It will be jollier travelling with them. They are big, strong fellows, every one of them has a revolver. Why do you look round and jump about as if you were sitting on a tack? Hey? See here, I – I – there is nothing about me worth looking at, there is nothing interesting about me in the least – unless it is my revolvers! Here, if you want to see them I'll take them out and show them to you – let me get them.'

The surveyor pretended to be searching in his pockets, and at that moment something happened which not even his worst fears had led him to expect. Klim suddenly threw himself out of the wagon and ran off on all fours through the forest.

'Help!' he shouted. 'Help! Take my horse, take my wagon, accursed one, only spare me my soul! Help!'

The sound of his hurrying footsteps died away, the dry leaves rustled, all was still. When this unexpected judgement fell on him, the surveyor's first act was to stop the horse; then he settled himself more comfortably in the wagon and began to think.

'So he has taken fright and made off, the fool! Well, what shall I do now? I don't know the way, so I can't go on alone, and, anyway, if I did, it would look as if I had stolen his horse. What shall I do? Klim! Klim!'

'Klim!' answered the echo.

At the idea of spending the whole night alone in a dark forest, listening to the wolves, the echo, and the snorting of the lean pony, the surveyor felt the gooseflesh running up and down his spine.

'Klim!' he yelled. 'Dear old Klim! Good old Klim! Where are you?'

For two hours he called, and it was not until he had lost his voice and resigned himself to the thought of a night in the forest that a faint breeze brought him the sound of a groan.

'Klim, is that you, old man? Come, Klim, let us start!'

'You – you'll kill me!'

'Why, Klim, I was only joking, old chap; upon my word I was. Fancy my carrying revolvers with me! I lied like that because I was afraid. Do let us start; I am frozen!'

Klim, thinking, no doubt, that a real robber would have made off long ago with the horse and wagon, came out of the forest and approached his fare with caution.

'What are you afraid of, idiot? I was only joking, and you are afraid of me! Get in!'

'Lord, Mister,' muttered Klim, climbing into the wagon, 'if I had foreseen this I wouldn't have taken you for a hundred roubles. You have nearly scared me to death!'

Klim beat his pony – the wagon shuddered; Klim beat him again – the wagon rocked; at the fourth stroke, as the wagon moved slowly away, the surveyor pulled his coat collar over his ears and abandoned himself to meditation.

Neither Klim nor the road seemed dangerous now.

The Night before Easter

I WAS STANDING on the bank of the Goltva waiting for the ferry-boat to come across from the other side. At most times the Goltva is a silent and pensive little river sparkling shyly behind a rank growth of rushes, but now a whole lake lay spread before me. The swelling spring floods had topped both banks and drowned the riverside for a long way inland, taking possession of gardens, meadows, and marshes, so that here and there only a solitary bush or poplar tree was seen sticking up above the surface like a rough rock in the darkness.

The weather, I thought, was gorgeous. The night was dark, but I could, nevertheless, distinguish the water, the trees, and anyone standing near me. The world was lit by stars, which were scattered without number over the whole sky. I don't remember ever having seen so many stars. You literally could not have inserted a fingertip between them. There were big ones the size of a goose's egg and little ones the size of a hemp-seed; they had all come out in the sky, to the last one, to celebrate Easter in holiday splendour, washed, fresh, and joyous, and all gently twinkled their rays. The sky was reflected in the river, and the stars bathed themselves in its depths and trembled on its ripples. The air was still and warm. Far away, in the impenetrable darkness on the other shore, burnt a few bright red fires.

A couple of steps away from me I made out the dark figure of a man, in a high sheepskin hat, carrying a gnarled stick.

'How slow the ferry is in coming!' I said.

'It is time it was here,' answered the dark figure.

'Are you waiting for it, too?'

'No; I am just waiting,' yawned the peasant. 'I want to see the 'lumination. I would go across, only I haven't five copecks for the ferry.'

'I'll give you five copecks.'

'No, thank you kindly; you can keep them and burn a candle for me when you reach the monastery. It will be better so, and I will stand here. And that ferry-boat hasn't come yet! Has it sunk?'

The peasant went down to the water's edge, took hold of the cable, and called out: 'Jerome! Je–rome!'

As if in answer to his cry, the slow booming of a great bell came to us from the other shore, a deep, muffled note, like the lowest string of a double bass, and it seemed as if the night itself were groaning. The next moment a cannon was fired. The sound of it rolled through the darkness and stopped somewhere behind my back. The peasant took off his hat and crossed himself.

'Christ has risen!' he said.

The vibrations of the first shot had hardly subsided before a second was heard, then a third one directly after that, and the darkness was filled with an incessant, shuddering rumble. New fires blazed up near the red ones, and all danced and flashed together turbulently.

'Je–rome!' came a faint, long-drawn cry.

'They are calling from the other shore,' said the peasant. 'That means that the ferry-boat isn't there, either. Jerome must be asleep.'

The fires and the velvet notes of the bell were calling; I was beginning to lose my patience and my temper; at last, peering into the thick darkness, I saw the shape of something that looked very much like a gallows. It was the long-expected ferry-boat. It came so slowly that if its outline had not gradually grown sharper one might have fancied it was standing still or moving toward the other shore.

'Jerome! Be quick!' shouted my peasant. 'A gentleman is waiting!'

The ferry-boat slipped up to the bank, rocked, creaked, and stopped. A tall man was standing on it holding the cable; he wore the cassock and conical hat of a monk.

'What made you so slow in coming?' I asked, jumping on board.

'Forgive me,' answered Jerome. 'Is there no one else?'

'No one.'

Jerome took the cable in both hands, bent himself into the form of a question-mark, and gave a grunt. The ferry-boat creaked and rocked; the form of the peasant in the high hat slowly disappeared; we were off. Jerome soon straightened himself and began to work with one hand. We were silent and fixed our eyes on the shore toward which we were floating. There the ''lumination' which the peasant was expecting had already begun. Great barrels of pitch blazed at the water's edge, and their reflection, red as from the rising moon, ran out in a broad streak to meet us. The burning barrels lit up the smoke that rose from them and the human figures that flashed in and out among them, but around and behind them, where the velvet notes came from, lay an impenetrable blackness. Suddenly, cleaving the night, a rocket shot up to heaven like a golden ribbon, curved, and, as if shattering against the sky, was spilled in sparks. A roar like distant cheering rose from the shore.

'How beautiful!' I exclaimed.

'Too beautiful for words,' sighed Jerome. 'It is the night, sir. At another time we would not notice a rocket, but tonight one rejoices at a trifle. Where are you from?'

I told him.

'Yes, this is a joyful night,' continued Jerome in the weak, sighing voice of one convalescing from an illness. 'Heaven and earth are rejoicing, all creation is celebrating the holiday. Can you tell me, kind master, why it is that even in the presence of great happiness a man cannot forget his grief?'

It seemed to me that this unexpected question was a challenge to one of those lengthy, soul-saving discussions that idle and weary monks like so well. I did not feel in the mood for talking much, so I only asked:

'What is your grief, brother?'

'Just an ordinary one, like everyone else's, kind master; today a special sorrow has fallen on the monastery; our Deacon Nicolas died at mass.'

'God's will be done!' said I, counterfeiting a monkish tone. 'We must all die. I even think you should rejoice, for they say that whoever dies on Easter eve goes straight to heaven.'

'That is true.'

We stopped speaking. The figure of the peasant in the sheepskin hat faded into the line of the shore, the barrels of pitch blazed brighter and brighter.

'And the Scriptures point clearly to the vanity of sorrow and regret,' Jerome broke silence. 'Then, why does the heart sorrow and refuse to listen to reason? Why does one want to cry so bitterly?'

Jerome shrugged his shoulders and, turning to me, began to speak rapidly:

'If I had died, or anyone else had died, it wouldn't have mattered, we shouldn't have been missed; but it was Nicolas who died – no one else but Nicolas! It is hard to believe that he is no longer on earth. As I stand here now on the ferry, it seems to me as if every moment I should hear his voice from the shore. He always came down to the river and called to me so that I should not feel lonely on the ferry. He used to leave his bed at night on purpose to do it. He was so good. Oh, dear, how good and kind he was! Even a mother is not to other men what Nicolas was to me. Have mercy on his soul, O Lord!'

Jerome gave the cable a pull, but immediately turned to me again:

'Your honour, how bright his mind was!' he said softly. 'How sweet and musical his voice was! Just such a voice as they will sing of now at mass: "Oh, most kind, most comforting is Thy voice." And, above all other human qualities, he had one extraordinary gift.'

'What gift?' I asked.

The monk glanced at me and, as if assured that he could entrust me with a secret, said, laughing gaily:

'He had the gift of writing akaphists!'* he said. 'It was a miracle, sir, nothing less. You will be astonished when I tell you about it. Our father archimandrite comes from Moscow, our father vicar has studied in Kazan, we have wise monks and elders, and yet – what do you think? – not one of them can write! And Nicolas, a plain monk, a deacon, who never learnt anything and had nothing to show – he could write! It was a miracle, truly a miracle!'

Jerome clasped his hands and, entirely forgetting the cable, continued with passion:

'Our father vicar has the greatest trouble over his sermons. When he was writing the history of the monastery, he tired out the whole brotherhood and made ten trips to town; but Nicolas could write *akaphists*, not just sermons and histories!'

'And are akaphists so hard to write?'

'Very hard,' nodded Jerome. 'Wisdom and saintliness will not help him to whom God has not given the gift. The monks who don't understand argue that you need only know the life of the saint of whom you are writing and follow the other akaphists, but that is not so, sir. Of course, to write an akaphist one must know the life of the saint down to the least detail, and of course, too, one must conform to the other akaphists so far as knowing where to begin and what to write about. To give you an example, the first hymn must always begin with "It is forbidden" or "It is elected", and the first ikos† must always begin with "Angel". If you are interested in hearing it, in the akaphist to the Lord Jesus the first ikos begins like this: "Angels of the Creator, might of the Lord"; in the akaphist to the Holy Virgin it begins, "An angel was sent, a messenger from heaven"; in the akaphist to Nicolas the Wonder-worker it begins, "An angel in form, a being of earth" – they all begin with "Angel". Of course, an akaphist must conform to other akaphists, but the important thing is not the life of the saint nor its conformity,

---

* Akaphist: a service of prayer to a special saint said or sung on that saint's day.
† Ikos. One of the short prayers included in an akaphist.

but its beauty, its sweetness. Everything about it must be graceful and brief and exact. Every line must be tender and gentle and soft; not a word must be harsh or unsuitable or rough. It must be written so that he who prays with his heart may weep with joy, that his soul may shudder and be afraid. In an akaphist to the Virgin he wrote: "Rejoice, exalted of men! Rejoice, beloved of the angels". In another part of the same akaphist he wrote: "Rejoice, holy-fruited tree that nourishest our faith; rejoice, tree of merciful leaves that coverest our sins"!'

Jerome bowed his head and covered his face with his hands, as if he had taken fright or were ashamed of something.

'Holy-fruited tree – tree of merciful leaves!' he muttered. 'Were there ever such words? How was it possible that the Lord should have given him such a gift? For brevity he used to combine many words and thoughts into one word, and how smoothly and truly his writing flowed! "Lambent Star of the world", he says in an akaphist to Jesus the all-merciful. "Lambent Star of the world!" Those words have never been spoken or written before; he thought of them himself; he found them in his own mind! But each line must not only be fluent and eloquent, it must be adorned with many things – with flowers and light and wind and sun and all the objects of the visible world. And every invocation must be written to fall softly and gratefully on the ear. "Rejoice in the land of the Kingdom of Paradise," he wrote in an akaphist to Nicolas the Wonder-worker, not simply "Rejoice in Paradise." It is smoother so and sweeter to the ear. And that is how Nicolas wrote; just like that. But I can't tell you how well he wrote.'

'Yes, in that case it is a pity he died,' I said; 'but still, brother, let us go ahead, or we shall be late.'

Jerome recollected himself and took hold of the cable. On the shore all the bells had begun to ring; the Procession of the Cross had probably started near the monastery, for now the dark space behind the bonfires was strewn with moving lights.

'Did Nicolas have his akaphists printed?' I asked Jerome.

'How could he have them printed?' he sighed. 'And then it would have been strange; why should he? No one in our monastery was interested in them; they didn't care for them. They knew that Nicolas wrote but never gave it any thought. No one sets any value on modern writing these days.'

'Are they prejudiced against it?'

'Exactly. If Nicolas had been an elder, perhaps the brothers might have been interested, but he wasn't even forty years old. Some laughed at him and even counted his writing a sin.'

'Then, why did he write?'

'Oh, chiefly for his own consolation. I was the only one of the brothers who read his akaphists. He used to throw his arms around me and smooth my hair and call me tender names, as if I were a little child. He used to open the door of his cell and make me sit by him, and we used to read – '

Jerome left his cable and came toward me.

'We were such friends,' he whispered with shining eyes. 'Wherever he went, I went. When I was not with him he was sad; he loved me more than all the others, and all because his akaphists made me cry. It is sad to remember. Now I am like an orphan or a widower. The brothers in our monastery are good and kind and pious, you know, but not one of them is gentle and tender. They are all noisy, and talk loudly, and cough, and walk heavily, but Nicolas always spoke quietly and gently, and if he saw that anyone was asleep or praying he would go by them as lightly as a fly or a gnat. His face was compassionate and tender – '

Jerome sighed deeply and pulled the cable. We were already nearing the shore. Out of the silence and darkness of the river we slowly drifted into a magician's land, smothered in choking smoke, uproarious with noise and light. Figures, seen clearly now, were moving among the fires; the light of the flames lent a strange, fantastic look to their red faces and forms. Here and there appeared the heads of horses, motionless as if cast in red copper.

'They will soon sing the Easter canon,' said Jerome. 'But Nicolas is dead, so there will be no one to penetrate its meaning. For him, no sweeter writing existed than this Easter canon. He used to listen to every word. You will be there, sir; listen to the singing.'

'What, won't you be in church?'

'I can't; I must run the ferry.'

'But won't they relieve you?'

'I don't know. I should have been relieved at nine o'clock, and, you see, I am still here. I must say, I should like to go to church.'

'Are you a monk?'

'Yes – that is, I am a lay brother.'

The ferry-boat ran against the bank and stopped. I slipped five copecks for my fare into Jerome's hand and jumped ashore. A wagon carrying a boy and a sleeping woman at once drove on to the ferry-boat. Jerome, faintly red in the firelight, bent to his rope and started the boat.

The first few steps I took were in the mud; farther on I came to a soft, freshly trampled path. This led to the dark, cave-like monastery gates, through clouds of smoke and a confused multitude of men and women, unharnessed horses, carts, and wagons. All chattered and snorted and laughed, gleaming in the crimson light through eddying shadows of smoke – chaos indeed! And amidst all this jostling there was found room to load a little cannon and sell gingerbread!

Not less activity but more order and decorum prevailed in the enclosure inside the walls. Here the air smelt of juniper and incense. The crowd talked loudly, but there was no laughing or neighing of horses. People carrying loaves and bundles stood huddled together among the crosses and tombstones; it was evident that many of them had come a long way to have their loaves blessed, and were tired. The strip of iron pavement that led from the gates to the church door rang loudly under the boots of the young lay brethren running busily along it; in the bell-tower there was hurrying and calling.

'What a busy night this is!' I thought. 'How good it is!'

Everything in nature seemed to reflect this activity, from the dark shadows to the iron pavement, the tombstones, and the trees under which the crowd was stirring. A turbulent contest was going on at the door between the ebbing and flowing throngs. Some were hurrying in, others were coming out, to return, stand for a moment, and again move on. They went from place to place, roaming about as if in search of something; waves started from the door and swept along the church, even stirring the front rows, where the more serious and solid folk were standing. Of regularly conducted prayer there could be no thought; there was no praying at all, only a kind of wholehearted, irresponsible, childish joy, seeking a pretext to break out and discharge itself in movement of any kind, even in disorderly pushing and crowding.

The same unusual activity struck one in the Easter service. The sanctuary gates of all the chapels were thrown wide open; dense clouds of incense floated around the lustres; everywhere were lights, brilliance, and the glitter of tapers. All reading was out of the question, and the singing went gaily and busily on without interruption. After every canon the priests changed their vestments and went out to scatter incense, and this took place nearly every ten minutes.

I had hardly succeeded in securing a place before a wave swept down from the front of the church and threw me back. Before me passed a tall, stout deacon, holding a long red taper, and behind him, carrying the incense, hurried a grey-haired archimandrite wearing a golden mitre. As they disappeared from sight the crowd pushed me back to my former place. But scarcely had ten minutes elapsed before another wave swept up and again the deacon appeared. This time he was followed by the father vicar, the same who, according to Jerome, had written the history of the monastery.

As I mixed with the crowd and caught the pervading, joyous excitement my heart ached unbearably for Jerome. Why did they not relieve him? Why should not someone less impressionable, with less feeling than he, go to the ferry?

'Lift up thine eyes, O Zion, and behold,' sang the choir. 'Thy Son, the Light of God, has come.'

I glanced at the faces around me. All wore a bright look of exaltation, but not a man 'penetrated the meaning' of the singing, and no one 'caught his breath' to hear. Why did they not relieve Jerome? In my imagination I could see him so clearly, standing quietly against the wall, bending forward, eagerly grasping the beauty of the sacred words. All that lay beyond the hearing of the people standing near me he would have drunk greedily with his quick ear, he would have grown drunk with rapture until he caught his breath, and in the whole church there would have been no happier man than he. Now he was rowing back and forth on the dark river, sorrowing for his dead brother and friend. A wave rolled up from behind, and a fat, smiling monk, looking back and fingering a rosary, came slipping sideways by me, forcing a passage for a lady in a hat and velvet cloak. Behind the lady hurried a servant of the monastery, holding a chair above our heads.

I left the church, wishing to see the dead Nicolas, unknown writer of akaphists. I passed through the enclosure where a row of monks' cells lay along the walls and looked into several windows but, seeing nothing, turned back. I do not regret now not having seen Nicolas. Who knows if in doing so I might not have dimmed the picture of him which my fancy now paints? I see him clearly, that lovable and poetical being who went out at night to call to Jerome, and, lonely and uncomprehended, strewed his akaphists with stars and rays of sunlight. He is shy and pale, with a gentle, pensive face, and in his eyes, beside intelligence, I see shining the tenderness and hardly repressed, child-like rapture which I had noticed in Jerome's voice when he recited to me quotations from the akaphists.

When we left the church after mass it was already light. Morning was here. The stars had faded and the sky looked blue-grey and dull; the iron pavement, the tombstones, and the buds on the trees were wet with dew; the air was piercing and damp. Outside the enclosure there was no activity such as I had seen the night before. Horses and men looked tired and sleepy; they scarcely stirred, and a few heaps of black ashes were all that remained of the barrels of pitch. When a man is tired and drowsy he thinks that nature, too, is in the same condition. The trees and the young grass seemed to me to be asleep, and even the bells seemed to ring less loudly and merrily than they had the night before. The bustle was over, and all that remained after the excitement was a pleasant lassitude and a desire for sleep and warmth.

I could now see the river from shore to shore. A light mist was drifting in little clouds across its surface, and a chilly dampness breathed from the water. When I jumped on to the ferry a wagon and about twenty men and women were already on it. The damp and, as it seemed to me, drowsy cable stretched across the broad river and was lost in places in the white mist.

'Christ is risen! Is there no one else?' asked a gentle voice.

I recognised it as Jerome's. The darkness no longer hid the monk from view, and I saw a tall, narrow shouldered man of thirty-five, with large, rounded features, half-closed, drowsy eyes, and a rough, wedge-shaped beard. He looked extraordinarily sad and tired.

'Haven't they relieved you yet?' I asked with surprise.

'Me?' he asked, smiling and turning his chilled, dew-drenched face to me. 'There won't be anyone to take my place till morning. Everybody has gone to the archimandrite now to break the Lenten fast.'

He pulled the cable, helped by a little peasant in a red fur hat that looked like the tubs honey is sold in; they grunted amicably and the ferry moved off.

We floated across the river, troubling on our passage the slowly rising mist. No one spoke. Jerome worked silently with one hand. For a long time he rested his dim, timid eyes on us all, and then at last fixed his gaze on the rosy face of a young merchant's wife standing beside me, shrinking in silence from the mist that enveloped her. He did not take his eyes off her face as long as the journey lasted.

There was little of the man in that long gaze; and it seemed to me as if Jerome were seeking in the woman's face the sweet and gentle features of his lost friend.

At Home

'SOMEBODY came from the Grigorieffs' to fetch a book, but I said you were not at home. The postman has brought the newspapers and two letters. And, by the way, sir, I wish you would give your attention to Seriozha. I saw him smoking today and also the day before yesterday. When I told him how wrong it was he put his fingers in his ears, as he always does, and began to sing loudly so as to drown my voice.'

Eugene Bikofski, an attorney of the circuit court, who had just come home from a session and was taking off his gloves in his study, looked at the governess who was making this statement and laughed.

'So Seriozha has been smoking!' he said with a shrug of his shoulders. 'Fancy the little beggar with a cigarette in his mouth! How old is he?'

'Seven years old. It seems of small consequence to you, but at his age smoking is a bad, a harmful habit; and bad habits should be nipped in the bud.'

'You are absolutely right. Where does he get the tobacco?'

'From your table.'

'He does? In that case, send him to me.'

When the governess had gone, Bikofski sat down in an easy-chair before his writing-table and began to think. For some reason he pictured to himself his Seriozha enveloped in clouds of tobacco smoke, with a huge, yard-long cigarette in his mouth, and this caricature made him smile. At the same time the earnest, anxious face of the governess awakened in him memories of days long past and half forgotten, when smoking at school and in the nursery aroused in masters and parents a strange, almost incomprehensible horror. It really was horror. Children were unmercifully flogged, and expelled from school, and their lives were blighted, although not one of the teachers nor fathers knew exactly what constituted the harm and offence of smoking. Even very intelligent people did not hesitate to combat the vice they did not understand. Bikofski called to mind the principal of his school, a highly educated, good-natured old man, who was so shocked when he caught a scholar with a cigarette that he would turn pale and immediately summon a special meeting of the school board and sentence the offender to expulsion. No doubt that is one of the laws of society – the less an evil is understood the more bitterly and harshly is it attacked.

The attorney thought of the two or three boys who had been expelled and of their subsequent lives, and could not but reflect that punishment is, in many cases, more productive of evil than crime itself. The living organism possesses the faculty of quickly adapting itself to every condition; if it were not so man would be conscious every moment of the unreasonable foundations on which his reasonable actions rest and of how little of justice and assurance are to be found even in those activities which are fraught with so much responsibility and which are so appalling in their consequences, such as education, literature, the law –

And thoughts such as these came floating into Bikofski's head; light, evanescent thoughts such as only enter weary, resting brains. One knows not whence they are nor why they come; they stay but a short while and seem to spread across the surface of the brain without ever sinking very far into its depths. For those whose minds for hours and days together are forced to be occupied with business and to travel always along the same lines, these homelike, untrammelled musings bring a sort of comfort and a pleasant restfulness of their own.

It was nine o'clock. On the floor overhead someone was pacing up and down, and still higher up, on the third storey, four hands were playing scales on the piano. The person who was pacing the floor seemed, from his nervous strides, to be the victim of tormenting thoughts or of the toothache; his footsteps and the monotonous scales added to the quiet of the evening something somnolent that predisposed the mind to idle reveries.

In the nursery, two rooms away, Seriozha and his governess were talking.

'Pa–pa has come!' sang the boy. 'Papa has co–ome! Pa! Pa! Pa!'

'*Votre père vous appelle, allez vite!*' cried the governess, twittering like a frightened bird.

'What shall I say to him?' thought Bikofski.

But before he had had time to think of anything to say his son Seriozha had already entered the study. This was a little person whose sex could only be divined from his clothes – he was so delicate, and fair, and frail. His body was as languid as a hot-house plant and everything about him looked wonderfully dainty and soft – his movements, his curly hair, his glance, his velvet tunic.

'Good-evening, papa,' he said in a gentle voice, climbing on to his father's knee and swiftly kissing his neck. 'Did you send for me?'

'Wait a bit, wait a bit, master,' answered the lawyer, putting him aside. 'Before you and I kiss each other we must have a talk, a serious talk. I am angry with you, and I don't love you any more; do you understand that, young man? I don't love you, and you are no son of mine.'

Seriozha looked steadfastly at his father and then turned his regard to the table and shrugged his shoulders.

'What have I done?' he asked, perplexed, and blinked. 'I didn't go into your study once today, and I haven't touched a thing.'

'Miss Natalie has just been complaining to me that you have been smoking; is that so? Have you been smoking?'

'Yes, I smoked once. That is so.'

'There! So now you have told a lie into the bargain!' said the lawyer, disguising his smile by a frown. 'Miss Natalie saw you smoking twice. That means that you have been caught doing three naughty things: smoking, taking tobacco that doesn't belong to you off my table, and telling a lie. Three accusations!'

'Oh, ye–es!' Seriozha remembered, and his eyes smiled. 'That is true, true! I did smoke twice – today and one other time.'

'There, you see, so it was twice and not once. I am very, very displeased with you. You used to be a good boy, but now I see you have grown bad and naughty.'

Bikofski straightened Seriozha's little collar and thought:

'What shall I say to him next?'

'Yes, it was very wrong,' he went on. 'I did not expect this of you. For one thing, you have no right to take tobacco that doesn't belong to you. People only have a right to use their own things; if a man takes other people's things he – he is bad. ('That isn't what I ought to say to him,' thought Bikofski.) For instance, Miss Natalie has a trunk with dresses in it. That trunk belongs to her, and we – that is, you and I – must not dare to touch it, because it isn't ours. You have your little horses and your pictures. I don't take them, do I? Perhaps I should like to, but they are not mine they are yours.'

'You can take them if you want to,' said Seriozha, raising his eyebrows. 'Don't mind, papa, you may have them. The little yellow dog that is on your table is mine, but I don't care if it stays there.'

'You don't understand me,' said Bikofski. 'You made me a present of that little dog; it belongs to me now, and I can do what I like with it; but I didn't give you the tobacco, the tobacco belongs to me. ('I'm not explaining it to him right,' thought the lawyer, 'not right at all.') If I want to smoke tobacco that isn't mine I must first get permission to do so – '

And so, slowly coupling sentence to sentence, and counterfeiting the speech of a child, Bikofski went on to explain to his son the meaning of possession. Seriozha's eyes rested on his father's chest, and he listened attentively (he liked to converse with his father in the evening); then he rested his elbows on the edge of the table and, half closing his near-sighted eyes, began contemplating the paper and the inkstand. His glance roamed across the table and was arrested by a bottle of glue.

'Papa, what is glue made of?' he suddenly asked, raising the bottle to his eyes.

Bikofski took the bottle away from him, put it where it belonged, and continued:

'In the next place, you have been smoking. That is very naughty indeed. If I smoke, it does not mean that smoking is good. When I smoke I know it is a stupid thing to do, and I am angry with myself and blame myself for doing it. ('Oh, what a wily teacher I am!' thought the lawyer.) Tobacco is very bad for the health, and men who smoke die sooner than they should. It is especially bad to smoke when one is as little as you are. Your chest is weak, you have not grown strong yet, and tobacco smoke gives weak people consumption and other diseases. Your Uncle Ignatius died of consumption; if he hadn't smoked he might have been living today.'

Seriozha looked thoughtfully at the lamp, touched the shade with his finger, and sighed.

'Uncle Ignatius used to play the violin,' he said. 'The Grigorieffs have his violin now.'

Seriozha again leaned his elbows on the edge of the table and became lost in thought. From the expression fixed on his pale features he seemed to be listening to something, or to be intent on the unfolding of his own ideas; sadness and something akin to fear appeared in his great, unblinking eyes; he was probably thinking of death, which such a little while ago had taken away his mother and his Uncle Ignatius. Death carries mothers and uncles away to another world, and their children and violins stay behind on earth. Dead people live in heaven, somewhere near the stars, and from there they look down upon the earth. Can they bear the separation?

'What shall I say to him?' thought Bikofski. 'He isn't listening. It is obvious that he doesn't attach any importance to his offence or to my arguments. What can I say to touch him?'

The lawyer rose and walked about the study.

'In my day these questions were settled with singular simplicity,' he reflected. 'If a youngster was caught smoking he was thrashed. This would, indeed, make a poor-spirited, cowardly boy give up smoking, but a clever and plucky one would carry his tobacco in his boot after the whipping and smoke in an outhouse. When he was caught in the outhouse and whipped again he would go down and smoke by the river, and so on until the lad was grown up. My mother used to give me money and candy to keep me from smoking. These expedients now seem to us weak and immoral. Taking up a logical standpoint, the educator of today tries to instil the first principles of right into a child by helping him to understand them and not by rousing his fear or his desire to distinguish himself and obtain a reward.'

While he was walking and meditating Seriozha had climbed up and was standing with his feet on a chair by the side of the table and had begun to draw pictures. A pile of paper cut especially for him and a blue pencil lay on the table so that he should not scribble on any business papers or touch the ink.

'Cook cut her finger today while she was chopping cabbage,' he said, moving his eyebrows and drawing a house. 'She screamed so that we were all frightened and ran into the kitchen. She was so silly! Miss Natalie told her to dip her finger in cold water, but she would only suck it. How could she put her dirty finger in her mouth! Papa, that wasn't nice, was it?'

Then he went on to narrate how an organ-grinder had come into the yard during dinner, with a little girl who had sung and danced to the music.

'He has his own field of thought,' the lawyer reflected. 'He has a little world of his own in his head, and knows what, according to him, is important and what is not. One cannot cheat him of his attention and consciousness by simply aping his language, one must also be able to think in his fashion. He would have understood me perfectly had I really regretted the tobacco, and been offended and burst into tears. That is why nothing can replace the mother in education, because she is able to feel and weep and laugh with her children. Nothing can be accomplished by logic and ethics. Well, what shall I say to him? What?'

And it seemed to Bikofski laughable and strange that an experienced student of justice like himself, who had spent half a lifetime in the study of every phase of the prevention and punishment of crime, should find himself completely at sea and unable to think of what to say to a boy.

'Listen! Give me your word of honour that you won't smoke again,' he said.

'Wo–ord of honour!' sang Seriozha. 'Wo–ord of ho–nour! nour! nour!'

'I wonder if he knows what word of honour means?' Bikofski asked himself. 'No, I'm a bad teacher. If one of our educationalists or jurists could look into my head at this moment he would call me a muddlehead and very likely accuse me of too much subtlety. But the fact is, all these confounded questions are settled so much more easily at school or in court than at home. Here, at home, one has to do with people whom one unreasoningly loves, and love is exacting and complicates things. If this child were my pupil or a prisoner at the bar, instead of being my son, I would not be such a coward and my thoughts would not wander as they now do.'

Bikofski sat down at the table and drew toward him one of Seriozha's drawings. The picture represented a crooked-roofed little house with smoke coming in zigzags, like lightning, out of the chimneys and rising to the edge of the paper. Near the house stood a soldier with dots for eyes and a bayonet that resembled the figure 4.

'A man cannot possibly be higher than a house,' said the lawyer. 'See here, your roof only reaches up to the soldier's shoulders.'

Seriozha climbed on to his father's lap and wriggled there a long time trying to get himself comfortably settled.

'No, papa,' he said, contemplating his drawing. 'If you made the soldier little, his eyes wouldn't show.'

What need was there to have corrected him? From daily observation of his son the lawyer had become convinced that children, like savages, have their own artistic view-point and their own odd requirements, which are beyond the scope of an adult intelligence. Under close observation, Seriozha might appear abnormal to an adult because he found it possible and reasonable to draw a man higher than a house, giving his pencil his own perceptions as well as a subject. Thus, the sounds of an orchestra he represented by round, smoky spots; a whistle, by a twisted thread; in his mind, sound was intimately connected with form and colour, so that in painting letters he invariably coloured the sound L, yellow; M, red; A, black; and so forth.

Throwing aside the drawing, Seriozha wriggled again, took a convenient position, and turned his attention to his father's beard. First he smoothed it carefully and then combed it apart in the form of side whiskers.

'Now you look like Ivan Stepanovitch,' he murmured, 'and now in a minute you're going to look like – our porter. Papa, why do porters stand at doors? To keep robbers from coming in?'

The lawyer felt the child's breath on his face, the soft hair brushed his cheek, and warmth and tenderness crept into his heart as if his whole soul, and not his hands alone, were lying on the velvet of Seriozha's tunic.

He looked into the boy's large, dark eyes and seemed to see mother and wife and everything he had once loved gazing out of those wide pupils.

'How could one whip him?' he thought. 'How could one bewilder him by punishment? No, we shouldn't pretend to know how to educate children. People used to be simpler; they thought less and so decided their problems more boldly; but we think too much; we are eaten up by logic. The more enlightened a man is the more he is given to reflection and hair-splitting; the more undecided he is, the more full of scruples, and the more timidly he approaches a task. And, seriously considered, how much bravery, how much self-reliance must a man not have to undertake teaching, or judging, or writing a big book!'

The clock struck ten.

'Come, boy, time for bed!' said the lawyer. 'Say good-night and then go.'

'No, papa,' pouted Seriozha. 'I want to stay a little longer. Tell me something; tell me a story.'

'Very well; but as soon as the story is told – off we go!'

On his free evenings the lawyer was in the habit of telling Seriozha stories. Like most busy people, he did not know one piece of poetry by heart, nether could he remember a single story, so he was forced to improvise something new every time. He generally took for his key-note 'Once upon a time,' and then went heaping one bit of innocent nonsense on another, not knowing, as he told the beginning, what the middle or the end would be. The scenes, the characters, and the situations he would seize at random, and the plot and the moral would trickle in of their own accord, independent of the will of the story-teller. Seriozha loved these improvisations, and the lawyer noticed that the more modest and uncomplicated the plot turned out to be the more deeply it affected the boy.

'Listen,' he began, raising his eyes to the ceiling. 'Once upon a time there lived an old, a very old king who had a long, grey beard and – and – whiskers as long as this. Well, this king lived in a palace of crystal that sparkled and flashed in the sunlight like a great big block of pure ice. The palace, little son, stood in a great big garden, and in this garden, you know, there grew oranges and bergamot pears and wild cherry trees; and tulips and roses and lilies-of-the-valley blossomed there and bright-coloured birds sang. Yes, and on the trees there hung little crystal bells that rang so sweetly when the wind blew that one never grew tired of listening to them. Crystal gives out a softer, sweeter tone than metal. Well, and what do you think? In that garden there were fountains. Don't you remember – you saw a fountain once at Aunt Sonia's summer house? Well, there were fountains just like that in the king's garden, only they were ever so much larger and their spray reached right up to the tip of the highest poplar trees – '

Bikofski reflected an instant and continued:

'The old king had only one son, who was heir to the kingdom, a little boy, just as little as you are. He was a good boy; he was never capricious, and he went to bed early, and never touched anything on his father's table – and – and was as nice as he could be in every way. He had only one failing – he smoked.'

Seriozha was listening intently, looking steadily into his father's eyes. The lawyer thought to himself: 'How shall I go on?' He ruminated for a long time and then ended thus:

'Because he smoked, the king's son fell ill of consumption and died when he was twenty years old. The old man, decrepit and ill, was left without anyone to take care of him, and there was no one to govern the kingdom or to protect the palace. Foes came and killed the old man and destroyed the palace, and now there are no wild cherry trees left in the garden, and no birds and no bells, and so, sonny – '

An ending like this seemed to Bikofski artless and absurd, but the whole tale had made a deep impression on Seriozha. Once more sadness and something resembling terror crept into his eyes; he gazed for a minute at the dark window and said in a low voice:

'I won't smoke any more – '

When he had said good-night and gone to bed, his father walked softly back and forth across the floor and smiled.

'It will be said that beauty and artistic form were the influences in this case,' he mused. 'That may be so, but it is no consolation. After all, those are not genuine means of influence. Why is it that morals and truth must not be presented in their raw state but always in a mixture, sugar-coated and gilded, like pills? It is not right. That sort of thing is falsification, trickery, deceit – '

He remembered the jurymen who invariably had to be harangued in an 'address'; the public who could only assimilate history by means of legends and historical novels and poems.

'Medicine must be sweet, truth must be beautiful; this has been man's folly since the days of Adam. Besides, it may all be quite natural, and perhaps it is as it should be. Nature herself has many tricks of expediency and many deceptions – '

He sat down to his work, but the idle, homelike thoughts long continued to flit through his brain. The scales could no longer be heard overhead, but the dweller on the second floor still continued to walk back and forth.

Champagne

IN THE YEAR in which my story begins I was working as station-master at a little flag-station on one of our southwestern railways. Whether my life there was gay or tedious you can decide for yourself when I tell you that there was not one human habitation within twenty miles of the place, not one woman, not one respectable dram-shop, and I was young and strong at that time, ardent and hot-headed and foolish. My only distractions were seeing the windows of the passenger-trains and drinking foul vodka, which the Jews adulterated with thorn-apple. It happened, sometimes, that a woman's head would flash by at a car-window, and then I would stand as still as a statue, holding my breath, staring after the train until it changed into an almost imperceptible dot. Or sometimes I would drink myself tight on the sickening vodka and remain unconscious of the flight of the long hours and days. On me, a son of the North, the steppes had the same effect as the sight of a neglected Tartar cemetery. In summer the solemn peace, the monotonous, strident chirping of the grasshoppers, the clear moonlight nights from which there was no concealment wrought in me a mournful sadness; in winter the immaculate whiteness of the plains, their cold remoteness, the long nights, and the howling of the wolves oppressed me like a painful nightmare.

There were several of us living at the little station – my wife and I, a deaf and scrofulous telegraph-operator, and three watchmen. My assistant, a consumptive young man, went often to the city for treatment, and there he would stay for months at a time, leaving me his duties as well as the right to his salary. I had no children, and nothing on earth could tempt a guest to stay with us. I myself could never visit anyone except my fellow employees along the line, and this I could only do once every month. On the whole, it was a very tedious existence.

I remember, my wife and I were waiting to see the New Year in. We sat at the table munching lazily, listening to the deaf telegraph-operator as he monotonously hammered his instrument in an adjoining room.

I had already had five glasses of vodka with thorn-apple and sat with my heavy head in my hands, thinking about this unconquerable, this inevitable tedium. My wife sat beside me with her eyes fixed on my face. She was gazing at me as only a woman gazes for whom nothing exists on earth but her good-looking husband. She loved me madly, servilely; she loved not only my good looks but my sins and my wickedness and my sadness, and even the cruelty with which I tormented her, heaping reproaches on her in my drunken wanderings, not knowing on whom to vent my spleen.

Notwithstanding that this melancholy was eating into my soul, we were preparing to welcome the New Year with unwonted solemnity and were waiting with considerable impatience for midnight.

The fact was, we had saved up two bottles of champagne, champagne of the real sort, with the label 'Veuve Clicquot' on the bottle. I had won this treasure that autumn in a bet at a christening party. It sometimes happens that during an arithmetic lesson, when the very atmosphere seems heavy with tedium, a butterfly will flutter into the classroom from out-of-doors. Then the urchins will all crane their necks and follow its flight with curiosity, as if they saw before them something strange and new and not simply a butterfly. We were amused in just such a way by this ordinary champagne which had dropped by chance into the midst of our dull life at the station. We said not a word and kept looking first at the clock and then at the bottles.

When the hands pointed to five minutes to twelve I slowly began to uncork one of the bottles. Whether I was weak from the effects of the vodka or whether the bottle was moist, I know not; I only remember that when the cork flew up to the ceiling with a pop the bottle slipped from my hands and fell to the floor. Not more than half a glassful of wine was spilled, for I was able to catch the bottle and to stop its fizzing mouth with my finger.

'Well, a happy New Year!' I cried, pouring out two glasses. 'Drink!'

My wife took the glass and stared at me with startled eyes. Her face had grown pale and was stamped with horror.

'Did you drop the bottle?' she asked.

'Yes; what of it?'

'That is bad,' she said, setting down her glass. 'It is a bad omen. It means that some disaster will befall us this year.'

'What a peasant you are!' I sighed. 'You are an intelligent woman, but you rave like an old nurse. Drink!'

'God grant I may be raving, but – something will surely happen. You'll see.'

She did not finish her glass but went off to one side and lost herself in thought. I made a few time-honoured remarks on the subject of superstition, drank half the bottle, walked back and forth across the room, and went out.

The silent, frosty night reigned outside in all its cold and lonely beauty. The moon and two downy white clouds hung motionless in the zenith over the station, as if they were glued to the sky and were waiting for something. They shed a faint, diaphanous light that touched the white earth tenderly, as if fearing to offend its modesty, and lit up everything – the snowdrifts and the embankment. The air was very still.

I walked along the embankment.

'A silly woman!' I thought, looking at the heavens, which were strewn with brilliant stars. 'Even if one admits that omens sometimes come true, what disaster could befall us? The misfortunes which we have encountered and which are now upon us are so great that it would be difficult to imagine anything worse. What further harm can be done to a fish after it has been caught, roasted, and served up with sauce at table?'

A poplar covered with snow looked, in the bluish mist, like a giant in a winding-sheet. It gazed austerely and sadly at me, as if, like myself, it knew its own loneliness. I looked at it a long time.

'My youth has been cast aside like a useless cigar stump,' I pursued the thread of my thoughts. 'My parents died when I was a child; I was taken away from school. I am gently bred, and yet I have had no better education than a labourer. I have no home, no kindred, no friends, no favourite occupation. I am not capable of anything, and at the height of my powers I am only fit to fill the position of station-master. Besides being a failure, I am poor and have been poor all my life. What further misfortune could befall me?'

A ruddy light appeared in the distance. A train was coming toward me. The awakening plains heard the noise of it. My meditations had been so bitter that it seemed to me as if I had been thinking aloud and that the moan of the telegraph wires and the roar of the train were the voice of my thoughts.

'What further misfortune could befall me? The loss of my wife?' I asked myself. 'Even that would not be terrible. I cannot conceal it from myself: I do not love her! I married her when I was still a boy. Now I am young and strong, and she has grown thin and old and stupid and is crammed with superstitions from her head to her heels. What is there beautiful in her mawkish love, her sunken chest, her faded eyes? I endure her, but I do not love her. What could happen? My youth will go, as they say, for a pinch of snuff. Women only flash by me in the car-windows like shooting stars. I have no love now and have never known it. My manhood, my courage, all will be lost. All will be thrown away like so much litter, and what riches I have are not worth one copper farthing here on these plains.'

The train flew noisily by me, and its lights shone on me unconcernedly out of the ruddy windows. I saw it halt near the green station lamps; it stopped there for a minute and then rolled on. After I had walked for two miles I turned homeward. My sad thoughts still pursued me. Bitter as my mood was, I remember I seemed to try to make myself gloomier and sadder. Shallow, self-centred people, you know, have moments when the consciousness that they are unhappy gives them a certain pleasure, and they will even coquet with their own sufferings. There was much that was just in my reflections and also much that was conceited and foolish, and there was something childish in the challenge: 'What further misfortune could befall me?'

'Yes, what could befall me?' I asked myself as I walked homeward. 'It seems to me that I have lived through everything. I have been ill. I have lost my money. I am reprimanded every day by the administration of the railway. I am starving, and a mad wolf has run into the station yard. What else could happen? I have been degraded and wronged, and I, too, have wronged others. There is only one thing that I have not done. I have never committed a crime, and I believe I am incapable of it; I am afraid of the law.'

The two clouds had quitted the moon and were sailing at a distance with an air of whispering together about something which the moon must not hear. A light breeze skimmed across the plains, carrying the faint sound of the departing train.

My wife met me at the threshold of our house. Her eyes were smiling merrily, and delight shone from her whole face.

'I have news!' she whispered. 'Go quickly to your room and put on your new coat; we have a guest!'

'What guest?'

'My aunt Natalia Petrovna has just come in on the train.'

'Which Natalia Petrovna?'

'My uncle Simeon's wife. You don't know her. She is very kind and very pretty.'

I must have frowned, for my wife's face grew suddenly serious, and she whispered quickly:

'Of course, it is strange that she should have come, but don't be angry, Nicolas; make allowances for her. You see, she is unfortunate.

My uncle is really a tyrant and very bad-tempered, and it is hard to live in peace with him. She says she is only going to stay with us three days, until she hears from her brother.'

My wife whispered a lot more nonsense about her tyrannical uncle, about the weakness of human beings in general and of young women in particular, about its being our duty to shelter everyone, even sinners, and so on. Without comprehending a thing, I donned my new coat and went to make the acquaintance of my 'aunt.'

A little woman with large black eyes was sitting at the table. Our board, the grey walls, the rough ottoman, everything down to the least grain of dust seemed to have become younger and gayer in the presence of this fresh young being, exhaling some strange perfume, beautiful and depraved. That our guest was depraved I knew from her smile, from her perfume, from the particular way she had of glancing and of using her eyelashes, and from the tone in which she addressed my wife, a respectable woman. There was no need for her to tell me that she had run away from her husband, that he was old and tyrannical, that she was merry and kind. I understood everything at her first glance; there are few men in Europe who cannot recognise a woman of a certain temperament on sight.

'I did not know I had such a big nephew,' said my aunt, holding out her hand to me.

'And I didn't know I had such a pretty aunt,' said I.

We recommenced our supper. The cork flew with a pop from the second bottle of champagne, and my aunt drank half a glass at a draught. When my wife left the room for a moment she was under no restraint and finished the rest of it. The wine and the presence of the woman went to my head. Do you remember the words of the song:

> Eyes passionate and darkling,
> Eyes beautiful and sparkling,
> Oh, but I love you!
> Oh, but I fear you!

I do not remember what happened next. If anyone wants to know how love begins let him read romances and novels; I shall only say a little, and that in the words of the same foolish song:

> When I first saw you,
> Evil was the hour –

Everything went head over heels to the devil. I remember a terrible, mad hurricane that whirled me away like a leaf. For a long time it whirled me, and wiped off the earth my wife and my aunt and my strength. From a little station on the plains it cast me, as you see, on to this dark street.

Now tell me, what further misfortune could befall me?

The Malefactor

A TINY, very thin little peasant stood before the examining magistrate. He wore a striped shirt and patched trousers; his shaggy beard, his pockmarked face, his eyes scarcely visible under their bushy, overhanging brows gave him a harsh and forbidding expression, to which a mane of matted, unkempt hair added a spider-like ferocity. He was barefoot.

'Denis Grigorieff,' began the magistrate, 'come nearer and answer my questions. While patrolling the track on the seventh of last July, Ivan Akinfoff, the railroad watchman, found you at the one hundred and forty-first verst unscrewing one of the nuts that fasten the rails to the ties. Here is the nut you had when he arrested you. Is this true?'

'What's that?'

'Did everything happen as Akinfoff reports?'

'Yes; just as he reports.'

'Very well. Now, what was your object in unscrewing that nut?'

'What's that?'

'Stop your "What's that?" and answer my question; why did you unscrew that nut?'

'If I hadn't needed the nut I wouldn't have unscrewed it,' grunted Denis, glancing at the ceiling.

'What did you need it for?'

'What for? We make sinkers out of nuts.'

'Whom do you mean by "we"?'

'We – the people, the peasants of Klimoff.'

'Look here, man, no playing the idiot! Talk sense, and don't lie to me about sinkers!'

'I never lied in my life,' muttered Denis, blinking. 'How can one possibly fish without sinkers, your honour? If you baited your hook with a shiner or a roach, do you think it would sink to the bottom without a sinker? You tell me I am lying!' laughed Denis. 'A fine bait a shiner would make, floating on the top of the water! Bass and pike and eels always take ground bait; a floating bait would only be taken by a garfish, and they won't often take it. Anyway, we haven't any garfish in our river; they like the open.'

'Why are you talking to me about garfish?'

'What's that? Didn't you ask me about fishing? All the gentlemen with us fish like that. The smallest boy knows more than to fish without a sinker. Of course, there are some people who don't know anything, and they go fishing without sinkers. Fools obey no laws.'

'So you tell me you unscrewed this nut to use as a weight?'

'What else should I have unscrewed it for? To play knuckle-bones with?'

'But you might have made a weight out of a piece of lead or a bullet or a nail or something.'

'Lead does not grow on every bush; it has to be bought; and a nail wouldn't do. There is nothing so good to make a weight of as a nut. It is heavy and has a hole in it.'

'What a fool he is pretending to be! You act as if you were one day old or had just dropped from the clouds. Don't you see, you donkey, what the consequences of this unscrewing must be? If the watchman hadn't found you, one of the trains might have run off the track and killed everybody, and you would have killed them!'

'God forbid, your honour! Do you think we are wicked heathen? Praise be to God, kind master, not only have we never killed anybody, we have never even thought of it! Holy Mother preserve us and have mercy upon us! How can you say such things?'

Denis smirked and winked incredulously at the magistrate. 'Huh! For how many years has the whole village been unscrewing nuts, and not an accident yet? If I were to carry a rail away, or even to put a log across the track, then, perhaps, the train might upset, but, Lord! a nut – pooh!'

'But can't you understand that the nuts fasten the rails to the ties?'

'Yes, we understand that, and so we don't unscrew them all; we always leave some; we do it carefully; we understand.'

Denis yawned and made the sign of the cross over his mouth.

'A train ran off the track not far from here last year,' said the magistrate. 'Now I know why.'

'What did you say?'

'Now, I say, I know why that train ran off the track last year.'

'Yes; you have been educated to know these things, kind master; you can understand just why everything is; but that watchman is a peasant who doesn't know anything; he just grabbed me by the coat collar and dragged me away. One ought to judge first and drag afterward. But a peasant has the sense of a peasant. You might write down, your honour, that he hit me twice – in the mouth and in the chest.'

'Another nut was found when your house was searched. Where did you unscrew that one, and when?'

'Do you mean the nut that was lying under the little red chest?'

'I haven't any idea where it was lying, but it was found. Where did you unscrew it?'

'I didn't unscrew it; it was given to me by Ignashka, the son of one-eyed Simon. That is, I am speaking of the nut under the little chest; the one in the sleigh in the courtyard, Mitrofan and I unscrewed together.'

'Which Mitrofan?'

'Mitrofan Petroff. Haven't you heard of him? He's the man that makes fishing-nets and sells them to the gentlemen. He needs a lot of nuts in his business – a dozen to every net.'

'Listen! In Article 1081 of the Code it says that "Whoever intentionally commits an act of injury to a railroad, whereby an accident might result to the trains, and who knows that such an accident might result" – do you hear that? "who *knows*" – "shall be severely punished." You could not but have known what this unscrewing would lead to. The sentence is exile and hard labour.'

'Of course, you know that better than I do. We people live in darkness. How can we know such things?'

'You know all about it perfectly well. You are lying and shamming ignorance.'

'Why should I lie? Ask anybody in the village if you don't believe me. They never catch a thing but roach without a sinker; even gudgeons hardly ever bite unless you use one.'

'Now you are going to begin on those garfish again!' smiled the magistrate.

'We don't have garfish in our river. If we let the bait float on the top without a sinker we sometimes catch a perch, but not often.'

'Oh, stop talking!'

Silence fell. Denis stood first on one leg and then on the other and stared at the table, winking rapidly as if he saw the sun before his eyes and not a green tablecover. The magistrate was writing quickly.

'I shall have to arrest you and send you to prison.'

Denis stopped winking, raised his heavy eyebrows, and looked inquiringly at the magistrate.

'How do you mean – to prison? Your honour, I haven't time! I have to go to the fair to collect the three roubles that Gregory owes me for tallow.'

'Stop talking! Don't interrupt!'

'To prison! If there was any reason, of course I'd go, but, living as I do – what is it for? I haven't robbed anyone; I haven't even been fighting. If it's the payment of my rent you are thinking about, you mustn't believe what the bailiff says, your honour. Ask any one of the gentlemen; that bailiff is a thief, sir!'

'Stop talking!'

'I'll stop,' mumbled Denis. 'All the same, I'll swear under oath that the bailiff has muddled his books. There are three brothers in our family – Kuzma and Gregory and I – '

'You are interrupting me. Here, Simon!' called the magistrate, 'take this man away.'

'There are three brothers in our family,' murmured Denis as two strapping soldiers took hold of him and led him out of the room. 'I can't be responsible for my brother. Kuzma won't pay his debts, and I, Denis, have to suffer! You call yourselves judges! If our old master, the general, were alive he would teach you judges your business. You ought to be reasonable, and not condemn so wildly. Flog a man if he deserves it – '

Murder Will Out

BEHIND three native horses, preserving the strictest incognito, Peter Posudin was hurrying along by back roads to the little county town of N—, whither he had been summoned by an anonymous letter.

'I'm hidden; I've vanished like smoke – ' he mused, burying his face in the collar of his coat. 'Having hatched their dirty plots, those low brutes are now, no doubt, patting themselves on the back at the thought of how cleverly they have covered their tracks – ha! ha! I can just see their horror and surprise as, at the height of their triumph, they hear: "Bring Liapkin Tiapkin to me."* What a rumpus there will be! Ha! ha!'

When he had wearied of musing, Posudin entered into conversation with his driver. As a man will who has a thirst for renown, he first of all inquired about himself.

'Tell me, do you know who Posudin is?' he asked.

'How should I not know?' grinned the driver. 'We know who he is.'

'What makes you laugh?'

'It's so funny. To think of not knowing who Posudin is, when one knows every little clerk! That's what he's here for, to be known by everyone.'

'Very well – and what do you think of him? Is he a good man?'

'Not bad,' yawned the peasant. 'He's a good gentleman; he understands his business. It isn't two years yet since he was sent here, and he has already done things.'

'What has he done, exactly?'

'He has done a lot of good, the Lord bless him. He has brought the railroad in and has sent Hohrinkoff out of our county. That Hohrinkoff was too much; he was a rascal and a fox. The former ones have always played into his hand, but, when Posudin came, away went Hohrinkoff to the devil as if he had never existed. Yes, sir! Posudin you never could

* Liapkin Tiapkin: one of the characters in Gogol's *Inspector General*.

bribe – no, sir! If you were to give him a hundred, a thousand roubles, you couldn't get him to saddle his conscience with a sin. No, indeed!'

'Thank Heaven, at least I am understood in that quarter!' exulted Posudin. 'That's splendid!'

'He's a well-mannered gentleman. Some of our men went to him once with some grievances and he treated them exactly as if they had been gentlemen. He shook hands with them all and said: "Please be seated." He's a quick, hot-headed kind of a gentleman; he never takes time to talk quietly; it's always – snort! snort! As for walking at a foot-pace, Lord, no! He's always on the run – on the run. Our men had hardly time to get out a word before he had called out: "My carriage!" and had come straight over here. He came, and settled everything, and never even took a copeck. He's a thousand times better than the last one, though, of course, that one was good, too. He was fine and important-looking, and no one in the whole county could shout louder than he could. When he was on the road you could hear him for ten miles, but when it comes to business the present one is a thousand times sharper. The present one has a brain in his head one hundred times as large as the other. He's a fine man in every way; there's only one trouble about him – he's a drunkard!'

'The devil!' thought Posudin.

'How do you know,' he asked, 'that I – that he is a drunkard?'

'Oh, of course, your honour, I have never seen him drunk myself. I'll not say what's not true, but people have told me – and they haven't seen him drunk, either; but that is what is said about him. In public, or when he is visiting, or at a ball, or in company he never drinks; it's at home that he soaks. He gets up in the morning, rubs his eyes, and his first thought is vodka! His valet brings him one glass and he at once asks for another, and so he keeps pouring it down all day. And I'll tell you a funny thing: for all that drinking he never turns a hair! He must know how to keep an eye on himself. When our Hohrinkoff used to drink, not only the people, even the dogs would howl; but Posudin – his nose doesn't even turn red! He shuts himself up in his study and laps. He has arranged a little kind of box on his table with a tube, so that no one can know what he's up to, and this box he keeps full of vodka. All one has to do is to stoop down to the little tube, suck, and get drunk. And out driving, too, in his portfolio – '

'How do they know that?' thought the horror-stricken Posudin. 'Good Lord, even that is known! How perfectly awful!'

'And then, with the female sex, too, he's a rascal!' The driver laughed and wagged his head. 'It's a scandal, it is! He has a bunch of ten of them.

Two of them live in his house. One is Nastasia Ivanovna; he has her for a sort of a housekeeper; another is – what the devil is her name? – oh, yes, Liudmila Semionovna. She's, as it were, his secretary. The head of them all is Nastasia. She has a great deal of power; people aren't nearly as much afraid of him as they are of her. Ha! ha! The third scatterbrain lives on Katchalna Street. It's disgraceful.'

'He even knows them by name,' thought Posudin, turning scarlet. 'And who is this that knows? A peasant, a carrier who has never even been to the city. Oh, how abominable! How disgusting! How vulgar!'

'How did you find all this out?' he asked irritably.

'People have told me. I haven't seen it myself, but I have heard of it from people. Is it so hard to find out? You can't stop the mouth of a valet or a coachman, and then, probably, Nastasia herself goes up and down all the side streets boasting of her good luck to the women. No one can hide from human eyes. Another thing, this Posudin has got a way now of making his trips of inspection in secret. In the old days, when he decided to go anywhere, he used to make it known a month beforehand, and there'd be such a rowing and thundering and ringing when he went – the Lord preserve us! He'd have men galloping ahead and men galloping behind and men galloping on either side. When he reached the place he was bound for he would take a nap and eat and drink his fill and then begin bawling his official business. He'd bawl and stamp his feet and then take another nap, and go back in the same way he came. But now when anything comes to his ears he watches for a chance to go off like a flash, secretly, so that no one shall see or know. Oh, it's a joke! He slips out of his house, so the officials won't see him, and into the train. When he reaches the station he's going to he doesn't take post-horses or anything high class but hustles round and hires some peasant to drive him. He wraps himself all up like a woman and growls all the way like an old hound, so that his voice won't be recognised. You'd split your sides laughing to hear people tell of it. The donkey drives along and thinks no one can tell who he is. But anyone can recognise him who has any sense – bah!'

'How do they recognise him?'

'It's very easy. In the old days, when our Hohrinkoff used to travel we used to know him by his heavy hands. If the man you were driving hit you on the mouth it meant that it was Hohrinkoff. But one can tell it's Posudin at first sight. A simple passenger acts simply, but Posudin isn't the man to care for simplicity. When he reaches, we'll say, a post-house, he begins right away. It's either too smelly or too hot or too cold; he sends for young chickens and fruits and jams of all kinds. That's how he's recognised at the post-houses; if anyone asks for young chickens and fruit in winter, that's Posudin. If anyone carefully says, "My dear fellow," and then makes everyone chase around on all sorts of fool's errands, you can swear to it it's Posudin. And he doesn't smell like other people, and he has his own way of lying down to sleep. At post-houses he lies down on the sofa, squirts scent all about him, and orders three candles to be put by his pillow. Then he lies down and reads papers. Even a cat, let alone a person, who sees that can tell who the man is.'

'That's right,' thought Posudin. 'Why didn't I know that before?'

'But, if necessary, he can be recognised without the fruit and the chickens. Everything is known by telegraph. He can muffle up his face there and hide himself all he likes; they know here that he's coming. They're expecting him. Before Posudin has so much as left home, here, by your leave, everything is ready for him! He comes to nab some man on the spot and arrest him, or to discharge another, and here they are laughing at him. "Yes, your Excellency," they say, "even though you did come unexpectedly, see, everything is in order!" He turns round and round and finally goes off the way he came. Yes, and he even praises everyone and shakes hands all round and begs pardon for having disturbed us. That's a fact! Didn't you know that? Ho! ho! Your Excellency, we people are sharp here. Every one of us is sharp. It's a pleasure to see what devils we are! Take, for instance, what happened today. As I was driving along this morning with an empty wagon, I saw the Jew restaurant keeper come flying toward me. "Where are you going, your Jewish honour?" says I. "I'm taking some wine and some delicacies to the town of N——" says he. "They're expecting Posudin there today." Wasn't that clever? And Posudin, perhaps, was only just getting ready to start, and perhaps he was muffling up his face so that no one should know him. Perhaps he is on his way now and is thinking that no one knows he is coming; and yet there are the wine and the salmon and the cheese all ready for him. What do you think of that? He is thinking as he drives: "Now, boys, you'll catch it!" And little the boys are caring. They've hidden everything long ago.'

'Turn back!' cried Posudin hoarsely. 'Turn round and drive back, you beast!'

And the astonished driver turned round and drove back.

The Trousseau

MANY are the houses I have seen in my day – big ones and little ones, stone ones and wooden ones, old ones and new ones, but, more deeply than any I have seen, one has engraved itself upon my memory.

It is not really a house, but a tiny cottage of one low storey and three windows, and bears a strong resemblance to a little, old, hunchbacked woman in a nightcap. Its stuccoed walls are painted white, the roof is of tiles and the chimney dilapidated, and it is all smothered in the foliage of mulberries, acacias, and poplar trees planted there by the grandparents and great-grandparents of the present inhabitants. This dense mass of verdure completely hides it from view but does not prevent it from considering itself a little town house. Alongside its broad garden lie other broad, green gardens, and the result is named Moscow Street.

The shutters of the little house are always closed; its inhabitants do not need light. They have no use for it. The windows are never opened because its inmates dislike fresh air. People living among mulberry trees, acacias, and burdocks are indifferent to nature; it is only to summer visitors that God has vouchsafed a capacity for appreciating her beauties. In regard to them the rest of mankind stagnates in profoundest ignorance. People do not value what they are rich in. We do not care for what we possess; we even dislike it. Outside the house lay an earthly paradise of verdure inhabited by happy birds; inside, alas! in summer it was stifling and hot and in winter warm as in a Turkish bath, and tedious, oh, so tedious!

I first visited the little house on business many years ago. I brought a message from its owner, Colonel Tchikamassoff, to his wife and daughter. I remember the first visit perfectly. I could never forget it.

Picture to yourself a stout little lady of forty years looking at you with surprise and fear as you enter the parlour from the hall. You are a 'strange guest,' a 'young man,' and this alone is enough to arouse astonishment and terror. You do not carry a cudgel or an axe or a revolver, and you are smiling pleasantly, but you are received with trepidation.

'Whom have I the honour and pleasure of meeting?' asks the little lady in a trembling voice, and you know her to be the wife of Tchikamassoff.

You introduce yourself and explain why you have come. Surprise and fear end in a shrill and joyful exclamation which echoes from the hall to the parlour, from the parlour to the dining-room, from the dining-room to the kitchen, and so into the very cellar. The whole house is soon filled with joyous little exclamations in various keys. Five minutes later, as you sit in the parlour on a large, soft, warm sofa, you can hear the whole of Moscow Street exclaiming.

The air smelled of moth balls and of a pair of new kid shoes that lay wrapped in a little cloth on a chair beside me. On the window-sills scraps of muslin lay among the geranium pots. Over them crawled lazy flies. On the wall hung an oil-portrait of a bishop, covered with glass, of which one corner was broken. Next to the bishop hung a row of ancestors with lemon-yellow, gypsy-looking faces. On the table lay a thimble, a spool of thread, and a half-darned stocking; on the floor lay dress patterns and a half-finished black blouse. In the next room two flustered and startled old women were hastily gathering up scraps of material from the floor.

'You must forgive this dreadful disorder,' said the old lady.

As she talked with me she glanced in confusion at the door behind which the old women were still picking up the scraps of cloth. The door, too, seemed embarrassed, and now opened a few inches, now shut again.

'What do you want?' asked Madame Tchikamassoff of the door.

'*Où est mon cravate, lequel mon père m'avait envoyé de Koursk?*' asked a soft little female voice behind the door.

'*Ah, est ce-que Marie, que* – oh, how can you? – *nous avons donc chez nous un homme très peu connu par nous* – ask Lukeria.'

'How well we talk French!' I read in Madame Tchikamassoff's eyes as she blushed with pleasure.

The door soon opened and there appeared a tall, thin girl of nineteen, in a muslin dress with a gold belt, from which hung, I remember, a mother-of-pearl fan. She came in, sat down, and blushed. First her long, slightly freckled nose blushed; from there the colour spread to her eyes and from her eyes to her temples.

'My daughter,' said Madame Tchikamassoff; 'and this, Manetchka, is the young man who – '

I introduced myself and expressed my surprise at seeing so many scraps of cloth about. Mother and daughter cast down their eyes.

'We had the fair here on Ascension Day,' said the mother, 'and we always buy all our materials then and sew all the rest of the year until the next fair. We never give our sewing out. My Peter does not make very much and we can't allow ourselves any luxury. We have to do our own sewing.'

'But who wears such quantities of clothes? There are only two of you!'

'Oh, do you think we shall wear them? They are not to wear; this is – a trousseau!'

'Oh, maman, how can you? What are you saying?' cried the daughter, flushing. 'He might really think – I shall never marry! Never!'

She spoke thus, but at the very word 'marry' her eyes sparkled.

Tea was brought, with biscuits and jam and butter, and then I was treated to raspberries and cream. At seven we had a supper of six courses, and during supper I heard a loud yawn from the next room. I glanced at the door with surprise; only a man could have yawned like that.

'That is Gregory, my husband's brother,' Madame Tchikamassoff explained, seeing my surprise. 'He has been living with us since last year. You must excuse him, he can't come out to see you; he is a great recluse and is afraid of strangers. He is planning to enter a monastery. His feelings were very much hurt when in the service, and so, from mortification – '

After supper Madame Tchikamassoff showed me a stole which Gregory had embroidered as an offering for the church. Manetchka cast aside her timidity for a moment and showed me a tobacco pouch which she had embroidered for her papa. When I pretended to be thunderstruck by her work she blushed and whispered something in her mother's ear. The mother beamed and invited me to come with her into the linen-closet. There I found five large chests and a great quantity of small trunks and boxes.

'This is – the trousseau!' the mother whispered. 'We made it all ourselves.'

While still looking at these enormous chests, I began to take leave of my hospitable hostesses. They made me promise to come again someday.

I kept this promise seven years later, when I was sent to the little town as an adviser in a lawsuit. As I entered the familiar cottage I heard the same exclamations; they recognised me! Of course they did! My first visit had been a great event in their lives, and events, when they are few and far between, are long remembered. The mother, stouter than ever and now growing grey, was on the floor cutting out some blue material; the daughter was sitting on the sofa embroidering. There were the same scraps of cloth, the same smell of moth balls, the same portrait with the broken corner.

But there were changes, nevertheless. A portrait of Peter Tchikamassoff hung beside that of the bishop, and the ladies were in mourning. He had died one week after his promotion to the rank of general.

We recalled old times and the general's widow began to weep.

'We have had a great sorrow,' she said. 'Peter – have you heard it? – is no longer with us. We are all alone now and have to shift for ourselves. Gregory is still alive, but we can't say anything good of him. He couldn't get into the monastery on account of – of drink, and he drinks more than ever now, from grief. I am going to the marshal very soon to lodge a complaint against him. Only think, he has opened the chests several times and – and has taken out Manetchka's trousseau and given it away to the pilgrims! He has taken all there was in two chests! If this goes on my Manetchka will be left with no trousseau at all.'

'What are you saying, mother?' cried Manetchka in confusion. 'He might really think that – I shall never, never be married!'

Manetchka looked upward at the ceiling with hope and inspiration in her eyes, and it was clear that she did not believe what she had said.

A little man darted into the hall and slipped by like a mouse. He was bald and wore a brown coat and goloshes instead of boots. 'Probably Gregory,' I thought.

I looked at the mother and daughter. Both had aged greatly. The hair of the mother was streaked with silver, and the daughter had faded and drooped, so that the mother now looked not more than five years older than her child.

'I am going to the marshal soon,' said the old lady, forgetting that she had already spoken of this. 'I want to lodge a complaint against Gregory. He takes everything that we sew and gives it away for the salvation of souls. My Manetchka has been left without a trousseau!'

Manetchka blushed, but this time she did not utter a word.

'We shall have to make it all over again, and we are not very rich; we are all alone now, she and I.'

'We are all alone,' Manetchka repeated.

Last year fate again took me to the little house. Going into the parlour, I saw the old lady Tchikamassoff. She was dressed all in black, and was sitting on the sofa and sewing. By her side sat a little old man in a brown coat with goloshes instead of boots. At the sight of me he jumped up and ran out of the room.

In answer to my greeting the little old lady smiled and said: '*Je suis charmée de vous revoir, monsieur*.'

'What are you sewing?' I asked after a pause.

'This is a chemise,' she answered. 'When it is finished I shall take it to the priest's house or else Gregory will carry it off. I hide everything now at the priest's,' she said in a whisper. And, glancing at a picture of her daughter that stood on the table before her, she sighed and said:

'You see, we are all alone now.'

But where was the daughter? Where was Manetchka? I did not ask. I did not want to ask the old lady dressed in deep mourning, and during all my visit in the little house and while I was afterward taking my leave, no Manetchka came in to see me, neither did I hear her voice nor her light, timid step. I understood now, and my heart grew sad.

The Decoration

Leo Pustiakoff, a teacher in a military school, lived next door to his friend Lieutenant Ledentsoff. Toward him he bent his steps one New Year's morning.

'The thing is this, Grisha,' he said after the customary New Year's greetings had passed between them, 'I wouldn't trouble you unless it were on very important business. Won't you please lend me your Order of St Stanislas for today? You see, I am dining at Spitchkin, the merchant's; you know what that old wretch Spitchkin is; he simply worships a decoration, and anyone who doesn't sport something round his neck or in his buttonhole is pretty nearly a scoundrel in his opinion, Besides, he has two daughters, Anastasia, you know, and Zina. I ask you as a friend – you understand, don't you, old man? Let me have it, I implore you!'

Pustiakoff uttered all this stammering and blushing and glancing apprehensively at the door. The lieutenant scolded a bit and then gave his consent.

At two o'clock Pustiakoff drove to the Spitchkin's in a cab, and, unbuttoning his fur coat as he drove, looked down at his chest. There shone the gold and gleamed the enamel of the borrowed decoration.

'Somehow, one seems to feel more self-respecting,' thought the teacher, clearing his throat. 'Here's a trifle not worth more than five roubles, and yet what a furor it will create!'

On reaching Spitchkin's house he threw open his coat and slowly paid off the cabman. The man, so it seemed to him, was petrified at the sight of his epaulets, his buttons, and his decoration. Pustiakoff coughed with self-satisfaction and entered the house. As he took off his coat in the hall he looked into the dining-room. There, at the long table, sat fifteen people at dinner. He heard talking and the clattering of dishes.

'Who rang the bell?' he heard the host ask. 'Why, it's you, Pustiakoff! Come in! You're a little bit late, but no matter; we have only just sat down.'

Pustiakoff puffed out his chest, threw up his head, and, rubbing his hands together, entered the room. But there something perfectly terrible met his sight. At the table next to Zina sat his colleague, the French teacher Tremblant! To let the Frenchman see the decoration would be to expose himself to a host of the most disagreeable questions, to disgrace himself for ever, to ruin his reputation. Pustiakoff's first impulse was to tear it off or else to rush from the room, but it was tightly sewn on, and retreat was now out of the question. Hastily covering the decoration with his right hand, he bowed awkwardly to the company and, without shaking hands with anyone, dropped heavily into an empty chair. This happened to be exactly opposite his colleague, the Frenchman.

'He must have been drinking,' thought Spitchkin, seeing him overwhelmed with confusion.

A plate of soup was put before Pustiakoff. He took up his spoon with his left hand, but, remembering that one can't eat with one's left hand in polite society, he explained that he had already had dinner and was not at all hungry.

'*Merci* – I – I have already eaten,' he stammered. 'I went to call on my uncle Elegeff the priest, and he begged me – to – to have dinner.'

The soul of Pustiakoff was filled with agony and vexation, his soup exhaled the most delicious aroma, and an extraordinarily appetising steam rose from the boiled sturgeon. The teacher tried to set his right hand free by covering the decoration with his left, but this was too inconvenient.

'They would be sure to catch sight of it,' he thought, 'and my arm would be stretched right across my chest as if I were about to sing a song. Lord! If only this meal might soon be over! I shall go and have dinner at the tavern.'

At the end of the third course he glanced timidly out of the corner of his eye at the Frenchman. For some reason Tremblant, too, was overcome with embarrassment; he kept looking at him and was not eating anything, either. As their glances met they became still more confused and dropped their eyes to their empty plates.

'He must have seen it, the beast!' thought Pustiakoff. 'I can see by his ugly face that he has! The wretch is a sneak and will report it to the director tomorrow.'

The hosts and their guests finished a fourth course and then, as fate would have it, a fifth.

A tall man with wide, hairy nostrils, a hooked nose, and eyes that were by nature half closed rose from his seat. He smoothed his hair and began:

'I – er – I – er – propose that we drink to the health of the ladies here present!'

The diners rose noisily and took up their glasses. A mighty 'hurrah!' filled the house. The ladies smiled and held out their glasses. Pustiakoff got up and took his in his left hand.

'Pustiakoff, may I trouble you to pass this to the lady next you?' said some man, handing him a glass. 'Make her drink it!'

This time, to his unspeakable horror, Pustiakoff found himself obliged to bring his right hand into action. The decoration, with its crumpled red ribbon, glittered as it saw the light at last. The teacher turned pale, dropped his head, and threw a terrified glance in the direction of the Frenchman. The latter was looking at him with wondering, curious eyes. A sly smile curved his lips and the embarrassment slowly faded from his face.

'Monsieur Tremblant,' said the host, 'pass the bottle, if you please!'

Tremblant stretched out his hand irresolutely toward the bottle, and – oh, rapture! Pustiakoff saw a decoration on his breast! And it was not just a plain St Stanislas, it was actually the Order of St Anne! So the Frenchman, too, had been duping them! Pustiakoff collapsed in his chair and laughed with delight. There was no need now to conceal his decoration! Both were guilty of the same sin; neither could give the other away.

'Ah-hem!' roared Spitchkin as his eyes caught the Order of St Stanislas on the teacher's breast.

'Yes,' said Pustiakoff, 'it's a strange thing, Tremblant, how few presentations were made these holidays. You and I are the only ones of all that crowd that have been decorated. A re-mark-able thing!'

Tremblant nodded gaily and proudly exhibited the left lapel of his coat on which flaunted the Order of St Anne.

After dinner Pustiakoff made the round of all the rooms and showed his decoration to the young ladies. His heart was easy and light even if hunger did pinch him a bit at the waistline.

'If I had only known,' he thought, looking enviously at Tremblant chatting with Spitchkin on the subject of decorations, 'I would have gone higher and swiped a Vladimir. Oh, why didn't I have more sense!'

This was the only thought that tormented him. Otherwise he was perfectly happy.

The Man in a Case

ON THE OUTSKIRTS of the village of Mironitski, in a shed belonging to the bailiff Prokofi, some belated huntsmen were encamped for the night. There were two of them: the veterinary surgeon Ivan Ivanitch and the schoolteacher Burkin. Ivan Ivanitch had a rather strange, hyphenated surname, Tchimsha-Himalaiski, which did not suit him at all, and so he was known all over the province simply by his two Christian names. He lived on a stud-farm near the town and had now come out hunting to get a breath of fresh air. Burkin, the school-teacher, had long been at home in this neighbourhood, for he came every year as the guest of Count P—.

They were not asleep. Ivan Ivanitch, a tall, spare old man with a long moustache, sat at the door of the shed, with the moon shining on him, smoking his pipe. Burkin lay inside on the hay and was invisible in the shadows.

They were telling stories. Among other things, they spoke of Mavra, the bailiff's wife, a healthy, intelligent woman who had never in her life been outside of her native village and who had never seen the town nor the railway; they remembered that she had sat beside the stove now for the last ten years, never going out into the street except after nightfall.

'There is nothing so very surprising in that,' said Burkin. 'There are not a few people in this world who, like hermit crabs and snails, are always trying to retire into their shells. Perhaps this is a manifestation of atavism, a harking back to the time when man's forebears were not yet gregarious animals but lived alone in their dens, or perhaps it is simply one of the many phases of human character – who can say? I am not an anthropologist and it is not my business to meddle with such questions; I only mean to say that people like Mavra are not an uncommon phenomenon. Here! We don't have to go far to seek an illustration. Two months ago a certain Byelinkoff died in our town, a colleague of mine, a teacher of Greek. You must have heard of him. He was remarkable for one thing: no matter how fine the weather was, he always went out in goloshes, carrying an umbrella and wearing a warm, wadded overcoat. And his umbrella he always kept in a case and his watch was in a case of grey chamois, and when he took out his penknife to sharpen a pencil that, too, was in a little case. Even his face seemed to be in a case, for he always kept it concealed behind the turned-up collar of his coat. He wore dark spectacles and a warm waistcoat, and he kept cotton-wool in his ears and he had the hood raised whenever he got into a cab. In a word, one saw in this man a perpetual and irresistible longing to wrap some covering around himself – one might call it a case – which would isolate him from external impressions. Reality chafed and alarmed him and kept him in a state of perpetual apprehension, and it was, perhaps, to justify his timidity and his aversion to the present that he always exalted the past and things which had never existed. The ancient languages which he taught were at bottom the goloshes and umbrella behind which he hid himself from the realities of existence.

' "Oh, how musical, how beautiful is the Greek tongue!" he would cry with a beaming look, and, as if in proof of what he had said, he would half shut his eyes, hold up one finger, and pronounce the word "anthropos"!

'And his opinions, too, Byelinkoff tried to confine in a case. Only bulletins and newspaper articles in which something was prohibited were clear to him. If he saw a bulletin forbidding the scholars to go out on the street after nine o'clock, or if he read an article enjoining him from carnal love, that was fixed and clear to him – and basta! For to him there was always an element of doubt, something unspoken and confused, concealed in licence and liberty of action. When it was permitted to start a dramatic or reading club in the town he would shake his head and say softly:

' "That is all very well and very fine, but I shouldn't wonder if something unpleasant would come of it."

'Every transgression and deviation from the right plunged him into dejection, although one wondered what business it was of his. If one of his colleagues came late to prayers, or if he heard rumours of some prank of the schoolboys, or if one of the lady superintendents was seen late at night with an officer, he would grow tremendously excited and always insist that something unpleasant would come of it. At the teachers' meetings he used to drive us absolutely mad by his prudence and his scruples and his absolutely case-like reflections. "Oh," he would cry, "the boys and girls in the school behave so very badly and make such a noise in the classrooms! Oh, what if this should reach the governor's ears, and what if something unpleasant should come of it? If only Petroff could be expelled from the second class and Yegorieff from the fourth, how good it would be!" And what was the result? We would grow so oppressed with his sighing and his moaning and his dark spectacles on his white face that we would give in – give Petroff and Yegorieff bad-conduct marks, put them under arrest, and finally expel them.

'He had a strange habit – he used to make the tour of our rooms. He would come into a master's room and just sit and say nothing, as if he were looking for something. He would sit like that for an hour or so and then would go out. This he called "keeping on good terms with his comrades", but it was plainly a heavy burden for him to come and sit with us, and he only did it because he considered it his duty as our comrade. All of us teachers were afraid of him. Even the director feared him. Our teachers are all a thoughtful and thoroughly steady lot, brought up on Turgenieff and Shedrin, and yet this man, with his goloshes and his umbrella, held the whole school in the hollow of his hand for fifteen years. The whole school, did I say? The whole town! The ladies did not dare to get up little plays on Saturday evenings for fear he should hear of it, and the clergy were ashamed to eat meat and play cards in his presence. Under the influence of men like Byelinkoff the people of our town in the last ten or fifteen years have begun to fear everything. They are afraid of sending letters, of making acquaintances, of speaking aloud, of reading books, of helping or teaching the poor – '

Ivan Ivanitch coughed as a sign that he wanted to make a remark, but he first finished his pipe, then gazed at the moon, and then at last, pausing at intervals, said:

'Yes, they are thoughtful and steady; they read Shedrin and Turgenieff and others, and therefore they have submitted patiently – that is just it.'

'Byelinkoff lived in the same house that I did,' Durkin went on, 'on the same floor. His door was opposite mine. We often met, and I was familiar with his domestic life. It was the same old story when he was at home. He wore a dressing-gown and a nightcap and had shutters to his windows and bolts to his doors – a perfect array of restraints and restrictions and of "oh-something-unpleasant-might-come-of-its". Lenten fare was bad for the health, but to eat flesh was impossible because somebody might say that Byelinkoff did not keep the fasts; therefore he ate perch fried in butter, which was not Lenten fare, but neither could it be called meat. He would not keep a woman servant for fear that people might think ill of him, so he employed as a cook an old man named Afanasi, a besotted semi-idiot of sixty who had once been an officer's servant and could cook after a fashion. This Afanasi would stand at the door with folded arms, sigh deeply, and always mutter one and the same thing:

' "There's a whole lot of *them* out today!"

'Byelinkoff's bedroom was like a little box and curtains hung round his bed. When he went to sleep he would pull the blankets over his head. The room would be stuffy and hot, the wind rattle the closed doors and rumble in the stove, and sighs, ominous sighs, would be heard from the kitchen; and he would shake under his bedclothes. He was afraid that something unpleasant might come of it – that Afanasi might murder him, that burglars might break in. All night he would be a prey to alarming dreams, and in the morning, as we walked to the school together, he would be melancholy and pale, and one could see that the crowded school toward which he was going dismayed him and was repugnant to his whole being, and that it was burdensome for a man of his solitary disposition to be walking beside me.

' "There is so much noise in the classrooms," he would say as if seeking an explanation of his depression.

'And think of it, this teacher of Greek, this man in a case, once very nearly got married!'

Ivan Ivanitch looked quickly round into the shed and said:

'You're joking!'

'Yes, he nearly got married, strange as it may appear. A new teacher of history and geography was appointed to our school, a certain Little Russian named Kovalenko. He did not come alone but brought his sister Varenka with him. He was young and tall and dark, with huge hands and a face from which it could be guessed that he possessed a bass voice. As a matter of fact, when he spoke his voice did sound as if it were coming out of a barrel – boo – boo – boo – . As for her, she was no longer young, thirty perhaps, but she was tall, too, and graceful, dark-eyed and red-cheeked – a sugar-plum of a girl, and so boisterous and jolly! She was always singing Little Russian songs and ha–ha-ing. At the slightest provocation she would break into loud peals of laughter – ha! ha! ha! I remember the first time we met the Kovalenkos; it was at a birthday party at the director's. Among the stern, tiresome teachers who go to birthday parties out of a sense of duty, we suddenly beheld a new Aphrodite risen from the waves, strolling about with her arms akimbo, laughing, singing, and dancing. She sang "The Wind Blows" with feeling, and then another song, and then another, and fascinated us all, even Byelinkoff. He sat down beside her and said with a sweet smile:

' "The Little Russian tongue with its tenderness and pleasant sonorousness reminds me of ancient Greek."

'This flattered her, and she began earnestly and with feeling to tell him that she had a farm in the province of Gadiatch, that her mamma lived there and that there were such pears and such melons there and such inns! Little Russians call gourds "inns", and make a soup out of the little red ones and the little blue ones that is "so good, so good it is simply – awful!"

'We listened and listened, and the same thought suddenly crossed the minds of all of us.

' "How nice it would be to make a match between them!" said the director's wife to me quietly.

'For some reason we all remembered that our Byelinkoff was unmarried, and it now seemed strange to us that until this moment we had not noticed, had somehow quite overlooked this important detail in his life. By the way, how does he regard women? we asked ourselves. How does he solve this daily problem? This had not interested us before at all; perhaps we had not even entertained the idea that a man who wore goloshes in all weathers and slept behind bed curtains could possibly fall in love.

' "He is already long past forty, but she is thirty herself," the director's wife expressed her opinion. "I think she would marry him."

'How many wrong and foolish deeds are committed in our country towns because we are bored! What need was there to have tried to marry off Byelinkoff, whom one could not even conceive of as being married? The director's wife and the inspector's wife and all the ladies of our school brightened and bloomed as if they had suddenly discovered the object of their existence. The director's wife takes a box at the theatre, and, behold! in it sits Varenka waving a fan, radiant and happy, and beside her is Byelinkoff, small and depressed, as if they had pulled him out of his room with a pair of pincers. I give an evening party, and the ladies insist that I shall invite both Byelinkoff and Varenka. In a word, the mills were grinding. It appeared that Varenka was not averse to marriage. It was not particularly cheerful for her living at her brother's, for they scolded and squabbled the day long. Here's a picture for you: Kovalenko is stalking down the street, a tall, lusty fellow in an embroidered shirt with his forelock hanging down over his forehead from under the brim of his cap. In one hand he carries a bundle of books, in the other a thick, knotted stick. Behind him walks his sister, also carrying books.

' "But you haven't read it, Mihailik!" she argues loudly. "I tell you, I swear to you, you haven't read it at all!"

' "But I tell you I have read it!" shouts Kovalenko, rattling his stick on the sidewalk.

' "Oh, Lord have mercy, Mintchik! What are you getting so angry about; does it matter?"

' "But I tell you that I have read it!" shouts Kovalenko still louder.

'And at home, as soon as an outsider came in they would open fire at each other. A life like that was probably growing wearisome for her; she wanted a nook of her own; and then her age should be taken into account; at her years there's little time for picking and choosing – a woman takes what she can get, even if the man be a teacher of Greek. And, as a matter of fact, the majority of our young ladies will marry whom they can, only to get married. Well, be it as it may, Varenka began to show our Byelinkoff marked favour.

'And what about Byelinkoff? He called on the Kovalenkos as he did on the rest of us. He would go to their rooms and sit and say nothing. He would say nothing, but Varenka would sing "The Wind Blows" for him, or gaze at him pensively out of her dark eyes, or suddenly break into peals of merry laughter – ha! ha! ha!

'In affairs of the heart, and especially in marriage, a large part is played by suggestion. Everyone – both the ladies and Byelinkoff's colleagues – all began to assure him that he ought to get married, that there was nothing for him to do but to marry. We all congratulated him and said all sorts of silly things with grave faces – that marriage was a serious step, and so forth. Besides that, Varenka was pretty and attractive; she was the daughter of a state councillor and owned a farm of her own; and, above all, she was the first woman who had treated him kindly and affectionately. His head was turned and he fancied that he really must marry.'

'Now would have been the time to get rid of his goloshes and his umbrella,' said Ivan Ivanitch.

'Will you believe it? That proved to be impossible. He put a photograph of Varenka on his table, and kept coming to me and talking to me about Varenka and family life, and about what a serious step marriage was; he was much at the Kovalenkos, but he did not change his way of living one atom. On the contrary, his resolve to get married affected him painfully; he grew thin and pale and seemed to shrink still farther into his case.

' "I like Miss Varenka," he said to me once with a wry smile, "and I know every man ought to marry, but – all this has happened so suddenly; I must think it over a bit."

' "What is there to think over?" I answered. "Marry her! That's all there is to it."

' "No, marriage is a serious step; one must first weigh the consequences and duties and responsibilities – so that nothing unpleasant shall come of it. All this worries me so that I can't sleep any more at night. And, to tell you the truth, I am alarmed: she and her brother have such a queer way of thinking; they reason somehow so strangely, and she has a very bold character. One might marry her and, before one knew it, get mixed up in some scandal."

'And so he did not propose, but still kept putting it off, to the deep chagrin of the director's wife and of all of our ladies; he still kept weighing those duties and responsibilities, though he went walking every day with Varenka, thinking, no doubt, that this was due to a man placed as he was. He still kept coming to me to discuss family life.

'But in all probability he would have proposed at last, and one of those bad and foolish matches would have been consummated, as so many thousands are, simply because people have nothing better to do with themselves, had we not been suddenly overwhelmed by a colossal scandal.

'I must tell you that Varenka's brother could not abide Byelinkoff.

' "I can't understand," he would say to us with a shrug of his shoulders, "I can't imagine how you can stomach that sneak with his horrid face. Oh, friends, how can you live here? Your whole atmosphere here is stifling and nauseating. Are you instructors and teachers? No, you are sycophants, and this isn't a temple of learning; it's a detective office, stinking as sour as a police court. No, brothers, I'm going to stay here a little while longer, and then I'm going back to my farm to catch crawfish and teach young Little Russians. I am going, and you can stay here with your Judas."

'Or else he would laugh and laugh till the tears rolled down his cheeks, now in a deep voice, now in a high squeaky one, and demand of me, spreading out his hands:

' "What does he sit in my room for? What is he after? He just sits and stares."

'He even called Byelinkoff "the spider", and, of course, we avoided mentioning to him that his sister was thinking of marrying this "spider". When the director's wife once hinted to him that it would be a good idea to settle his sister with such a steady, universally respected man as Byelinkoff he frowned and growled:

' "That's none of my business. Let her marry a reptile if she likes. I can't endure interfering in other people's affairs."

'And now listen to what followed. Some wag made a caricature of Byelinkoff in goloshes and cotton trousers, holding up an umbrella, with Varenka on his arm. Underneath was written: "The Amorous Anthropos." His expression was caught to perfection. The artist must have worked more nights than one, for every teacher in our school, every teacher in the seminary, and every official received a copy. Byelinkoff got one, too. The caricature made the most painful impression on him.

'We were coming out of our house together. It was on a Sunday, the first of May, and all of us, teachers and pupils, had agreed to meet at the school and from there walk out beyond the town into the woods. So we came out together, and his face was absolutely green; he looked like a thunder-cloud.

' "What bad, what unkind people there are!" he burst out, and his lips quivered.

'I really felt sorry for him. As we walked along, we suddenly saw Kovalenko riding toward us on a bicycle, followed by Varenka, also on a bicycle. She was scarlet and dusty, but merry and gay nevertheless.

' "We are going on ahead!" she cried. "This weather is so glorious, so glorious, it's simply awful!"

'And they disappeared from view.

'Our Byelinkoff's face turned from green to white, and he seemed paralysed. He stopped and looked at me.

' "Allow me, what do I see?" he asked. "Or does my eyesight deceive me? Is it proper for schoolteachers and women to ride bicycles?"

' "What is there improper about it?" said I. "Let them ride to their hearts' content."

' "But how is it possible?" he shrieked, stupefied by my calmness. "What are you saying?"

'And he was so shocked that he did not want to go on any farther, but turned and went home.

'Next day he rubbed his hands nervously all the time and trembled, and we could see from his face that he was not well. He left his work – the first time in his life that this had happened to him – and did not come to dinner. Toward evening he dressed himself warmly, although the weather was now quite summer-like, and crawled over to the Kovalenkos. Varenka was not at home; he found her brother alone.

' "Sit down," said Kovalenko coldly and frowned. He looked sleepy; he had just had a nap after his dinner and was in a very bad humour.

'Byelinkoff sat for ten minutes in silence and then said:

' "I have come to you to relieve my mind. I am very, very much grieved. Some lampooner has made a picture of myself and a person who is near to us both in a ridiculous position. I consider it my duty to assure you that I have had nothing to do with this; I have never given any occasion for such a jest; I have always behaved with perfect propriety all the time."

'Kovalenko sat moodily without saying a word. Byelinkoff waited a few minutes and then went on in a sad, low voice:

' "And I have something else to say to you. I have been a teacher for many years, and your career is just beginning: I consider it my duty as an older man to give you a word of warning. You ride the bicycle – now, this amusement is quite improper for a teacher of the young."

' "Why?" asked Kovalenko in a deep voice.

' "Need I really explain that to you, Kovalenko? Isn't it obvious? If the master goes about on a bicycle, what is there left for the pupils to go about on? Only their heads! And if permission to do it has not been given in a bulletin, it must not be done. I was horrified yesterday. My head swam when I saw your sister – a woman or a girl on a bicycle – how terrible!"

' "What do you want, anyhow?"

' "I only want one thing: I want to caution you. You are a young man, the future lies before you, you must be very, very careful, or you will make a mistake. Oh, what a mistake you will make! You go about wearing embroidered shirts, you are always on the street with some book or other, and now you ride a bicycle! The director will hear of it; it will reach the ears of the trustees that you and your sister ride the bicycle – what is the use?"

' "It is nobody's business whether my sister and I ride the bicycle or not," said Kovalenko flushing deeply. "And whoever interferes in my domestic and family affairs I will kick to the devil."

'Byelinkoff paled and rose.

' "If you talk to me in that way I cannot continue," he said. "I must ask you never to refer to the heads of the school in that tone in my presence. You should have more respect for the authorities."

' "Did I say anything against the authorities?" asked Kovalenko, glaring angrily at him. "Please leave me alone! I am an honourable man, and I decline to talk to a person like you. I don't like sneaks!"

'Byelinkoff began nervously to bustle about and put on his things. You see, this was the first time in his life that he had heard such rudeness.

' "You can say what you like," he cried as he stepped out of the hall on to the landing of the stairs. "I must only warn you of one thing. Someone may have overheard our conversation and I shall have to report it to the director in its principal features, as it might be misinterpreted and something unpleasant might come of it. I shall be obliged to do this."

' "To report it? Go ahead, report it!"

'Kovalenko seized him by the nape of the neck and pushed, and Byelinkoff tumbled downstairs with his goloshes rattling after him. The staircase was long and steep, but he rolled safely to the bottom, picked himself up, and touched his nose to make sure that his spectacles were all right. At the very moment of his descent Varenka had come in with two ladies; they stood at the foot of the stairs and watched him, and for Byelinkoff this was the most terrible thing of all. He would rather have broken his neck and both legs than to have appeared ridiculous; the whole town would now know it, the director, the trustees would hear of it – oh, something unpleasant would come of it! There would be another caricature, and the end of it would be that he would have to resign.

'As he picked himself up Varenka recognised him. When she caught sight of his absurd face, his wrinkled overcoat, and his goloshes, not knowing what had happened but supposing that he had fallen downstairs of his own accord, she could not control herself and laughed till the whole house rang:

' "Ha! ha! ha!"

'This pealing and rippling "ha! ha! ha!" settled everything – it put an end to the wedding and to the earthly career of Byelinkoff.

'He did not hear what Varenka said to him; he saw nothing before his eyes. When he reached home he first took Varenka's picture off the table, then he went to bed and never got up again.

'Three days later Afanasi came to me and asked me whether he ought not to send for a doctor, as something was happening to his master. I went to see Byelinkoff. He was lying speechless behind his bed curtains, covered with a blanket, and when a question was asked him he only answered yes or no, and not another sound did he utter. There he lay, and about the bed roamed Afanasi, gloomy, scowling, sighing profoundly, and reeking of vodka like a tap-room.

'A month later Byelinkoff died. We all went to his funeral, that is, the boys' and girls' schools and the seminary. As he lay in his coffin the expression on his face was timid and sweet, even gay, as if he were glad to be put in a case at last out of which he need never rise. Yes, he had attained his ideal! As if in his honour, the day of his funeral was overcast and rainy, and all of us wore goloshes and carried umbrellas. Varenka, too, was at the funeral and burst into tears when the coffin was lowered into the grave. I have noticed that Little Russian women always either laugh or cry, they know no middle state.

'I must confess that it is a great pleasure to bury such people as Byelinkoff. On our way back from the cemetery we all wore sober, Lenten expressions; no one wished to betray this feeling of pleasure; the same feeling that we used to have long, long ago in childhood when our elders went away from home and we could run about the garden for a few hours in perfect liberty. Oh, liberty, liberty! Even a hint, even a faint hope of its possibility lends the soul wings, does it not?

'We returned from the cemetery in a good humour, but before a week had elapsed our life was trickling on as sternly, as wearily, as senselessly as before; a life not prohibited in a bulletin and yet not quite permitted – no better than it had been!

'And, as a matter of fact, though we had buried Byelinkoff, how many more people in cases there were left! How many more there will be!'

'Yes, so, so, quite right,' said Ivan Ivanitch smoking his pipe.

'How many more there will be!' Burkin repeated.

The schoolmaster stepped out of the shed. He was a small man, fat, quite bald, with a black beard that reached almost to his waist; two dogs followed him out.

'What a moon! What a moon!' he exclaimed looking up.

It was already midnight. To the right the whole village lay visible, its long street stretching away for three or four miles. Everything was wrapped in deep, peaceful slumber; not a movement, not a sound; it did not seem possible that nature could lie so silent. Peace fills the soul when one sees the broad street of a village on a moonlight night with its huts and its haystacks and its dreaming willows. It looks so gentle and beautiful and sad in its rest, screened by the shades of night from care and grief and toil. The stars, too, seem to be gazing at it with tenderness and emotion, and one feels that there is no evil in the world and that all is well. To the left the fields began at the edge of the village and were visible for miles down to the horizon; in all this broad expanse there was also neither movement nor sound.

'Yes, so, so, quite right,' Ivan Ivanitch repeated. 'But think how we live in town, so hot and cramped, writing unnecessary papers and playing vint – isn't that also a case? And isn't our whole life, which we spend among rogues and backbiters and stupid, idle women, talking and listening to nothing but folly – isn't that a case? Here! If you like I'll tell you a very instructive story.'

'No, it's time to go to sleep,' Burkin said. 'Tomorrow!'

Both men went into the shed and lay down on the hay. They had already covered themselves up and were half asleep when they suddenly heard light footsteps approaching – tip – tip. Somebody was walking by the shed. The footsteps went on and stopped, and in a minute came back again – tip – tip. The dogs growled.

'That was Mavra,' said Burkin as the sound died away.

'One hears and sees all this lying,' said Ivan Ivanitch, turning over on the other side. 'Nobody calls one a fool for standing it all, for enduring insults and humiliations without daring to declare oneself openly on the side of free and honest people. One has to lie oneself and smile, all for a crust of bread, a corner to live in, and a little rank, which is not worth a penny – no, a man can't go on living like this.'

'Oh, come, that's out of another opera, Ivan Ivanitch,' said the schoolmaster. 'Let's go to sleep!'

And ten minutes later Burkin was already asleep. But Ivan Ivanitch, sighing, still tossed from side to side, and at last got up and went out again and sat in the doorway smoking his pipe.

Little Jack

JACK JUKOFF was a little boy of nine who, three months ago, had been apprenticed to Aliakin, the shoemaker. On Christmas Eve he did not go to bed. He waited until his master and the foreman had gone out to church, and then fetched a bottle of ink and a rusty pen from his master's cupboard, spread out a crumpled sheet of paper before him, and began to write. Before he had formed the first letter he had more than once looked fearfully round at the door, glanced at the icon, on each side of which were ranged shelves laden with boot-lasts, and sighed deeply. The paper lay spread on the bench, and before it knelt Little Jack.

> DEAR GRANDPAPA – Constantine Makaritch [he wrote], I am writing you a letter. I wish you a merry Christmas and I hope God will give you all sorts of good things. I have no papa or mamma, and you are all I have.

Little Jack turned his eyes to the dark window, on which shone the reflection of the candle, and vividly pictured to himself his grandfather, Constantine Makaritch: a small, thin, but extraordinarily active old man of sixty-five, with bleary eyes and a perpetually smiling face; by day sleeping in the kitchen or teasing the cook; by night, muffled in a huge sheepskin coat, walking about the garden beating his watchman's rattle. Behind him, hanging their heads, pace the dogs Kashtanka and The Eel, so called because he is black and his body is long like a weasel's. The Eel is uncommonly respectful and affectionate; he gazes with impartial fondness upon strangers and friends alike; but his credit, in spite of this, is bad. Beneath the disguise of a humble and deferential manner he conceals the most Jesuitical perfidy. Nobody knows better than he how to steal up and grab you by the leg, how to make his way into the ice-house, or filch a hen from a peasant. His hind legs have been broken more than once; twice he has been hung, and every week he is thrashed within an inch of his life; but he always recovers.

At this moment, no doubt, grandfather is standing at the gate blinking at the glowing red windows of the village church, stamping his felt boots, and teasing the servants. His rattle hangs at his belt. He beats his arms and hugs himself with cold, and, giggling after the manner of old men, pinches first the maid, then the cook.

'Let's have some snuff!' he says, handing the women his snuff-box.

The women take snuff and sneeze. Grandfather goes off into indescribable ecstasies, breaks into shouts of laughter, and cries:

'Wipe it off! It's freezing on!'

Then they give the dogs snuff. Kashtanka sneezes and wrinkles her nose; her feelings are hurt, and she walks away. The Eel refrains from sneezing out of respect and wags his tail. The weather is glorious. The night is dark, but the whole village is visible; the white roofs, the columns of smoke rising from the chimneys, the trees, silvery with frost, and the snowdrifts. The sky is strewn with gaily twinkling stars, and the milky way is as bright as if it had been washed and scrubbed with snow for the holiday.

Little Jack sighed, dipped his pen in the ink, and went on:

I had a dragging yesterday. My master dragged me into the yard by my hair and beat me with a stirrup because I went to sleep without meaning to while I was rocking the baby. Last week my mistress told me to clean some herrings, and I began cleaning one from the tail, and she took it and poked its head into my face. The foreman laughs at me and sends me for vodka, makes me steal the cucumbers, and then my master beats me with whatever comes handy. And I have nothing to eat. I get bread in the morning, and porridge for dinner, and bread for supper. My master and mistress drink up all the tea and the soup. And they make me sleep in the hall, and when the baby cries I don't sleep at all because I have to rock the cradle. Dear grandpa, please take me away from here, home to the village. I can't stand it. I beg you on my knees; I will pray to God for you all my life. Take me away from here, or else I shall die . . .

Little Jack's mouth twisted; he rubbed his eyes with a grimy fist and sobbed.

I will grind your tobacco for you, he continued, and pray to God for you; and if I don't you can kill me like Sidoroff's goat. And if you think I ought to work I can ask the steward please to let me clean the boots, or I can do the ploughing in place of Teddy. Dear

Grandpa, I can't stand it; I shall die. I wanted to run away to the village on foot, but I haven't any boots, and it is so cold. And when I am big I will always take care of you and not allow anyone to hurt you at all, and when you die I will pray to God for you as I do for my mother, Pelagea.

Moscow is a big city. All the houses are manor houses, and there are lots of horses, but no sheep, and the dogs are not fierce. The children don't carry stars,* and they don't let anyone sing in church, and in one store I saw in the window how they were selling fish-hooks with the lines on them, and there was a fish on every hook, and the hooks were very large and one held a sturgeon that weighed forty pounds. I saw a store where they sell all kinds of guns just like our master's guns; some cost a hundred roubles. But at the butcher's there are grouse and partridges and hares; but the butcher won't tell where they were killed.

Dear Grandpa, when they have the Christmas tree at the big house, keep some gold nuts for me and put them away in the green chest. Ask Miss Olga for them and say they are for Little Jack.

Little Jack heaved a shuddering sigh and stared at the window again. He remembered how his grandfather used to go to the forest for the Christmas tree, and take his grandchild with him. Those were jolly days. Grandfather wheezed and grunted, and the snow wheezed and grunted, and Little Jack wheezed and grunted in sympathy. Before cutting down the tree grandfather would finish smoking his pipe and slowly take snuff, laughing all the time at little, shivering Jacky. The young fir trees, muffled in snow, stood immovable and wondered: 'Which of us is going to die?' Hares flew like arrows across the snow, and grandfather could never help crying: 'Hold on! Hold on! Hold on! Oh, the bobtailed devil!'

Then grandfather would drag the fallen fir tree up to the big house, and there they would all set to work trimming it. The busiest of all was Miss Olga, Jack's favourite. While Jack's mother, Pelagea, was still alive and a housemaid at the big house Miss Olga used to give Little Jack candy, and because she had nothing better to do had taught him to read and write and to count up to a hundred, and even to dance the quadrille.

When Pelagea died the little orphan was banished to the kitchen, where his grandfather was, and from there he was sent to Moscow, to Aliakin, the shoemaker.

* A Russian peasant custom at Christmas time.

Do come, dear grandpapa [Little Jack went on]. Please come; I beg you for Christ's sake to come and take me away. Have pity on your poor little orphan, because everyone scolds me, and I'm so hungry, and it's so lonely – I can't tell you how lonely it is. I cry all day long. And the other day my master hit me on the head with a boot tree, so that I fell down and almost didn't come to again. And give my love to Nelly and one-eyed Gregory and to the coachman, and don't let anyone use my accordion.

Your grandson,

JOHN JUKOFF

Dear Grandpapa, do come.

Little Jack folded the paper in four and put it in an envelope which he had bought that evening for one copeck. He reflected an instant, then dipped his pen in the ink and wrote the address:

To my Grandpapa in the Village.

Then he scratched his head, thought a moment, and added:

Constantine Makaritch.

Delighted to have finished his letter without interruption, he put on his cap and, without waiting to throw his little overcoat over his shoulders, ran out into the street in his shirt.

The butcher, whom he had asked the evening before, had told him that one drops letters into the mail-boxes, and that from there they are carried all over the world in mail wagons with ringing bells, driven by drivers who are drunk. Little Jack ran to the nearest mailbox and dropped his letter in the opening.

An hour later he was sound asleep, lulled by the sweetest hopes. He dreamed he saw a stove. On the stove sat his grandfather swinging his bare legs and reading his letter to the cook. Near the stove walked The Eel, wagging his tail.

Dreams

TWO SOLDIERS are escorting to the county town a vagrant who does not remember who he is. One of them is black-bearded and thickset, with legs so uncommonly short that, seen from behind, they seem to begin much lower down than those of other men; the other is long, lank, spare, and straight as a stick, with a thin beard of a dark-reddish hue. The first waddles along, looking from side to side and sucking now a straw and now the sleeve of his coat. He slaps his thigh and hums to himself, and looks, on the whole, light-hearted and care-free. The other, with his lean face and narrow shoulders, is staid and important looking; in build and in the expression of his whole person he resembles a priest of the Starover Faith or one of those warriors depicted on antique icons. 'For his wisdom God has enlarged his brow,' that is to say, he is bald, which still more enhances the resemblance. The first soldier is called Andrew Ptaka, the second Nikander Sapojnikoff.

The man they are escorting is not in the least like what everyone imagines a tramp should be. He is small and sickly and feeble, with little, colourless, absolutely undefined features. His eyebrows are thin, his glance is humble and mild, and his whiskers have barely made their appearance though he is already past thirty. He steps timidly along, stooping, with his hands thrust into his sleeves. The collar of his threadbare, unpeasant-like little coat is turned right up to the brim of his cap, so that all that can venture to peep out at the world is his little red nose. When he speaks, it is in a high, obsequious little voice, and then he immediately coughs. It is hard, very hard to recognise in him a vagabond who is hiding his name. He looks more like some impoverished, Godforsaken son of a priest, or a clerk discharged for intemperance, or a merchant's son who has essayed his puny strength on the stage and is now returning to his home to play out the last act of the parable of the prodigal son. Perhaps, judging from the dull patience with which he battles with the clinging autumn mud, he is a fanatic;

some youth trained for a monk who is wandering from one monastery to another all over Russia, doggedly seeking 'a life of peace and freedom from sin', which he cannot find.

The wayfarers have been walking a long time, but for all their efforts they cannot get away from the same spot of ground. Before them lie ten yards of dark-brown, muddy road, behind them lies as much; beyond that, wherever they turn, rises a dense wall of white fog. They walk and walk, but the ground they walk on is always the same; the wall comes no nearer; the spot remains a spot. Now and then they catch glimpses of white, irregular cobblestones, a dip in the road, or an armful of hay dropped by some passing wagon; a large pool of muddy water gleams for a moment, or a shadow, vaguely outlined, suddenly and unexpectedly appears before them. The nearer they come to this, the smaller and darker it grows; they come nearer still, and before them rises a crooked mile-post with its numbers effaced, or a woebegone birch tree, naked and wet, like a wayside beggar. The birch tree is whispering something with the remains of its yellow foliage; one leaf breaks off and flutters sluggishly to the ground, and then again there come fog and mud and the brown grass by the roadside. Dim, evil tears hang on these blades – not the tears of quiet joy that the earth weeps when she meets and accompanies the summer sun, and with which at dawn she quenches the thirst of quail and rails and graceful, long-billed snipe! The feet of the travellers are caught by the thick, sticky mud; every step costs them an effort.

Andrew Ptaka is a trifle provoked. He is scrutinising the vagrant and trying to understand how a live, sober man could forget his name.

'You belong to the Orthodox Church, don't you?' he asks.

'I do,' answers the tramp briefly.

'H'm – have you been christened?'

'Of course I have; I'm not a Turk! I go to church and observe the fasts and don't eat flesh when it's forbidden to do so – '

'Well, then, what name shall I call you by?'

'Call me what you please, lad.'

Ptaka shrugs his shoulders and slaps his thigh in extreme perplexity. The other soldier, Nikander, preserves a sedate silence. He is not so simple as Ptaka, and evidently knows very well reasons which might induce a member of the Orthodox Church to conceal his identity. His expressive face is stern and cold. He walks apart and disdains idle gossip with his companions. He seems to be endeavouring to show to everyone and everything, even to the mist, how grave and sensible he is.

'The Lord only knows what to think about you!' pursues Ptaka. 'Are you a peasant or not? Are you a gentleman or not? Or are you something between the two? I was rinsing out a sieve in a pond one day and caught a little monster as long as my finger here, with gills and a tail. Thinks I – it's a fish! Then I take another look at it – and I'll be blessed if it didn't have feet! It wasn't a fish and it wasn't a reptile – the devil only knows what it was! That's just what you are. What class do you belong to?'

'I am a peasant by birth,' sighs the tramp. 'My mother was a house serf. In looks I'm not a peasant, and that is because fate has willed it so, good man. My mother was a nurse in a gentleman's house and had every pleasure the heart could desire, and I, as her flesh and blood, belonged, in her lifetime, to the household. They petted me and spoiled me and beat me till they beat me from common to well-bred. I slept in a bed, had a real dinner every day, and wore trousers and low shoes like any little noble. Whatever my mother had to eat, I had. They gave her dresses and dressed me, too. Oh, we lived well! The candy and cake I ate in my childhood would buy a good horse now if I could sell them! My mother taught me to read and write, and from the time I was a baby instilled the fear of God into me and trained me so well that to this day I couldn't use an impolite, peasant word. I don't drink vodka, boy, and I dress cleanly and can make a respectable appearance in good society. God give her health if she is still alive; if she is dead, take her soul, O Lord, to rest in thy heavenly kingdom where the blessed find peace!'

The tramp uncovers his head, with its sparse bristles, casts his eyes upward, and makes the sign of the cross twice.

'Give her peace, O Lord, in green places!' he says in a drawling voice, more like an old woman's than a man's. 'Keep thy slave Keenia in all thy ways, O Lord! If it had not been for my good mother I should have been a simple peasant now, not knowing a thing. As it is, lad, ask me what you please; I know everything: the Holy Scriptures, all godly things, all the prayers, and the Catechisms. I live according to the Scriptures; I do wrong to no one, I keep my body pure, I observe the fasts and eat as it is ordered. Some men find pleasure only in vodka and brawling, but when I have time I sit in a corner and read a book, and as I read I cry and cry – '

'Why do you cry?'

'Because the things they tell of are so pitiful. Sometimes you pay only five copecks for a book and weep and wail over it to despair – '

'Is your father dead?' asks Ptaka.

'I don't know, lad. It's no use hiding a sin; I don't know who my father was. What I think is that I was an illegitimate son of my mother's. My mother lived all her life with the gentry and never would marry a common peasant.'

'So she flew higher, up to his master!' laughs Ptaka.

'That is so. My mother was pious and godly, and of course it is a sin, a great sin, to say so, but, nevertheless, maybe I have noble blood in my veins. Maybe I am a peasant in station only and am really a highborn gentleman.'

The 'high-born gentleman' utters all this in soft, sickly sweet voice, wrinkling his narrow brows and emitting squeaky noises from his cold, red, little nose.

Ptaka listens to him, eyes him with astonishment, and still shrugs his shoulders.

After going four miles the soldiers and the tramp sit down on a little knoll to rest.

'Even a dog can remember his name,' mutters Ptaka. 'I am called Andrew and he is called Nikander; every man has his God-given name and no one could possibly forget it – not possibly!'

'Whose business is it of anyone's to know who I am?' sighs the tramp, leaning his cheek on his hand. 'And what good would it do me if they knew? If I were allowed to go wherever I liked I should be worse off than I am now. I know the law, my Christian friends – now I am a vagrant who does not remember his name, and the worst they could do to me would be to send me to eastern Siberia with thirty or forty lashes, but if I should tell them my real name and station I should be sent to hard labour again – I know!'

'You mean to say you have been a convict?'

'I have, my good friend. My head was shaved and I wore chains for four years.'

'What for?'

'For murder, good man. When I was still a boy, about eighteen years old, my mother put arsenic into our master's glass by mistake instead of soda. There were a great many different little boxes in the storeroom and it was not hard to mistake them.'

The tramp sighs, shakes his head, and continues:

'She was a godly woman, but who can say? The soul of another is a dark forest. Maybe she did it by mistake. Maybe it was because her master had attached another servant to himself and her heart could not forgive the insult. Perhaps she did put it in on purpose – God only knows! I was young then and couldn't understand everything. I remember now that our master did, in fact, take another mistress at that time and that my mother was deeply hurt. Our trial went on for two years after that. My mother was condemned to twenty years' penal servitude and I to seven on account of my youth.'

'And what charge were you convicted on?'

'For being an accomplice. I handed our master the glass. It was always that way: my mother would prepare the soda and I would hand him the glass. But I am confessing all this before you, brothers, as before God. You won't tell anyone – '

'No one will ever ask us,' says Ptaka. 'So that means you ran away from prison, does it?'

'Yes, I ran away, good friend. Fourteen of us escaped. God be with them! They ran away and took me along, too. Now judge for yourself, lad, and tell me honestly whether I have any reason for telling my name? I should be condemned to penal servitude again; and what sort of a convict am I? I am delicate and sickly; I like cleanliness in my food and in the places where I sleep. When I pray to God I like to have a little shrine lamp or a candle burning, and I don't like to have noises going on round me when I'm praying. When I prostrate myself I don't like to have the floor all filthy and spat over, and I prostrate myself forty times morning and night for my mother's salvation.'

The tramp takes off his cap and crosses himself.

'But let them send me to eastern Siberia if they want to!' he cries. 'I'm not afraid of that.'

'What? Is that better?'

'It is an entirely different affair. At hard labour you are no better off than a crab in a basket. You are crowded and pushed and hustled; there's not a quiet corner to take breath; it's a hell on earth – the Mother of God forbid it! A ruffian you are, and a ruffian's treatment you receive – worse than any dog's. You get nothing to eat; there is nowhere to sleep and nowhere to say your prayers. In exile it's different. You first enrol yourself in the company, as everyone else does. The government is compelled by law to give you your share of land. Yes, indeed! Land, they say, is cheap there, as cheap as snow. You can take all you want! They would give me land for farming, lad, and land for a garden, and land for a house. Then I would plough and sow, as other men do, raise cattle and bees and sheep and dogs – I'd get myself a Siberian cat to keep the rats and mice from eating my property, I'd build me a house, brothers, and buy icons; and, God willing, I'd marry and have children – '

The tramp is murmuring to himself now and has ceased looking at his listeners; he is gazing off somewhere to one side. Artless as his reveries are, he speaks with such sincerity and such heartfelt earnestness that it is hard not to believe what he says. The little mouth of the vagrant is twisted by a smile, and his whole face, his eyes, and his nose are numbed and paralysed by the foretaste of far-off happiness. The soldiers listen and regard him earnestly, not without compassion. They also believe what he says.

'I am not afraid of Siberia,' the tramp murmurs on. 'Siberia and Russia are the same thing. They have the same God there as here, and the same Czar, and they speak the language of Orthodox Christians, as I am speaking with you; only there is greater plenty, and the people are richer. Everything is better there. Take, for example, the rivers. They are a thousand times finer than ours. And fish! The fishing in them is simply beyond words! Fishing, brothers, is the greatest joy of my life. I don't ask for bread; only let me sit and hold a fishing-line! Indeed, that is true! I catch fish on a hook and line and in pots and with bow nets, and when the ice comes I use cast nets. I am not strong enough to fish with a cast net myself; so I have to hire a peasant for five copecks to do that for me. Heavens, what fun it is! It's like seeing your own brother again to catch an eel or a mudfish! And you have to treat every fish differently, I can tell you. You use a minnow for one, and a worm for another, and a frog or a grasshopper for a third; you've got to know all that. Take, for example, the eel. The eel isn't a dainty fish; it will take even a newt. Pikes like earthworms – garfish, butterflies. There is no greater joy on earth than fishing for chubs in swift water. You bait your hook with a butterfly or a beetle, so that it will float on the surface; and you let your line run out some twenty or thirty yards without a sinker; then you stand in the water without your trousers and let the bait float down with the current till – tug! and there's a chub on the hook! Then you have to watch ever so closely for just the right moment to hook it or the confounded thing will go off with your bait. The moment it twitches the line you've got to pull; there isn't a second to lose! The number of fish I have caught in my life is a caution! When we were escaping and the other convicts were asleep in the forest, I couldn't sleep and would go off in search of a river. The rivers there are so wide and swift and steep-banked – it's a caution. And all along their shores lie dense forests. The trees are so high that it makes your head swim to look up to the top of them. According to prices here every one of those pine trees is worth ten roubles – '

Under the confused stress of his imagination, the dream pictures of the past, and the sweet foretaste of happiness, the piteous little man stops speaking and only moves his lips as if whispering to himself. The feeble, beatific smile does not leave his face. The soldiers say nothing.

Their heads have sunk forward on to their breasts, and they are lost in meditation. In the autumn silence, when a chill, harsh fog from the earth settles on the soul and rises like a prison wall before one to testify to the narrow limits of man's freedom, ah! then it is sweet to dream of wide, swift rivers with bold, fertile banks, of dense forests, of boundless plains! Idly, peacefully, the fancy pictures to itself a man, a tiny speck, appearing on the steep, uninhabited bank of a river in the early morning, before the flush of dawn has faded from the sky. The summits of the everlasting pines rise piled high in terraces on either side of the stream and, muttering darkly, look sternly at that free man. Roots, great rocks, and thorny bushes obstruct his path, but he is strong of body and valiant of heart and fears neither the pines nor the rocks nor the solitude nor the rolling echoes that reiterate every footfall.

The imagination of the soldiers is painting for them pictures of a free life which they have never lived. Is it that they darkly recall images of things heard long ago? Or have these visions of a life of liberty come down to them with their flesh and blood as an inheritance from their remote, wild ancestors? God only knows!

The first to break the silence is Nikander, who until now has not let fall a word. Perhaps he is jealous of the vagrant's visionary happiness; perhaps he feels in his heart that dreams of bliss are incongruous amidst surroundings of grey mist and brown-black mud – at any rate, he looks sternly at the tramp and says:

'That is all very well, brother; that is all very fine, but you'll never reach that land of plenty! How could you? You would go thirty miles and then give up the ghost – a little half-dead creature like you! You've only walked four miles today and yet, look at you! You can't seem to get rested at all!'

The tramp turns slowly to Nikander and the blissful smile fades from his face. He looks with dismay at the grave countenance of the soldier as if he had been caught doing wrong and seems to have recollected something, for he nods his head. Silence falls once more. All three are busy with their own thoughts. The soldiers are trying to force their minds to grasp what perhaps God alone can conceive of: the terrible expanse that lies between them and that land of freedom. Images more clear, precise, and terrifying are crowding into the vagrant's head – courts of justice, dungeons for exiles and for convicts, prison barracks, weary halts along the road, the cold of winter, illness, the death of his companions – all rise vividly before him.

The tramp blinks, and little drops stand out upon his brow. He wipes his forehead with his sleeve, draws a deep breath as if he had just jumped out of a hot oven, wipes his forehead with the other sleeve, and glances fearfully behind him.

'It is quite true that you could never get there,' Ptaka assents. 'You're not a walker! Look at yourself – all skin and bone! It would kill you, brother.'

'Of course it would kill him; he couldn't possibly do it,' declares Nikander. 'He'll be sent straight to the hospital, anyway, as it is. That's a fact!'

The nameless wanderer looks with terror at the stern, impassive faces of his evil-boding fellow travellers; then, lowering his eyes, he rapidly crosses himself without taking off his cap. He is trembling all over, his head is shaking, and he is beginning to writhe like a caterpillar that someone has stepped on.

'Come on! Time to go!' cries Nikander, rising. 'We have rested long enough!'

Another minute and the travellers are plodding along the muddy road. The tramp is stooping more than before and has thrust his hands still deeper into the sleeves of his coat. Ptaka is silent.

The Death of an Official

ONE BEAUTIFUL EVENING the not less beautiful minor government official Ivan Tcherviakoff was sitting in the second row of the orchestra looking through his opera-glasses at *Les Cloches de Corneville*. As he sat there he felt himself to be in the seventh heaven of happiness. But suddenly (in stories one often finds this 'suddenly'; authors are right – life is full of the unexpected), suddenly his face grew wrinkled, his eyes rolled, and he held his breath – he took down his opera-glasses, bent forward, and – ha-choo! He sneezed, as you see. Sneezing is not prohibited to anyone anywhere. Peasants sneeze, and chiefs of police sneeze, and even privy councillors sneeze sometimes; everyone sneezes. Tcherviakoff was in no wise embarrassed; he wiped his nose with his handkerchief and glanced about him politely to make sure that he had not disturbed anyone by his sneezing. And then he felt himself perforce abashed. He saw that an old man who was sitting in front of him in the first row was painfully wiping his bald spot and the back of his neck with his glove and muttering something. In this old man Tcherviakoff recognised General Brizjaloff of the Department of Highways.

'I sneezed on him!' thought Tcherviakoff. 'He is not my chief, but still it is awkward. I must apologise.'

Tcherviakoff cleared his throat, shifted himself forward, and whispered in the general's ear.

'I beg your pardon, your Excellency; I sneezed on you. I accidentally – '

'Never mind, never mind – '

'For Heaven's sake, excuse me. I – I didn't mean to – '

'Oh, sit down, please! Let me listen to what is being said.'

Tcherviakoff was overwhelmed with confusion. He smiled idiotically and began looking at the stage. He looked at it but no longer felt any sensation of bliss. Anxiety was beginning to torment him. During the next entr'acte he approached Brizjaloff, walked along at his side, and, conquering his timidity, murmured:

'I sneezed on your Excellency. Excuse me. You see, I – did not do it to – '

'Oh, enough of that! I had already forgotten it, and you keep on at the same thing!' the general said, impatiently twitching his lower lip.

'He says he has forgotten it, but there is malice in his eye,' thought Tcherviakoff, glancing at the general mistrustfully. 'He won't even speak. I must explain that I didn't mean to – that sneezing is a law of nature – or else he might think I was spitting. If he doesn't think so now he will later.'

On reaching his home Tcherviakoff told his wife of his rudeness. He thought she regarded what had happened too flippantly. She was only alarmed at first; when she learned that Brizjaloff was not their chief she felt reassured.

'Still, you must go and apologise,' she said. 'He might think you didn't know how to behave in society.'

'That's just it! I have apologised, but he acted so curiously; he didn't say anything sensible. But, then, there was no time for conversation.'

Next day Tcherviakoff shaved, donned his new undress uniform, and went to explain things to Brizjaloff. As he entered the general's reception-room his eye fell on a great crowd of petitioners assembled there, and in their midst was the general, who had already begun his reception. Having interrogated several of the petitioners, the general raised his eyes to Tcherviakoff.

'Yesterday, at the "Arcadian", if you remember, your Excellency – ' the little official began, 'I sneezed and – accidentally spattered you. Excu – '

'What nonsense! Rot! What can I do for you?'

'He won't speak to me!' thought Tcherviakoff, turning pale. 'He is angry; I must explain to him – '

When the general had finished his interview with the last petitioner and was going into an inner apartment, Tcherviakoff stepped up to him and murmured:

'Your Excellency! If I dare to trouble your Excellency, it is only, I can assure you, from a feeling of repentance. I did not do it on purpose. Your Excellency must know that – '

The general made a tearful face and waved his hand.

'You are simply joking, sir!' he said disappearing behind the door.

'He says I am joking!' thought Tcherviakoff. 'But there is no joke about this at all. He is a general and he can't see that! As that is the case, I'll not beg that swashbuckler's pardon again, confound him! I'll write him a letter, but I'll not come here again; I'll be hanged if I will!'

Thus Tcherviakoff reflected walking homeward. He did not write that letter to the general. He thought and thought and couldn't for the life of him think of anything to write. He had to go next day himself and explain.

'I came yesterday and troubled your Excellency,' he mumbled, as the general looked at him interrogatively, 'but not with the idea of joking, as your Excellency was good enough to remark. I wanted to beg your pardon because in sneezing I – I did not dream of joking. How could I dare to? To joke would be to show no respect for persons – it would – '

'Get out!' roared the general, suddenly quaking and growing purple in the face.

'Er – what?' whispered Tcherviakoff, swooning with horror.

'Get out!' repeated the general, stamping.

Something seemed to break in Tcherviakoff's breast. He stumbled through the door and out into the street, not seeing or hearing a thing, and crawled along the sidewalk. Going home mechanically, he lay down on a sofa, without taking off his undress uniform, and – died.

Agatha

DURING MY STAY in the province of S— I spent much of my time in the company of Sava Stukatch, or Savka for short, the watchman of the communal vegetable gardens of the village of Dubofka. These gardens on the bank of the river were my favourite resort for what may be called fishing 'in general' – when you leave home without knowing the hour or day of your return and take with you a supply of provisions and every conceivable article of fishing-tackle. To tell the truth, I cared less for the fishing than I did for the peaceful idling, the chatting with Savka, the eating at all hours, and the long watches in the quiet summer nights.

Savka was a young fellow of twenty-five, tall, handsome, and hard as a brick. He had a reputation for cleverness and good sense, could read and write, and seldom drank vodka; but, powerful and young as he was, as a workman he was not worth one copper copeck. Though as tough as whipcord, his strong muscles were impregnated with a heavy, invincible indolence. Like everyone else in the village, he had formerly lived in a hut of his own and had had his own share of the land, but he had neither ploughed nor sowed nor followed any trade. His old mother had gone begging from door to door while he lived like the birds of the air, not knowing in the morning what he would eat at noon. It was not will, nor energy, nor pity for his mother that were lacking; he simply felt no inclination for toil and did not see the necessity for it. A sense of peace and an inborn, almost artistic, passion for an idle, disorderly life emanated from his whole being. When his healthy young body craved muscular exercise the lad would abandon himself completely for a short time to some untrammelled but absurd occupation such as sharpening a lot of useless stakes or running races with the women. His favourite state was one of concentrated immobility. He was capable of remaining for hours in one place, motionless, and with his eyes fixed on the same spot. He moved when the fancy seized him, and then only when he saw a chance for some swift, impetuous action such as catching a running dog by the tail, snatching the kerchief from the head of a woman, or leaping across a broad ditch.

It follows that, being so stingy of movement, Savka was as poor as Job's turkey and lived worse than a vagabond. As time went on his arrears had accumulated and, young and strong as he was, he had been sent by the commune to take an old man's place as watchman and scarecrow in the village communal gardens. He did not care a snap of his finger how much he was laughed at for his untimely old age. This occupation, so quiet and so well adapted for motionless contemplation, exactly suited his tastes.

I happened to be visiting Savka one beautiful evening in May. I lay, I remember, on a worn, tattered rug near a shed from which came the thick, choking smell of dried grass. With my hands behind my head I lay staring before me. At my feet was a wooden pitchfork; beyond that a dark object stood out sharply – it was Savka's little dog Kutka – and not more than fifteen feet beyond Kutka the ground fell away abruptly to the steep bank of the river. I could not see the water from where I lay, only the tops of the bushes crowding along the bank and the jagged and winding contours of the opposite shore. Beyond the river, on a dark hill, the huts of the village where my Savka had lived lay huddled together like startled young partridges. The evening light was fading behind the hill, only a pale strip of crimson remained, and across this little clouds were gathering as ashes gather on dying embers.

To the right of the garden lay a dark alder wood whispering softly and shivering sometimes as a sudden breeze wandered by. A bright little fire was twinkling in the dusk, there, where the eye could no longer distinguish the fields from the sky. At a short distance from me sat Savka, cross-legged, his head bowed, thoughtfully gazing at Kutka. Our hooks had long since been baited and dropped into the stream, and there was nothing for us to do but surrender ourselves to the repose so much loved by the never-weary but eternally resting Savka. Though the sunset had not faded entirely the summer night had folded the world in its soothing, sleep-giving embrace.

Nature had sunk into her first profound slumber; only in the wood some night-bird unknown to me uttered a slow, lazy cry which sounded like, 'Is that Ni–ki–ta?' and then answered himself: 'Nikita! Nikita! Nikita!'

'Why aren't the nightingales singing this evening?' I asked.

Savka turned slowly toward me. His features were large but well formed and expressive and gentle as a woman's. He looked with kind, pensive eyes, first at the wood and then at the thicket, then quietly took out a little pipe from his pocket, put it to his lips, and blew a few notes like a hen nightingale. At once, as if answering his call, a rail-bird 'chucked' from the opposite shore.

'There goes a nightingale for you!' laughed Savka. 'Chuck-chuck! chuck-chuck! as if it were jerking at a hook, and yet it thinks it is singing!'

'I like those birds,' I said. 'Do you know that when the time for migrating comes the rail doesn't fly but runs along the ground? It only flies across rivers and the ocean and goes all the rest of the way on foot.'

'The little monkey!' murmured Savka, gazing with respect in the direction of the calling rail.

Knowing how much Savka loved listening, I told him all I had learned about rails from my sportsman's books. From rails we slipped imperceptibly into migration. Savka listened with rapt attention, not moving an eyelash, smiling with pleasure.

'In which country are the birds most at home, in ours or over there?' he asked.

'In ours, of course. They are hatched here and here they raise their young. This is their native land, and they only fly away to escape being frozen to death.'

'How strange!' Savka sighed, stretching. 'One can't talk of anything but what it is strange. Take that shouting bird over there, take people, take this little stone – there's a meaning in everything. Oh, if I had only known you were going to be here this evening, sir, I wouldn't have told that woman to come! She asked if she might.'

'Oh, you mustn't mind me!' I said. 'I shan't interfere. I can go and lie in the wood.'

'What an idea! It wouldn't have killed her to wait till tomorrow. If she were sitting here now and listening, we could do nothing but drivel. One can't talk sense when she is around.'

'Are you expecting Daria?'

'No, a new one asked to come here this evening; Agatha, the switchman's wife.'

Savka uttered this in his usual impassive way, in a dull voice, as if he were speaking of tobacco or porridge, but I jumped with astonishment. I knew Agatha well. She was still very young, not more than nineteen or twenty, and less than a year ago had married a railway switchman – a fine, bold young peasant. She lived in the village, and her husband came home to her every night from the railway.

'These affairs of yours with women will end badly someday,' I said sadly.

'Never mind!'

Then, after a moment's reflection, Savka added:

'So I have told the women, but they won't listen; the idiots don't care.'

Silence fell. The shadows deepened, the outlines of all objects faded into the darkness. The streak of light behind the hill was altogether extinguished, and the stars shone ever clearer and brighter. The mournful, monotonous chirping of the crickets, the calling of the rail-bird, and the whistling of the quail seemed not to break the nocturnal silence but rather to add to it a still greater depth. It was as if the stars, and not the birds and insects, were singing softly and charming our ears as they looked down from heaven.

Savka broke silence first. He slowly turned his regard from Kutka's black form to me, and said:

'This is tedious for you, sir, I can see. Let's have supper.'

Without waiting for my consent, he crawled on his stomach into the shed, rummaged about there until the whole building shook like a leaf, and crawled back with a bottle of vodka and an earthenware bowl, which he placed before me. In the bowl were baked eggs, fried cakes of rye flour, some pieces of black bread, and a few other things. We each had a drink out of a crooked glass that refused to stand up, and began our meal. Oh, that coarse, grey salt, those dirty, greasy cakes, those eggs as tough as India-rubber, how good they all tasted!

'You live the life of a tramp, and yet you have all these good things!' I exclaimed, pointing to the bowl. 'Where do you get them?'

'The women bring them,' grunted Savka.

'Why?'

'Oh, out of pity.'

Not only the bill of fare but Savka's clothes, too, bore traces of feminine 'pity'. I noticed that he wore a new worsted girdle that evening and that a little copper cross was suspended round his grimy neck by a bright crimson ribbon. I knew the weakness of the fair sex for Savka, and I knew, too, how unwilling he was to speak of it, so I did not pursue the subject. Besides, I had no time to say more. Kutka, who had been sitting near by in patient expectation of scraps, suddenly pricked up his ears and growled. We heard an intermittent splashing of water.

'Someone is crossing the ford,' said Savka.

In a few minutes Kutka growled again and emitted a sound like a cough.

'Here!' cried his master.

Light footsteps rustled in the night, and a woman's form came out of the wood. I recognised her in spite of the darkness; it was Agatha.

She came forward timidly, stopped, and breathed heavily. It was probably more fear at fording the river by night than her walk which had robbed her of breath. When she saw two men by the shed instead of one she gave a faint cry and fell back a step.

'Oh, is that you?' asked Savka, thrusting a cake into his mouth.

'I – I – ' she faltered, dropping a little bundle she carried and glancing at me. 'Jacob sent you his greetings, and told me to give you this – this – '

'Why do you tell a story? Jacob, indeed!' Savka laughed at her. 'No fibbing! Sit down and pay us a visit.'

Agatha cast another glance at me and irresolutely sat down.

'I had already given you up this evening,' said Savka after a long pause. 'What makes you sit there like that? Eat something. Or is it a drink of vodka you want?'

'What are you thinking about?' cried Agatha. 'Am I a drunkard?'

'Drink it! It warms the heart. Come on!'

Savka handed Agatha the crooked glass. She drank the vodka slowly, without eating anything after it, and only blew noisily through her lips.

'So you have brought something with you?' Savka continued as he undid the bundle. His voice took on a playfully indulgent tone. 'She can't come without bringing something. Aha! A pie and potatoes! These people live well,' he sighed, facing me. 'They are the only ones in the village who still have potatoes left over from winter.'

It was too dark to see Agatha's face, but from the movement of her shoulders and head I thought that she kept her eyes fixed on Savka's face. I decided to take a stroll so as not to make the third at a tryst, and rose to my feet. But at that moment a nightingale in the wood suddenly gave out two deep contralto notes. Half a minute later it poured forth a fine, high trill and, having tried its voice thus, began to sing.

Savka leaped up and listened. 'That is last night's bird!' he exclaimed 'Wait – '

'Let it alone!' I called after him. 'What do you want with it?'

Savka waved his hand as much as to say, 'Don't shout!' and vanished into the darkness. He could be a splendid hunter and fisherman when he liked, but this gift was as much wasted as his strength. He was too lazy to turn it to account, and his passion for the chase he expended on idle feats. He loved to seize nightingales in his hands, or to shoot pike with bird shot, or to stand by the river for hours at a time trying with all his might to catch a little fish on a large hook.

When she was left with me Agatha coughed and drew her hand several times across her brow. The vodka was already beginning to go to her head.

'How have you been, Agatha?' I asked after a long silence, when it seemed awkward not to say something.

'Very well, thank you – you won't tell anyone, will you, master?' she added suddenly in a whisper.

'No, no,' I reassured her. 'But you are very brave, Agatha. What if Jacob should find out?'

'He won't find out.'

'He might.'

'No, I shall get back before he does. He works on the railway now and comes home when the mail-train goes through, and I can hear it coming from here.'

Agatha again drew her hand across her brow and looked in the direction which Savka had taken. The nightingale was still singing. A night-bird flew by close to the ground; as it caught sight of us it swerved, rustled its wings, and flew away across the river.

The nightingale soon ceased, but still Savka did not return. Agatha rose to her feet, took two or three restless steps, and sat down again.

'Where is he?' she burst out. 'The train won't wait till tomorrow! I must go at once!'

'Savka!' I shouted. 'Savka!'

Not even an echo answered. Agatha stirred uneasily and rose once more.

'It is time to go!' she cried in a troubled voice. 'The train will be here in a moment. I know when the trains come.'

The poor girl was right. In less than ten minutes we heard a distant noise. Agatha looked long at the wood and impatiently wrung her hands.

'Oh, where is he?' she cried with a nervous laugh. 'I am going; indeed I am going!'

Meanwhile, the rumbling grew louder. The clanking of the wheels was distinguishable now from the deep panting of the engine. A whistle blew and the train thundered across a bridge. Another minute and all was still.

'I'll wait one second more,' sighed Agatha, sitting down resolutely. 'I don't care what happens, I'll wait.'

At last Savka appeared in the gloom. He was humming softly and his bare feet fell noiselessly on the mellow earth of the garden.

'Let me tell you the bad luck,' he cried with a merry laugh. 'Just as I reached the bush and stretched out my hand he stopped singing! Oh, you little rat! I waited and waited for him to begin again and finally snapped my fingers at him – '

Savka dropped awkwardly down beside Agatha and caught her round the waist with both arms to keep his balance.

'Why, you're as black as a thunder-cloud! What's the matter?' he asked.

For all his warm-hearted simplicity, Savka despised women. He treated them carelessly, in an offhand way, and even sank so low as to laugh with contempt at their feeling for himself. Heaven knows if this careless disdain may not have been one of the secrets of his charm for the village Dulcineas. He was graceful and comely, and a quiet caress always shone in his eyes even when they rested on the women he despised, but his outward appearance alone could not account for the fascination he exercised. Beside his happy exterior and his odd ways, it seems as if the touching role played by Savka must also have exerted its influence over the women. He was known to everyone as a failure, an unfortunate exile from his native hut.

'Ho-ho!' he cried. 'Let's have another drink, Brother Agatha!'

I rose and walked the length of the garden, picking my way among the beds of vegetables. They lay like large, flat graves, and an odour rose from them of fresh earth and moist, tender leaves newly wet with dew. The little red fire still gleamed and seemed to wink a smiling greeting.

I heard a blissful laugh. It was Agatha.

'And the train?' I remembered. 'It came long ago!'

I waited a little while and then went back to the shed. Savka was sitting motionless, with his legs crossed, softly, almost inaudibly, humming a monosyllabic song that sounded like:

'Oh, you   come you   you and I   '

Overpowered by the vodka, by Savka's careless caresses, and by the sultry heat of the night, Agatha lay on the ground with her head against his knees.

'Why, Agatha, the train came in long ago!' I cried.

Savka seized the suggestion. 'Yes, yes, it's time for you to go!' he said, raising his head.

Agatha started up and looked at me.

'It's long past the time!' I said.

Agatha turned and raised herself on one knee. She was suffering. For a minute her whole figure, as well as I could see in the darkness, expressed struggle and vacillation. There was a moment when she drew herself up to rise, as if she had summoned her strength, but here some irresistible, implacable force smote her from head to foot and she dropped again.

'Oh, what do I care?' she cried with a wild, deep laugh, and in that laugh rang reckless determination, impotence, pain.

I walked quietly into the wood and from there went down to the river. The stream lay asleep. A soft flower on a high stem brushed my cheek like a child who tries to show that he is still waking. Having nothing to do, I felt for one of the lines and pulled it in. It resisted feebly and then hung limp. Nothing had been caught. The village and the opposite shore were invisible. A light flashed in one of the huts but quickly went out. I searched along the bank and found a hollow which I had discovered in the daytime, and in this I ensconced myself as if in an easy-chair. I sat for a long time. I saw the stars begin to grow misty and dim; I felt a chill pass like a light sigh over the earth, stirring the leaves of the dreaming willows.

'A-ga-tha!' cried a faint voice on the other shore.

It was the frightened husband searching for his wife through the village. At the same moment a burst of laughter came from the garden, from the wife who was trying, in a few hours of happiness, to make up for the torture that awaited her on the morrow.

I fell into a doze.

When I awoke, Savka was sitting beside me lightly tapping my shoulder. The river, the wood, both shores, the green, newly washed trees and fields were flooded with bright morning light. The rays of the rising sun beat on my back from between the slender trunks of the trees.

'So you are fishing,' chuckled Savka. 'Get up!'

I rose, stretched myself blissfully, and my awakening lungs greedily drank in the moist, scented air.

'Has Agatha gone?' I asked.

'There she is.' Savka pointed in the direction of the ford.

I looked and saw Agatha. Dishevelled, her kerchief slipping from her hair, she was holding up her skirts and wading across the river. Her feet scarcely moved.

'She feels the shoe pinching,' murmured Savka, gazing at her with half-closed eyes. 'She is hanging her tail as she goes. They are as silly as cats and as timid as hares, those women. The idiot wouldn't go when she was told to last night, and now she will catch it, and I'll be had up! There'll be another row about women.'

Agatha stepped out on to the bank and started across the fields to the village. At first she walked boldly, but emotion and terror soon had their way with her; she looked back fearfully and stopped, panting.

'She is frightened,' Savka smiled sadly, with his eyes on the bright-green ribbon that stretched across the dewy grass behind Agatha. 'She doesn't want to go on. Her husband has been standing there waiting for her for an hour. Do you see him?'

Savka smiled as he spoke the last words, but my heart stood still. In the road, near one of the huts on the outskirts of the village, stood Jacob with his eyes fixed on his returning wife. He did not stir from one spot but stood as still as a post. What were his thoughts as he looked at her? What words had he prepared to receive her with? Agatha stood still for some time, looked back again as if expecting succour from us, and went on. Never have I seen anyone, whether drunk or sober, walk with such a gait. Agatha seemed to be writhing under her husband's gaze. First she zigzagged, and then stopped and trampled the ground in one spot, throwing out her arms, her knees bending under her, and then staggered back. After she had gone a hundred paces she looked back once more and sat down.

I looked at Savka's face. It was pale and drawn with that mixture of pity and aversion that men feel at the sight of a suffering animal.

'What is joy for the cat is tears for the mouse,' he sighed.

Suddenly Agatha jumped up, threw back her head, and advanced with firm footsteps toward her husband. She was resolved now, one could see, and had plucked up her courage.

The Beggar

'KIND SIR, have pity; turn your attention to a poor, hungry man! For three days I have had nothing to eat; I haven't five copecks for a lodging, I swear it before God. For eight years I was a village schoolteacher and then I lost my place through intrigues. I fell a victim to calumny. It is a year now since I have had anything to do –'

The advocate Skvortsoff looked at the ragged, fawn-coloured overcoat of the suppliant, at his dull, drunken eyes, at the red spot on either cheek, and it seemed to him as if he had seen this man somewhere before.

'I have now had an offer of a position in the province of Kaluga,' the mendicant went on, 'but I haven't the money to get there. Help me kindly; I am ashamed to ask, but – I am obliged to by circumstances.'

Skvortsoff's eyes fell on the man's overshoes, one of which was high and the other low, and he suddenly remembered something.

'Look here, it seems to me I met you the day before yesterday in Sadovaya Street,' he said; 'but you told me then that you were a student who had been expelled, and not a village schoolteacher. Do you remember?'

'N–no, that can't be so,' mumbled the beggar, taken aback. 'I am a village schoolteacher, and if you like I can show you my papers.'

'Have done with lying! You called yourself a student and even told me what you had been expelled for. Don't you remember?'

Skvortsoff flushed and turned from the ragged creature with an expression of disgust.

'This is dishonesty, my dear sir!' he cried angrily. 'This is swindling! I shall send the police for you, damn you! Even if you are poor and hungry, that does not give you any right to lie brazenly and shamelessly!'

The waif caught hold of the door-handle and looked furtively round the antechamber, like a detected thief.

'I – I'm not lying –' he muttered. 'I can show you my papers.'

'Who would believe you?' Skvortsoff continued indignantly. 'Don't you know that it's a low, dirty trick to exploit the sympathy which society feels for village schoolteachers and students? It's revolting!'

Skvortsoff lost his temper and began to berate the mendicant unmercifully. The impudent lying of the ragamuffin offended what he, Skvortsoff, most prized in himself: his kindness, his tender heart, his compassion for all unhappy beings. That lie, an attempt to take advantage of the pity of its 'subject', seemed to him to profane the charity which he liked to extend to the poor out of the purity of his heart. At first the waif continued to protest innocence, but soon he grew silent and hung his head in confusion.

'Sir!' he said, laying his hand on his heart, 'the fact is I – was lying! I am neither a student nor a schoolteacher. All that was a fiction. Formerly I sang in a Russian choir and was sent away for drunkenness. But what else can I do? I can't get along without lying. No one will give me anything when I tell the truth. With truth a man would starve to death or die of cold for lack of a lodging. You reason justly, I understand you, but – what can I do?'

'What can you do? You ask what you can do?' cried Skvortsoff, coming close to him. 'Work! That's what you can do! You must work!'

'Work – yes. I know that myself: but where can I find work?'

'By God, you judge harshly!' cried the beggar with a bitter laugh. 'Where can I find manual labour? It's too late for me to be a clerk because in trade one has to begin as a boy; no one would ever take me for a porter because they couldn't order me about; no factory would have me because for that one has to know a trade, and I know none.'

'Nonsense! You always find some excuse! How would you like to chop wood for me?'

'I wouldn't refuse to do that, but in these days even skilled wood-cutters find themselves sitting without bread.'

'Huh! You loafers all talk that way. As soon as an offer is made you, you refuse it. Will you come and chop wood for me?'

'Yes, sir; I will.'

'Very well; we'll soon find out. Splendid – we'll see – '

Skvortsoff hastened along, rubbing his hands, not without a feeling of malice, and called his cook out of the kitchen.

'Here, Olga,' he said, 'take this gentleman into the wood-shed and let him chop wood.'

The tatterdemalion scarecrow shrugged his shoulders, as if in perplexity, and went irresolutely after the cook. It was obvious from his gait that he had not consented to go and chop wood because he was hungry and wanted work, but simply from pride and shame, because he had been trapped by his own words. It was obvious, too, that his strength had been undermined by vodka and that he was unhealthy and did not feel the slightest inclination for toil.

Skvortsoff hurried into the dining-room. From its windows one could see the wood-shed and everything that went on in the yard. Standing at the window, Skvortsoff saw the cook and the beggar come out into the yard by the back door and make their way across the dirty snow to the shed. Olga glared wrathfully at her companion, shoved him aside with her elbow, unlocked the shed, and angrily banged the door.

'We probably interrupted the woman over her coffee,' thought Skvortsoff. 'What an ill-tempered creature!'

Next he saw the pseudo-teacher, pseudo-student seat himself on a log and become lost in thought with his red cheeks resting on his fists. The woman flung down an axe at his feet, spat angrily, and, judging from the expression of her lips, began to scold him. The beggar irresolutely pulled a billet of wood toward him, set it up between his feet, and tapped it feebly with the axe. The billet wavered and fell down. The beggar again pulled it to him, blew on his freezing hands, and tapped it with his axe cautiously, as if afraid of hitting his overshoe or of cutting off his finger. The stick of wood again fell to the ground.

Skvortsoff's anger had vanished and he now began to feel a little sorry and ashamed of himself for having set a spoiled, drunken, perchance sick man to work at menial labour in the cold.

'Well, never mind,' he thought, going into his study from the dining-room. 'I did it for his own good.'

An hour later Olga came in and announced that the wood had all been chopped.

'Good! Give him half a rouble,' said Skvortsoff. 'If he wants to he can come back and cut wood on the first day of each month. We can always find work for him.'

On the first of the month the waif made his appearance and again earned half a rouble, although he could barely stand on his legs. From that day on he often appeared in the yard and every time work was found for him. Now he would shovel snow, now put the wood-shed in order, now beat the dust out of rugs and mattresses. Every time he received from twenty to forty copecks, and once, even a pair of old trousers were sent out to him.

When Skvortsoff moved into another house he hired him to help in the packing and hauling of the furniture. This time the waif was sober, gloomy, and silent. He hardly touched the furniture, and walked behind the wagons hanging his head, not even making a pretence of appearing busy. He only shivered in the cold and became embarrassed when the carters jeered at him for his idleness, his feebleness, and his tattered, fancy overcoat. After the moving was over Skvortsoff sent for him.

'Well, I see that my words have taken effect,' he said, handing him a rouble. 'Here's for your pains. I see you are sober and have no objection to work. What is your name?'

'Lushkoff.'

'Well, Lushkoff, I can now offer you some other, cleaner employment. Can you write?'

'I can.'

'Then take this letter to a friend of mine tomorrow and you will be given some copying to do. Work hard, don't drink, and remember what I have said to you. Goodbye!'

Pleased at having put a man on the right path, Skvortsoff tapped Lushkoff kindly on the shoulder and even gave him his hand at parting. Lushkoff took the letter, and from that day forth came no more to the yard for work.

Two years went by. Then one evening, as Skvortsoff was standing at the ticket window of a theatre paying for his seat, he noticed a little man beside him with a coat collar of curly fur and a worn sealskin cap. This little individual timidly asked the ticket seller for a seat in the gallery and paid for it in copper coins.

'Lushkoff, is that you?' cried Skvortsoff, recognising in the little man his former wood-chopper. 'How are you? What are you doing? How is everything with you?'

'All right. I am a notary now and get thirty-five roubles a month.'

'Thank Heaven! That's fine! I am delighted for your sake. I am very, very glad, Lushkoff. You see, you are my godson, in a sense. I gave you a push along the right path, you know. Do you remember what a roasting I gave you, eh? I nearly had you sinking into the ground at my feet that day. Thank you, old man, for not forgetting my words.'

'Thank you, too,' said Lushkoff. 'If I hadn't come to you then I might still have been calling myself a teacher or a student to this day. Yes, by flying to your protection I dragged myself out of a pit.'

'I am very glad, indeed.'

'Thank you for your kind words and deeds. You talked splendidly to me then. I am very grateful to you and to your cook. God bless that good and noble woman! You spoke finely then, and I shall be indebted to you to my dying day; but, strictly speaking, it was your cook, Olga, who saved me.'

'How is that?'

'Like this. When I used to come to your house to chop wood she used to begin: "Oh, you sot, you! Oh, you miserable creature! There's nothing for you but ruin." And then she would sit down opposite me and grow sad, look into my face and weep. "Oh, you unlucky man! There is no pleasure for you in this world and there will be none in the world to come. You drunkard! You will burn in hell. Oh, you unhappy one!" And so she would carry on, you know, in that strain. I can't tell you how much misery she suffered, how many tears she shed for my sake. But the chief thing was – she used to chop the wood for me. Do you know, sir, that I did not chop one single stick of wood for you? She did it all. Why this saved me, why I changed, why I stopped drinking at the sight of her I cannot explain. I only know that, owing to her words and noble deeds a change took place in my heart; she set me right and I shall never forget it. However, it is time to go now; there goes the bell.'

Lushkoff bowed and departed to the gallery.

Children

PAPA, MAMMA AND AUNT NADIA are not at home. They have gone to a christening party at the old officer's – the one that always rides a little grey horse – and Grisha, Annie, Aliosha, Sonia and Andrew, the cook's son, are sitting at the dining-room table playing loto, waiting for their return. To tell the truth, it is already past bedtime, but how can they possibly go to sleep without first finding out from mamma what the baby looked like and what there had been for supper?

The table is lit by a hanging lamp and strewn with numbers, nutshells, scraps of paper, and counters. Before each player lie two cards and a little heap of counters with which to cover the figures on the cards. In the centre of the table gleams a little white dish containing five-copeck pieces, and near the dish lie a half-eaten apple, a pair of scissors, and a plate into which one is supposed to put one's nutshells. The children are playing for money and the stakes are five copecks. The agreement is that if anyone cheats he must go at once. The players are alone in the dining-room. Nurse is downstairs in the kitchen showing the cook how to cut out a dress and the oldest brother, Vasia, a schoolboy in the fifth class, is lying on the sofa in the drawing-room feeling bored.

The children are playing with fervour; it is Grisha's face that depicts the most acute feeling. He is a nine-year-old boy with a closely shaved head, fat cheeks, and lips as full as a negro's; he has already entered the preparatory class, and so he considers himself grown up and very clever. He is playing solely for the sake of the money; if it weren't for the copecks in the little dish he would have been asleep long ago. His brown eyes rove uneasily and jealously over the cards of his opponents. Terror lest he should lose, enmity, and the financial calculations which fill his shaved head won't let him sit still or concentrate his thoughts, and so he is wriggling as if he were sitting on pins and needles. When he wins he greedily grabs the money and immediately thrusts it into his pocket. His sister Annie, a child of eight with a pointed chin and bright, clever eyes, is also terrified lest somebody else should win. She alternately flushes and pales and keeps a watchful eye on the players. It isn't the money that interests her; her pleasure in the game comes from pride. Sonia, the other sister, is six. Her head is covered with curls and her cheeks are a colour that can only be seen on the faces of healthy children, expensive dolls, and on candy boxes. She is playing loto for the sake of the process involved in the playing. Her face is alive with emotion. She laughs and claps her hands no matter who wins.

Aliosha, a puffy, spherical little person, pants, snuffles, and makes round eyes at the cards. He is neither greedy of gain nor of success. They can't drive him away from the table, they can't put him to bed, and that is all there is to it; he looks phlegmatic, but at heart he is a little wretch. He has taken his place at the table not so much for the sake of the loto as for the sake of the quarrels that are inseparable from the game. He is horribly pleased if one child hits or abuses another. He only knows the figure one and those ending in zero, so Annie is covering his numbers for him.

The fifth player, Andrew, the cook's son, is a dark-faced, sickly boy. He wears a cotton shirt and a copper cross hangs round his neck. He is standing quite still, dreamily contemplating the cards, and is indifferent to his own success and that of the others because he is entirely absorbed in the mathematical side of the game and in its simple philosophy. 'It is strange,' he is thinking, 'how many different numbers there are in this world; how is it they don't get mixed up?'

With the exception of Sonia and Aliosha, the players take turns in calling out the numbers. Because the numbers are all so alike, they have, with practice, invented the funniest expressions and nicknames for them – seven they call 'the poker'; eleven, 'little sticks'; ninety, 'grandpa', and so forth. The game is moving along briskly.

'Thirty-two!' cries Grisha as he draws the yellow counters one by one from the paternal hat. 'Seventeen! A poker! Twenty-three – climb a tree!'

Annie notices that Andrew has missed the twenty-three. At any other time she would have pointed this out to him, but now, when her pride is lying in the little dish with her copeck, she rejoices to see it.

'Twenty-two!' continues Grisha. 'Grandpa! Nine!'

'Oh, a cockroach! a cockroach!' shrieks Sonia, pointing to a cockroach which is running across the table.

'Don't kill it!' says Aliosha in a deep voice. 'It may have babies!'

Sonia follows the cockroach with her eyes, thinking about its babies and wondering what little cockroach children can possibly look like.

'Forty-three! One!' continues Grisha in agony because Annie has already covered two lines. 'Six!'

'Game! I've won the game!' cries Sonia casting up her eyes coquettishly and laughing.

The faces of the players fall.

'We must make sure of it!' Grisha says, looking spitefully at her.

As the biggest and cleverest, Grisha has appropriated the right to be umpire; what he says is final.

They spend a long time carefully verifying Sonia's card and, to the great regret of all her opponents, find that she has not been cheating. Another game commences.

'I saw a funny thing yesterday,' Annie remarks, as if to herself. 'Philip Philipovitch turned his eyelids inside out, and his eyes were all red and horrid, just like a devil's.'

'I've seen that, too,' says Grisha. 'Eight! One of the boys at school can wiggle his ears. Twenty-seven!'

Andrew lifts his eyes to Grisha's face and says:

'I can wiggle my ears.'

'Come on, wiggle them!'

Andrew wiggles his eyes, his lips, his fingers, and thinks that his ears, too, are in motion. There is general laughter.

'That Philip Philipovitch isn't nice,' sighs Sonia. 'He came into the nursery yesterday, and I was only in my chemise. I was so ashamed!'

'Game!' shouts Grisha suddenly, grabbing the money out of the dish. 'Prove it if you want to!'

The cook's son looks up and turns pale.

'Then I can't go on playing,' he says in a low voice.

'Why?'

'Because my money's all gone.'

'You mayn't play without money!' Grisha declares.

As a last resort Andrew searches through his pockets once more and finds nothing but crumbs and the gnawed stump of a pencil. The corners of his mouth go down and he begins to blink painfully. He is just going to cry.

'I'll let you have the money!' exclaims Sonia, unable to endure his agonised glances. 'Only see that you give it back!'

The money is paid in, and the game goes on.

'I hear ringing!' says Annie, opening her eyes wide.

They all stop playing and gaze open-mouthed at the dark window. The light of the lamp is shining among the shadows outside.

'You just think you heard it.'

'At night they only ring bells in the churchyard,' says Andrew.

'Why do they ring them there?'

'To keep robbers from breaking into the church. Robbers are afraid of bells.'

'Why do robbers want to break into the church?' asks Sonia.

'Why? To kill the watchman, of course!'

A minute elapses in silence. They look at one another, shudder, and continue the game.

'He's cheating!' roars Aliosha suddenly, for no reason at all.

'You liar! I wasn't cheating!' Andrew turns white, makes a wry face, and thumps Aliosha on the head. Aliosha glares wrathfully, puts one knee on the table, and – biff! – slaps Andrew on the cheek! Each slaps the other once more, and then they begin to bawl. These horrors are too much for Sonia; she, too, bursts into tears, and the dining-room resounds with discordant wails.

But you need not imagine that this puts an end to the game. Before five minutes are over the children are laughing again and babbling as peacefully as ever. Their faces are wet with tears, but this does not prevent them from smiling. Aliosha is even radiant – there has been a quarrel!

Enter into the dining-room Vasia, the schoolboy, looking sleepy and bored.

'This is disgusting!' he thinks, seeing Grisha fumbling in his pocket, in which the coins are jingling. 'The idea of letting the children have money! The idea of letting them gamble! A fine education this is for them, I swear! It's disgusting!'

But the children are playing with such relish that he begins to want to take a seat beside them himself and try his own luck.

'Wait a minute! I'll play, too,' he exclaims.

'Put in a copeck!'

'In a minute,' he says, feeling through his pockets. 'I haven't any copecks, but here's a rouble. I'll put in a rouble.'

'No, no, no; put in a copeck!'

'You sillies, a rouble is worth more than a copeck,' the boy explains. 'Whoever wins can give me the change.'

'No; please go away.'

The schoolboy shrugs his shoulders and goes into the kitchen to get some change from the servants. It seems there is none to be had there.

'You change it for me,' he urges Grisha, coming back. 'I'll pay you a discount on it. You won't? Then sell me ten copecks for my rouble.'

Grisha eyes Vasia with suspicion. He scents a plot or foul play of some sort.

'No, I won't,' he says, clutching his pocket.

Vasia loses his temper and calls the players idiots and donkeys.

'Vasia, I'll put it in for you,' cries Sonia. 'Sit down!'

The boy takes his seat and lays down two cards before him. Annie begins calling out the numbers.

'I've dropped a copeck!' Grisha suddenly declares in a troubled voice. 'Wait a minute!'

The children take down the lamp and crawl under the table to look for the coin.

They seize nutshells and trash in their hands and bump their heads together, but the copeck is not to be found. They renew the search and continue it until Vasia snatches the lamp out of Grisha's hands and puts it back in its place. Grisha continues to search in the dark.

But now, at last, the copeck is found. The players take their seats at the table with the idea of resuming the game.

'Sonia is asleep!' cries Annie.

With her curly head on her arms, Sonia is wrapped in slumber as peaceful and profound as if she had gone to sleep an hour ago. She fell asleep suddenly while the others were looking for the copeck.

'Come and lie down on mamma's bed!' says Annie, leading her out of the dining-room. 'Come!'

The whole crowd go with her, and some five minutes later mamma's bed offers a remarkable spectacle. On it sleeps Sonia. Aliosha is snoring beside her. Lying with their heads to her heels sleep Grisha and Annie. And here, too, the cook's son, Andrew, has found room for himself. The coins lie scattered beside them, powerless until the beginning of a new game.

Good-night!

The Troublesome Guest

In a low, lopsided hut inhabited by the forester, Artem, sat two men. One of them was Artem himself, a short, lean peasant with a senile, wrinkled face and a beard growing out of his neck; the other was a passing hunter, a tall young fellow wearing a new shirt and large, muddy boots.

In the dark night outside the windows roared the wind with which nature lashes herself before a thunderstorm. The tempest howled fiercely and the stooping trees moaned with pain. Flying leaves rattled against the sheet of paper that patched a broken window-pane.

'I'll tell you what, boy,' half whispered Artem, in a hoarse, squeaky voice, staring at the hunter with fixed and startled eyes, 'I am not afraid of wolves nor witches nor wild animals, but I am afraid of men. You can guard yourself against wild animals with guns or other arms, but there is no protection against a bad man.'

'Of course not. You can shoot an animal, but if you shot a robber you would have to answer for it by going to Siberia.'

'I have been a forester here for close on thirty years, and I have had more trouble with bad men than I can begin to tell you. I have had them here by the score. This hut being in a clearing and the road passing so near brings the wretches this way. One of the ruffians will come along and, without troubling to take off his cap, will just rush up and order me. "Here, give me some bread!" Where can I get bread from? What right has he to ask for it? Am I a millionaire that I should feed every drunkard that passes by? But his eyes are glistening with wickedness, and without a moment's hesitation he shouts in my ear: "Give me some bread!" Then I give it to him. I wouldn't want to fight the heathen brute. Some of them have shoulders a yard wide and great fists as big as your boot, and I – you see what I am! You could knock me down with your little finger. Well, I give him his bread and he gorges himself and lies all over the hut, and as for saying a word of thanks – not he! Then there come some that want money; then it's "Tell me where your money is!" But what money have I got? Where should I get money from?'

'Was there ever a forester that didn't have money?' laughed the hunter. 'You get your wages every month and sell wood on the sly, too, I'll be bound.'

Artem stared in terror at the hunter and wagged his beard as a magpie wags its tail.

'You are too young to say such things to me,' said he. 'You will have to answer for those words before God. Who are you? Where are you from?'

'I am Nethed, the bailiff's son, from Viasofka.'

'Yes, out larking with your gun. I used to like to go larking with a gun, too, when I was younger. Well, well – oh – oh!' yawned Artem. 'It's a great misfortune, good people are scarce and robbers and murderers too plentiful to count.'

'You speak as if you were afraid of me.'

'What an idea! Why should I be afraid of you? I can see; I can understand. You didn't burst in; you came in quietly and bowed and crossed yourself like an honest man. I know what's what. I don't mind letting you have bread. I am a widower. I never light the fire in the stove, and I have sold my samovar and am too poor to have meat and such things, but bread – you are welcome to that!'

At that moment something under the bench growled and the growling was followed by hissing. Artem jumped and drew up his feet, looking inquiringly at the hunter.

'That is my dog insulting your cat,' said the hunter. 'You devils, you,' he shouted to the animals under the bench. 'Lie down or you'll get a whipping! Why, uncle, how thin your cat is! Nothing but skin and bones!'

'She is getting old; it is time she was killed. So you say you are from Viasofka?'

'You don't give her anything to eat, I can see that. She is a living creature even if she is a cat. It's a shame!'

'Viasofka is a wicked place,' continued Artem as if he hadn't heard the hunter. 'The church there was robbed twice in one year. Can you believe that there are such heathen? They not only don't fear man; they don't even fear God! To steal God's property! To hang for that is too little! In the old days the governors used to have such knaves beheaded.'

'You can punish them as you like, thrash them, or sentence them to anything you please, you'll only be wasting your time. You can't knock the bad out of a bad man.'

'The Holy Virgin have mercy on us and save us,' sighed the forester in a trembling voice, 'save us from our enemies and evil-wishers! Last week, at Bolovich, one of the haymakers struck another in the chest and beat him to death. Thy will be done, O Lord! How do you think it began? One haymaker came out of a tavern drunk and met another, also drunk – '

Hearkening to something the hunter suddenly craned his neck forward and strained his ears to catch some sound.

'Stop!' he interrupted the forester. 'I thought I heard someone calling.'

The hunter and the forester both fixed their eyes on the dark window and listened attentively. Above the noise of the trees they caught the sounds that strike an attentive ear during a storm, and it was hard to distinguish whether someone was really calling or whether it was only the wind sobbing in the chimney. But now a gust that tore at the roof and rattled the paper in the window brought a distinct cry: 'Help!'

'Talking about murderers, here they are!' cried the hunter. He paled and got up. 'Someone is being robbed.'

'The Lord preserve us!' whispered the forester, also turning pale and rising.

The hunter looked aimlessly out of the window and strode across the hut.

'What a night, what a night!' he muttered. 'As black as pitch and just the time for a robbery. Did you hear that? Someone screamed again.'

The forester looked at the icon, then at the hunter, and sank feebly on to a bench, like a man who has been shocked by sudden news.

'Oh, son,' he wailed, 'go into the hall and bolt the outside door! And the light ought to be put out!'

'What for?'

'They might come in here. Who knows? Oh, we are all miserable sinners!'

'We have got to go out, and you want to bolt the door! Come, shall we start?'

The hunter threw his gun across his shoulder and seized his cap.

'Put on your coat! Get your gun! Here, Flerka, here!' he called to his dog. 'Flerka!'

A long-eared dog, a cross between a setter and a mastiff, came out from under the bench and lay down at his master's feet, wagging his tail.

'Why don't you get up?' cried the hunter to the forester. 'Aren't you coming?'

'Where to?'

'To help.'

'Why should I go?' The forester made a gesture of indifference and huddled himself together. 'Let him alone!'

'Why won't you come?'

'After those blood-curdling stories, I refuse to go one step into the darkness. Let him alone! I've seen dreadful things happen in those woods.'

'What are you afraid of? Haven't you got a gun? Come along; it's scary work going alone; it will be jollier together. Did you hear that? There's that screaming again! Get up!'

'What do you take me for, boy?' groaned the forester. 'Do you think I'm going out there like a fool, to be murdered?'

'So you won't go?'

The forester was silent. The dog, probably hearing the human cries, began to bark dismally.

'Will you come, I say?' shouted the hunter, glaring angrily.

'You worry me,' the forester said, frowning. 'Go yourself!'

'You – you dirty beast!' muttered the hunter, turning toward the door. 'Here, Flerka!'

He went out, leaving the door open. The wind swept through the hut, the candle flame flickered, flared brightly, and went out.

As he closed the door after the hunter the forester saw the pools of water in the clearing, the pines, and the retreating form of his guest lit up by a flash of lightning. The thunder growled in the distance.

'Holy, holy, holy!' he whispered, hurriedly throwing the heavy bolt into place. 'What weather the Lord has sent us!'

Re-entering the room, he felt his way to the stove, climbed up, and covered his head. Lying under his sheepskin coat, he strained his ears to listen. The screams had stopped, but now the thunder was roaring louder and louder, clap on clap. A heavy, driving rain beat fiercely against the glass and the paper pane of the window.

'What a storm!' he thought, and pictured to himself the hunter, soaking wet and stumbling over the stumps. 'His teeth must be chattering with fear!'

Not more than ten minutes had elapsed before he heard footsteps, followed by loud knocking at the door.

'Who is there?' he called.

'It is I!' answered the hunter's voice. 'Open the door!'

The forester climbed down from the stove, felt for the candle, lit it, and went to open the door. The hunter and his dog were drenched to the skin. They had been caught in the fiercest and heaviest of the rain and were streaming like wet rags.

'What happened out there?' asked the forester.

'A woman in a wagon had got off the road,' answered the hunter, trying to catch his breath, 'and had fallen into a ditch.'

'What a fool! And got scared, I suppose. Did you put her back on the road?'

'I refuse to answer such a coward as you.'

The hunter threw his wet cap on the bench and continued: 'Now I know that you are a coward and the scum of the earth. And you are supposed to be a watchman, and you get wages for it! You worthless trash, you!'

The forester crawled guiltily to the stove, groaned, and lay down. The hunter sat down on the bench, thought an instant, and then threw himself, wet as he was, full length along it. Next moment he jumped up again, blew out the candle, and again lay down. Once, at an unusually loud thunderclap, he turned over, spat, and muttered:

'So he was afraid – and what if someone had been murdering the woman? Whose business was it to go to her help? And he's an old man, too, and a Christian! He's a pig, that's what he is!'

The forester grunted and heaved a deep sigh. Flerka shook herself violently in the darkness and scattered drops of water everywhere.

'I don't suppose you would have cared one bit if the old woman had been murdered!' continued the hunter. 'By God, I didn't know you were a man like that!'

Silence fell. The storm had blown over and the thunder now rumbled in the distance, but it was still raining.

'What if it had been you calling for help and not a woman?' the hunter burst out. 'How would you have liked it, you beast, if no one had run to your rescue? You drive me crazy with your chicken-hearted ways, damn you!'

Then, after another long entr'acte, the hunter said:

'If you are as afraid of people as you seem to be, you must have money somewhere. A poor man doesn't get frightened like that.'

'You will answer for those words before God,' croaked Artem from the stove. 'I haven't a penny.'

'Huh! Nonsense! Cowards always have money. Why are you so afraid of people? Of course you have money. I believe I'll just rob you on purpose to teach you a lesson!'

Artem silently slipped down from the stove, lit the candle, and sat down under the icon. He was pale and did not take his eyes off the hunter.

'Yes, I shall certainly rob you,' continued the hunter. 'What do you think? Shouldn't one give one's brother a lesson? Tell me where you have hidden the money!'

Artem drew his feet up under him and blinked.

'What are you hugging yourself for? Have you lost your tongue, you clown? Why don't you answer?'

The hunter jumped up and strode toward the forester.

'There he sits with his eyes popping out of his head like an owl! Well! Give me the money or I'll shoot you with my gun!'

'Why do you torment me?' whimpered the forester, and great tears rolled out of his eyes. 'What have I done to you? God is witness to everything. You will have to answer for your words before God. You have no right to ask me for money.'

The hunter looked at Artem's weeping face, frowned, marched across the hut, angrily clapped on his cap, and seized his gun.

'Bah! You're too sickening to look at!' he muttered between his teeth. 'I can't endure the sight of you! I couldn't sleep here, anyway! Goodbye! Here, Flerka!'

The door slammed and the troublesome guest went out with his dog. Artem locked the door behind him, crossed himself, and lay down.

Not Wanted

IT IS SEVEN O'CLOCK of a June evening. A throng of summer residents, just alighted from the train, is crawling along the road that leads from the little station of Kilkovo. They are mostly the fathers of families and are laden with hand-bags, portfolios, and feminine bandboxes. They all look weary and hungry and cross, as if it were not for them that the sun was shining and the grass was so green.

Crawling there, among others, is Paul Zaikin, a member of the circuit court, tall and round-shouldered, perspiring, scarlet, and glum.

'Do you come out into the country every day?' asks another summer resident in carroty-red trousers.

'No, not every day,' rejoins Zaikin with gloom. 'My wife and son live here all the time, but I only come twice a week. I have no time to make the trip every day, and, besides, it's too costly.'

'You're right about the expense,' sighs he of the carroty trousers. 'One can't go to the station on foot in the city, one has to hire a cab; then the ticket costs forty-two copecks; and then one buys a newspaper to read on the way and a glass of vodka to keep up one's strength – all these are trivial expenses, but before you know it the copecks have mounted up to two hundred roubles by the end of the summer. Of course the lap of nature is worth more than that, and the idylls and all – I won't attempt to deny it – but, with our salaries as government officials, every copeck counts, as you know. If you are careless enough to waste a copeck it will keep you awake all night. Yes, indeed. I, my dear sir (I have not the honour of knowing your name), get a salary of a little less than two thousand roubles a year. State councillor is my rank, and yet I only smoke second-rate tobacco and haven't a rouble to spare to buy myself Vichy water which the doctors prescribe for my gravel.'

'It's absolutely atrocious,' says Zaikin after a long pause. 'I, sir, am convinced that suburban life was invented by devils and women; the devil invented it from malice and the women from unbounded folly.

Good Lord! This isn't life; this is penal servitude; this is hell. It's so sweltering and hot here one scarcely can breathe, and yet one is driven from one place to another like a thing accursed, with never a corner to take refuge in. And in town you've no furniture left and no servant; everything has been dragged to the country. You feed Heaven knows how; you never have tea because there is no one to light the samovar; you never wash, and then you come here, into the lap of nature, and have to tramp through the dust, on foot, in this heat – bah! Are you married?'

'Yes; I have three children,' sigh the red trousers.

'Atrocious! It's astonishing to me that we are still alive.'

At last the two men reach the summer colony. Zaikin bids farewell to the red trousers and goes to his own house. There he is met by a dead silence. He hears only the buzzing of mosquitoes and the supplications for help of a fly that is making a spider's dinner. Muslin curtains hang before the windows and behind these gleam faded red geranium blossoms. Flies are dozing on the unpainted wooden walls among the cheap coloured prints. There is not a soul in the hall, in the kitchen, in the dining-room. At last, in the room which does duty as living-room and drawing-room both, Zaikin discovers his son Peter, a small boy of six. Peter is sitting at the table, snuffling loudly and hanging his lower lip, and with a pair of scissors is cutting the knave of diamonds out of a card.

'Oh, is that you, papa?' he asks without turning round. 'Good-evening!'

'Good-evening! Where is your mother?'

'Mamma? Oh, she has gone with Miss Olga to a rehearsal. They're going to act a play the day after tomorrow. And they're going to take me. Are you going?'

'H'm. And when is she coming back?'

'She said she would be back this evening.'

'Where is Natalia?'

'Mamma took Natalia with her to help her dress at the rehearsal, and Akulina has gone to the woods to get mushrooms. Papa, why do mosquitoes' stomachs get red when they bite?'

'I don't know. Because they suck blood. So there is no one at home?'

'No, no one but me.'

Zaikin sinks into a chair and for a minute looks dully out of the window.

'Who's going to give us our dinner?' he asks.

'They didn't cook any dinner today, papa. Mamma thought you

wouldn't come home today, and so she said for them not to cook dinner. She and Miss Olga are going to have dinner at the rehearsal.'

'How delightful! And what have you had to eat?'

'I've had some milk. They bought some milk for me for six copecks. But, papa, why do mosquitoes suck blood?'

Zaikin suddenly feels as if some heavy object had rolled down on his liver and were beginning to gnaw it. He feels so vexed and injured and bitter that he trembles and breathes heavily and longs to leap up, bang on the floor with some heavy weight, and break into recriminations. But he remembers that the doctor has sternly forbidden him excitement; so he gets up and, making a great effort to control himself, begins whistling an air from 'The Huguenots.'

He hears Peter's voice: 'Papa, can you act plays?'

Zaikin's temper is going.

'Oh, leave me alone with your stupid questions!' he cries. 'You stick like a wet leaf. You're six already, and yet you're as silly as you were three years ago. You're a stupid, rowdy boy. What do you mean by destroying those cards, for instance? How dare you destroy them?'

'They're not your cards,' says Peter, turning round. 'Natalia gave them to me.'

'That's a fib, a fib, you good-for-nothing boy!' cries Zaikin, more and more incensed. 'You're always fibbing! You need a whipping, you little puppy. I'll pull your ears for you!'

Peter jumps up, thrusts out his neck, and stares intently at his father's red, angry face. His large eyes first blink and then are clouded with moisture, and he screws up his face.

'What are you scolding me for?' wails Peter. 'Why can't you let me alone, donkey? I don't bother anyone, and I'm not naughty, and I do as I'm told, and you – you get angry! Why do you scold me?'

The boy spoke with conviction and wept so bitterly that Zaikin grew ashamed of himself.

'Yes, really, what am I trying to pick a quarrel with him for?' he reflects. 'Come, that will do!' he says, touching Peter's shoulder. 'I'm sorry, Peterkin; forgive me! You're a good little boy, a nice little boy, and I love you.'

Peter wipes his eyes on his sleeve, resumes his former seat with a sigh, and starts cutting out a queen. Zaikin goes into his study, stretches himself out on the sofa, and begins to muse with his hands behind his head.

The boy's recent tears have softened his anger, and his liver is, little by little, beginning to feel easier. He now only feels hungry and tired.

'Papa!' he hears on the other side of the door. 'Shall I show you my collection of insects?'

'Yes, show it to me.'

Peter comes into the study and hands his father a long green box. Even before raising it to his ear Zaikin hears a despairing buzzing and the scratching of tiny feet on the sides of the box. As he lifts the cover he sees a great number of butterflies, beetles, grasshoppers, and flies fixed by pins to the bottom of the box. All, with the exception of two or three butterflies, are alive and wriggling.

'And that little grasshopper is still alive!' exclaims Peter, astonished. 'We caught him yesterday morning, and he isn't dead yet!'

'Who taught you to stick them down like that?'

'Miss Olga.'

'Miss Olga ought to be stuck down herself,' says Zaikin with disgust. 'Take them away! It's shameful to torture animals.'

'Heavens! How atrociously he is being brought up!' he thinks as Peter departs.

Zaikin has forgotten his hunger and fatigue and is thinking only of the fate of his boy. The daylight has gradually faded outside the windows; the summer residents can be heard coming home in little groups from their evening bath. Someone takes up his stand below the open window and cries: 'Mushrooms! Who wants mushrooms?' Receiving no answer, he shuffles on farther with his bare feet. And now, when the twilight has deepened so that the geraniums have lost their outlines behind the muslin curtains and the freshness of evening has begun to draw in at the window, the door into the hall opens noisily and sounds of rapid footsteps, laughter, and talk can be heard.

'Mamma!' shrieks Peter.

Zaikin peeps out of the study and sees his wife Nadejda, buxom and rosy as ever. Miss Olga is with her, a bony blonde with large freckles, and two unknown men: one young and lank, with curly red hair and a large Adam's apple; the other short and dumpy, with an actor's clean-shaven face and a crooked, blue chin.

'Natalia, light the samovar!' cries the wife, her dress rustling noisily. 'I hear that the master has come home! Paul, where are you? Good-evening, Paul!' she says, and runs panting into the study. 'So you've come? I'm so glad! Two of our amateurs have come home with me; come, I'll introduce you to them! There, the tallest one, yonder, is Koromisloff; he sings divinely; the other, the little one, is a certain Smerkaloff; he's an actor by profession and recites most wonderfully! Whew! I'm so tired! We have just had a rehearsal. Everything's going finely. We are giving "The Lodger with the Trombone" and "She Expects Him". The performance will be the day after tomorrow – '

'Why did you bring them here?'

'I simply had to, dear. We must go through our roles once more after tea and sing a song, too. Koromisloff and I are singing a duet together. Oh, I nearly forgot! Dearie, do send Natalia for some sardines and vodka and cheese and things – they will probably stay to supper, too. Oh, how tired I am!'

'H'm. I haven't any money!'

'Oh, really, dear, how can you? How awkward! Don't make it embarrassing for me!'

In half an hour Natalia has been sent for vodka and other delicacies, and Zaikin, having drunk his fill of tea and eaten a whole loaf of French bread, has retired to his bedroom and lain down on the bed, while Nadejda and her guests, with laughter and noise, have once more fallen to rehearsing their roles. Paul listens for a long time to the hideous recitations of Koromisloff and the theatrical shouts of Smerkaloff. The recitations are followed by a long conversation, which is rent by the shrieking laughter of Miss Olga. Smerkaloff, by right of being a real actor, is explaining their roles to them with heat and assurance.

Next follows a duet, and after the duet comes the clattering of dishes. In his dreams Zaikin hears Smerkaloff reciting 'The Sinner', hears him beginning to rant as he struts before his audience. He hisses, he beats his breast, he weeps, he guffaws in a hoarse bass voice.

Zaikin groans and buries his head under the blanket.

'You have a long way to go, and it's dark,' he hears his wife's voice saying an hour later. 'Why don't you spend the night with us? Koromisloff can sleep here in the drawing-room on the sofa, and you, Smerkaloff, can have Peter's bed. Peter can go in my husband's study. Do stay!'

As the clock strikes two silence falls at last. Then the bedroom door opens, and Nadejda appears.

'Paul, are you asleep?' she whispers.

'No, what do you want?'

'Darling, go to your study and lie down on the sofa there, I want to put Miss Olga into your bed. Go, dear! I would put her in the study, but she is afraid to sleep alone. Do get up!'

Zaikin gets up, throws a dressing-gown over his shoulders, seizes a pillow, and crawls into the study. Feeling his way to the sofa, he strikes a match and sees Peter lying on it! The boy is awake and is gazing with wide eyes at the flame.

'Papa, why don't mosquitoes go to sleep at night?' he inquires.

'Because – because,' mutters Zaikin, 'because you and I are not wanted here. We haven't even a place to sleep!'

'Papa, why does Miss Olga have freckles on her face?'

'Oh, shut up! I'm tired of you!'

After a few moments' reflection Zaikin dresses and steps out into the road to get some fresh air. He looks up at the grey morning sky, the motionless clouds, hears the lazy cry of a sleepy rail, and muses on the morrow when, in town once more, he will return after the day's business and throw himself down to sleep. All at once there appears from round the corner the form of a man.

'The watchman, no doubt,' thinks Zaikin.

But as they catch sight of one another and approach more closely he recognises yesterday's acquaintance of the carroty-red trousers.

'What, not asleep?' he asks.

'No, I somehow can't sleep,' sigh the red trousers 'I am enjoying nature. A beloved guest came to stay with us, you know, on the night train – my wife's mamma. My nieces came with her; such fine little girls! I am delighted, although – it is rather damp. And you, too, are enjoying nature?'

'Yes,' bellows Zaikin, 'I, too, am enjoying – I say, don't you know some – isn't there any bar or something of the sort near here?'

The red trousers raise their eyes to heaven in profound meditation.

The Robbers

ERGUNOFF, the doctor's assistant, was a man of frivolous character who had the reputation in the district of a windbag and a great drinker. One evening before Christmas he was returning from the hamlet of Repin with some purchases for the hospital. To bring him back more quickly, the doctor had lent him his very best horse.

At first the weather was fair, but toward eight o'clock a violent snowstorm sprang up and, with some seven versts more to go, Ergunoff completely lost his way.

He did not know which way to guide the horse, as the road was strange, so he went on at random wherever his fancy led him, hoping that the horse would find the way home. Two hours passed; the horse was exhausted and he himself was freezing. He imagined he was going back to Repin instead of toward home, when he suddenly heard the faint barking of a dog above the noise of the storm and saw a dim red light ahead. A high gate and a long wooden fence surmounted by a bristling row of spikes gradually appeared; behind them rose the crooked windlass of a well. The wind swept aside the clouds of snow and a squat little cottage with a high roof took shape around the ruddy light. Of its three windows, one had a red curtain hanging before it and behind this a light was burning.

What was this dwelling? The doctor remembered that there was said to be an inn, formerly owned by Andrew Tchirikoff, lying to the right of the road some six or seven versts from the hospital. He remembered, too, that Tchirikoff had been murdered by carriers not long since, leaving behind him an old wife and a daughter, Liubka, who had come to the hospital for medicine two years ago. The house had an evil reputation, and to come there late in the evening, and with somebody else's horse, too, was not unfraught with danger.

But there was nothing else to be done now; the doctor felt for the revolver in his saddle-bag, coughed sternly, and knocked on the window with his whip.

'Hey! Is anyone there?' he shouted. 'Let me in to warm myself, good woman!'

With a hoarse bark a black dog whirled out under the feet of his horse, then came a white one, then another black one – a whole dozen of them. The doctor picked out the biggest, brandished his whip, and brought it down with all his might across the dog's back. The little, long-legged cur threw up its sharp muzzle and gave a thin, piercing howl.

The doctor stood and knocked a long time at the window. At last a light glowed on the frosted trees near the house, the gate creaked, and the muffled form of a woman appeared with a lantern in her hand.

'Let me in to warm myself, granny!' cried the doctor. 'I am on my way to the hospital and have lost the road. This weather is frightful. Don't be afraid; I am a friend.'

'Our friends are all inside and we don't want any strangers,' answered the form roughly. 'Why do you knock when you don't have to? The gate isn't locked.'

The doctor entered the yard and stopped on the threshold of the house.

'Tell someone to look after my horse, old woman,' he said.

'I am not an old woman,' said the figure, and, indeed, this was so. Her face was lit for an instant as she blew out the lantern, and the doctor saw her black eyes and recognised Liubka.

'I can't get a man now,' she said as she went into the house. 'Some are drunk and asleep and the others have been away in Repin since morning. This is a holiday.'

While tying his horse in the shed, Ergunoff heard whinnying and made out another horse in the darkness. He put out his hand and felt a Cossack saddle. This meant that there was someone besides the two women in the house. In any case, the doctor unsaddled his horse and took his saddle and purchases in with him.

The first room he entered was almost empty. The air was hot and smelled of freshly scrubbed boards. At a table under the icons sat a small, thin peasant of forty with a little red beard and wearing a blue shirt. It was Kalashnikoff, a notorious ruffian and horse thief, whose father and uncle kept a tavern at Bogolofka where they carried on a trade in stolen horses. He had been to the hospital more than once, not for medicine but to talk about horses with the doctor. Hadn't his honour the doctor a horse for sale? And wouldn't he trade the brown mare for the dun gelding? Tonight he had plastered his hair with pomade and silver ear-rings shone in his ears – he was in holiday garb. Frowning, his lower lip hanging, he was attentively studying a large, untidy picture-book. Stretched on the floor by the stove lay another peasant; his face, shoulders, and chest were covered with a fur coat; he seemed to be asleep. Two pools of melted snow lay at his feet which were shod in new boots with shining steel under the heels.

Kalashnikoff greeted the doctor as he caught sight of him.

'What awful weather!' answered Ergunoff, rubbing his cold knees with his hands. 'The snow has gone down my neck, and I am wet through, and I think my revolver – '

He took out his revolver, looked at it from all sides, and put it back in the saddle-bag; but it did not make the slightest impression; the peasant went on looking at his book.

'Yes, this is awful weather. I lost my way, and if it had not been for the dogs here I should have been frozen to death. Where are the keepers of the inn?'

'The old woman has gone to Repin. The girl is getting supper,' answered Kalashnikoff.

Silence fell. The doctor, all huddled up, shivered and grunted, blew on his hands, and pretended to be dreadfully frozen and miserable. The excited dogs still howled in the yard. The silence grew wearisome.

'You come from Bogolofka, don't you?' asked the doctor severely.

'Yes, from Bogolofka,' answered the peasant.

Because he had nothing better to do, the doctor began to think about Bogolofka. It is a large village lying in a deep ravine, and to anyone travelling along the highroad at night, looking down into the dark gorge and then up at the sky, it seems as if the moon were hanging over a bottomless abyss and as if this were the jumping-off place of the earth. The road leading down is so steep, so winding and narrow, that when he was called to Bogolofka during an epidemic, or to vaccinate the people for smallpox, the doctor would have to whistle and shout with all his might the whole way down, for to pass a wagon on that road was impossible.

The peasants of Bogolofka enjoy a great reputation as gardeners and horse thieves; their orchards are magnificent, and in the springtime the whole village is sunk in a sea of white cherry blossoms. In summer a bucketful of cherries can be had for three copecks – you just pay your money and help yourself. The men and women are handsome and prosperous. They love finery and do nothing, not even on working days, but sit on their beds and clean one another's heads.

But now, at last, footsteps were heard and Liubka came in. She was a young girl of twenty, barefoot and in a red dress. She cast a sidelong glance at the doctor and crossed the room twice from corner to corner, not walking simply but mincing and throwing out her chest; it was obvious that she liked to shuffle her bare feet on the freshly scrubbed boards and had taken off her shoes and stockings on purpose to do it.

Kalashnikoff burst out laughing and beckoned her to him; she went to the table and he pointed to a picture of the prophet Elijah driving a span of three horses to heaven. Liubka rested her elbows on the table and her long, red-brown braid, tied at the end with a bit of red ribbon, fell across her shoulder and hung almost to the floor. She, too, laughed.

'What a perfectly beautiful picture!' exclaimed Kalashnikoff. 'Beautiful!' he repeated, and made a motion as if he wanted to take the reins into his own hands.

The wind rumbled in the stove; something growled and squealed there as if a large dog were killing a rat.

'The evil ones are going by!' said Liubka.

'That was the wind,' said Kalashnikoff. He was silent for a while and then raised his eyes to the doctor's face and asked: 'According to you, sir, according to the ideas of educated people, are there any devils in the world or not?'

'What shall I say, old man?' answered the doctor, shrugging one shoulder. 'Of course, scientifically speaking, devils don't exist because they are only a superstition, but, talking it over simply, as you and I are doing, I should say that they did. I have been through a great deal in my life. After finishing school I decided to be a doctor in a dragoon regiment, and of course I went to the war and have received the Red Cross medal. After the peace of San Stefano I came back to Russia and entered the civil service. I can truthfully say that I have seen more marvels in my roving life than most people have seen in their dreams, and so, of course, I have met devils too, not devils with horns and tails – they are all nonsense – but devils something on that order – '

'Where?' asked Kalashnikoff.

'In various places. Though it shouldn't be mentioned at night, I met one right here once, near this very house. I was on my way to Golishino to do some vaccinating, driving along in a racing cart. I had my instruments with me, and my watch and so forth, and then the horse and all – well, I was hurrying along at a smart pace; you never can tell what might happen with so many tramps about. I had got as far as that confounded Snaky Hollow and had started going down when I suddenly saw someone coming toward me. His hair and eyes were black and his whole face was black as soot. He went straight up to my horse, took hold of the left rein, and ordered me to stop. He looked at the horse and then at me, and then threw down the rein and, without any suspicious words, said: "Where are you going?" But he was grinning and his eyes looked wicked. "You're a sly bird!" I thought, and answered, "I am going to do some vaccinating. What business is it of yours?" "If that's so," said he, "you can vaccinate me," and with that he bared his arm and thrust it under my nose. Of course I didn't argue with him. I just vaccinated him then and there to get rid of him. When I looked at my lancet afterward it was all rusty.'

The peasant who had been lying asleep by the stove suddenly turned over and threw off his coat, and, to his great surprise, the doctor recognised the stranger whom he had encountered in Snaky Hollow. The man's hair, eyebrows, and eyes were black as coal, his face was swarthy, and in addition he had a black spot the size of a lentil on his right cheek. He looked mockingly at the doctor and said:

'I took hold of the left rein, that is true, but you are raving about the vaccination, mister. We never even mentioned smallpox.'

The doctor was embarrassed. 'I wasn't talking about you,' he said. 'Lie down, since that's what you were doing.'

The dark peasant had never been to the hospital, and the doctor did not know who he was nor where he came from, but now, observing him, he decided that he must be a gypsy. The man got up, yawned loudly, and, sitting down beside Liubka and Kalashnikoff at the table, began looking at the pictures. Jealousy and emotion were depicted on his sleepy face.

'There, Merik!' Liubka said to him. 'If you'll bring me some horses like those I'll go to heaven!'

'Sinners can't go to heaven,' said Kalashnikoff. 'Heaven is for the saints.'

Liubka got up and began to lay the table. She fetched a great chunk of hog's fat, some salted cucumbers, a wooden plate of boiled beef, and finally a pan in which a sausage and cabbage were frying. There also appeared on the table a glass decanter of vodka which, when it was poured out, filled the room with the scent of orange-peel.

The doctor felt angry with Kalashnikoff and the dark Merik for talking together all the time without taking any more notice of him than if he had not been in the room. He wanted to talk and brag and drink and eat his fill, and if possible to romp with Liubka, who had sat down beside him and got up five times during supper and, with her hands on her broad hips, nudged him as if accidentally with her handsome shoulders. She was a lusty, merry wench, boisterous, and never still for an instant. She was continually sitting down and then jumping up again, and when she sat down beside you would turn first her breast and then her back toward you, like a naughty child, invariably jostling you with her elbow or knee.

The doctor didn't like it, either, that the peasants drank only one glass of vodka apiece and then stopped. It was awkward to drink alone, but at last he could resist it no longer and took a second glass, then a third, and then ate the whole sausage. He decided to flatter the peasants so that they would stop holding him at a distance and take him into their company.

'You are great fellows at Bogolofka,' he said, wagging his head.

'How do you mean?' asked Kalashnikoff.

'Well, about horses; you are experts at stealing.'

'That was in the old days,' said Merik after a pause. 'Not one of the old crowd is left now but Filia, and his hair is grey.'

'Yes, only old Filia,' sighed Kalashnikoff. 'He must be seventy now. The German immigrants put out one of his eyes and he is almost blind in the other. He has a cataract. Whenever the police saw him in the old days they used to call out, "Hello, Shamil!"* and all the peasants called him Shamil, too, but now it's only "One-eyed Filia". What a great chap he used to be! He and Andrew Grigoritch and I met one night near Rogovna, where a regiment of cavalry was encamped, and drove away ten of the best horses in the regiment, and the sentries never suspected a thing. Next morning we sold the whole bunch to Afonka, the gypsy, for twenty roubles. Yes, sir! But thieves these days don't rob a man unless he's either drunk or asleep, and without fear of God will even pull off his boots if he's drunk; and then they go ten versts with the horse, scared to death all the time, and haggle with the Jews at the bazaar till the police nab them, the fools! That kind of thing isn't a spree, it's a mess! They're a rotten lot, and that's the truth.'

'What about Merik?' asked Liubka.

'Merik isn't one of us,' Kalashnikoff answered. 'He comes from Kharkoff. He's a fine fellow, there's no doubt about that; he's all right, is Merik.'

Liubka glanced slyly and gaily at Merik and said:

'It wasn't for nothing they dipped him in the ice hole!'

'How was that?' asked the doctor.

'This way,' answered Merik with a grin. 'Filia once stole three horses belonging to the Samoiloff tenants, and their suspicions fell on me. There were ten tenants on the place – thirty men in all, counting the workmen – all big, husky fellows. Well, one of them comes up to me at

---

* A famous Circassian chieftain.

the bazaar one day and says: "Come on, Merik, and see the new horses we've brought from the fair!" I want to see them, of course, so off I go to where the fellows are, all thirty of them. They grabbed me and tied my hands behind my back, and led me down to the river. One hole in the ice had already been made; they cut another about ten feet away. "Come on!" they said. "We'll show you the horses." Then they made a noose out of rope and fastened it under my arms, tied a crooked pole to the other end, long enough to reach from hole to hole, pushed it into the water, and pulled. Down I went – splash! – just as I was, fur coat, boots, and all. They stood and prodded me and kicked me, and finally dragged me under the ice and out through the other hole.'

Liubka shivered and shrank together.

'At first the cold threw me into a glow,' Merik continued, 'but when they pulled me out, my strength had all gone, and I lay helpless on the snow while the fellows stood over me and beat my knees and elbows with sticks. It hurt like the mischief. When they had finished thrashing me they went away. And now everything on me began to freeze; my clothes turned into a block of ice. I raised myself and fell down again. Then – thank goodness! – a woman came by and took me away with her.'

During this story the doctor had drunk five or six glasses of vodka, and his heart was growing merry. He, too, wanted to tell some wonderful yarn to show that he was as brave a fellow as they were and afraid of nothing.

'Once, in the province of Penza – ' he began, but, because he had drunk a great deal and perhaps also because they had caught him telling a lie, the peasants paid no attention to him, and even stopped answering his questions. Worse than that: they completely ignored his presence and launched into such openhearted confidences that his blood ran cold and his hair stood straight on end.

Kalashnikoff's manner was staid, as became a sober-minded man of his position. He spoke authoritatively and made the sign of the cross over his mouth whenever he yawned. No one would have suspected him of being a brigand, a merciless brigand, the scourge of the unfortunate, a man who had been in jail twice and who would have been sent to Siberia had not his father and uncle, thieves like himself, bought him off. Merik swaggered like a young dandy. He saw that Liubka and Kalashnikoff were admiring him and thought himself a very fine fellow; so he stuck his arms akimbo, threw out his chest, and stretched himself till the bench cracked.

After supper Kalashnikoff said a short prayer before the icon without getting up and shook hands with Merik; Merik, too, said a prayer and returned the hand-shake. Liubka cleared away the remains of the supper, scattered gingerbread cakes, roasted nuts, and pumpkin-seeds on the table, and brought out two bottles of sweet wine.

'Eternal peace to the soul of Andrew Grigoritch!' said Kalashnikoff, and he and Merik touched glasses. 'We used to meet here or at my brother Martin's when he was alive, and, Lord, Lord, what fellows we were! What talks we had! Such wonderful talks! There were Martin and Filia and noisy Theodore; everything was so pleasant and nice; and, heavens, what sprees we used to go on! Oh, what sprees!'

Liubka went out and came back in a few minutes with a string of beads around her neck and a green kerchief on her head.

'Merik, look what Kalashnikoff brought me today!' she cried.

She looked at herself in the glass and nodded her head so that the beads tinkled. Then she opened the chest and took out first a cotton dress with red and blue spots, then another with flounces that rustled and crackled like paper, and lastly a blue kerchief shot with the colours of the rainbow. These she showed, laughing and clapping her hands as if amazed at owning so many treasures.

Kalashnikoff tuned a balalaika and began to play, and the doctor could not for the life of him make out whether the tune were merry or sad; at times it was so dreadfully sad that it made him want to cry, and then the next moment it was gay. Merik suddenly jumped up, beat on the floor with his iron-shod boots, and then, spreading his arms, crossed the room on his heels from the table to the stove and from the stove to the chest. Here he leaped up as if he had been stung, clapped his feet in the air, dropped down, and, sitting on his heels, danced helter-skelter across the floor.

Liubka waved both arms, gave a despairing shriek, and followed after him. She danced sideways at first, stealthily, as if trying to steal up on someone and hit him from behind; then she drummed with her heels as Merik did, spun round like a top, and dropped down so that her red dress floated up about her like a bell. Looking at her fiercely, and showing his teeth, Merik danced toward her, crouching on his heels, as if longing to destroy her with his terrible feet; but she jumped up, threw back her head, and, waving her arms as a great bird flaps its wings, flew about the room, hardly touching the floor.

'What a glorious girl!' sighed the doctor, sitting on the chest and watching the dancers. 'All lightning and fire! What would I not give – ' and he wished he were a peasant instead of a doctor. Why did he wear a coat and a chain with a gilt key and not a blue shirt and a rope girdle?

Then he might sing boldly and dance and throw his arms around Liubka as Merik did.

The fierce stamping and yelling and huzzaing rattled the dishes in the cupboard, the candle flame leaped and flickered.

The string broke around Liubka's neck, and the beads scattered across the floor; her kerchief slipped from her head, and, instead of a girl, all that could be seen was a red cloud and the flash of dark eyes. As for Merik, it looked as if every instant his arms and legs would fly off.

But now he struck the floor for the last time with his heel and stopped as if struck by lightning. Exhausted, scarcely able to breathe, Liubka leaned against him and clutched him as if he had been a post. He threw his arms around her and, looking into her eyes, said tenderly and softly as if in play:

'I'm going to find where the old woman keeps her money, and then I'll kill her and cut your little throat with a knife and set fire to the inn. Everyone will think you were burned to death, and I'll take your money and go to Kuban, and there I'll herd horses and keep sheep.'

Liubka did not answer anything to this, she only looked wistfully at Merik and said:

'Is it nice in Kuban, Merik?'

He did not answer her but went across to the chest, sat down, and was lost in thought – he was probably dreaming of Kuban.

'It's time for me to go,' said Kalashnikoff. 'Filia is probably waiting for me. Goodbye, Liubka.'

The doctor went out to see that Kalashnikoff did not ride away on his horse. The storm was still raging. White clouds of snow, catching their long tails in the bushes and tall grass, swept across the yard, and on the far side of the fence great giants in white shrouds with wide sleeves whirled and fell and rose again, wrestling and waving their arms. What a wind there was! The naked birches and cherry trees, unable to resist its rough caresses, bent to the ground and moaned: 'For what sins, O Lord, hast thou fastened us to the earth, and why may we not fly away free?'

'Get along!' said Kalashnikoff roughly as he mounted his horse. One half of the gate was open and a huge snowdrift had piled up beside it. 'Come up, will you?' cried Kalashnikoff, and the little short-legged pony started forward and buried itself to the belly in the drift. Kalashnikoff was whitened with snow and soon he and his horse faded out of sight beyond the gate.

When the doctor re-entered the house he found Liubka on the floor picking up her beads; Merik was gone.

'What a stunning wench!' thought the doctor, lying down on the bench and putting his coat under his head. 'If only Merik weren't here!'

It teased him to have Liubka creeping about on the floor near the bench, and he thought that if it weren't for Merik he would certainly get up and kiss her and then see what would happen next. It was true that she was only a girl, but she could hardly be honest; and, even if she were, why need he be squeamish in a robber's den? Liubka picked up her beads and went away. The candle burned out, and the flame caught the bit of paper in the socket. The doctor laid his revolver and a box of matches beside him and blew out the light. The lamp before the icon flickered so brightly that it hurt his eyes; splashes of light danced across the ceiling, the floor, and the cupboard, and among them the doctor seemed to see Liubka, deep-chested and strong, now whirling like a top, now breathing heavily, exhausted with the dance.

'Oh, if the devil would only take Merik!' he thought.

The lamp flared up for the last time, winked and went out. Someone, probably Merik, came into the room and sat down on the bench. He pulled at his pipe, and his swarthy cheeks with their black spot were lit for a second. The vile tobacco smoke tickled the doctor's throat.

'What horrible tobacco you smoke, confound it!' the doctor said. 'It makes me sick.'

'I always mix my tobacco with the flowers of oats,' answered Merik; 'it is better for the chest.'

He smoked, spat, and went out. Half an hour passed. A light flashed in the hall. Merik came back in his hat and coat, followed by Liubka carrying a candle.

'Stay here, Merik!' she said in a beseeching voice.

'No, Liubka, don't detain me.'

'Listen, Merik,' said Liubka, and her voice grew tender and soft, 'I know you will find my mother's money and kill her and me, and then go to Kuban and love other girls; but I don't care. I only ask one thing, dearie – stay here!'

'No, I want to be off on a spree,' said Merik, tightening his belt.

'How can you go off on a spree? You came here on foot.'

Merik stooped down and whispered something in Liubka's ear; she looked at the door and laughed through her tears.

'The old windbag is asleep,' she said.

Merik took her in his arms, gave her a great kiss, and went out-of-doors. The doctor slipped his revolver into his pocket, jumped up quickly, and ran after him.

'Let me get by!' he cried to Liubka as she slammed and bolted the front door, planting herself in front of it. 'Let me get by! What are you standing there for?'

'Why do you want to get by?'

'To look at my horse.'

Liubka fixed her eyes on him with an expression both tender and sly.

'Why do you want to look at your horse? Look at me!' she said, and bent down and touched the gold key on his chain with her finger.

'Let me get by; he is going away on my horse!' cried the doctor. 'Let me get by, damn you!' he shouted and struck her furiously on the shoulder as he threw his whole weight against her in order to shove her aside. But she clung to the bolt as tightly as if she were made of steel.

'Let me pass!' he yelled, struggling. 'I tell you he's going!'

'Nonsense! He won't go.' She breathed heavily and, stroking her aching shoulder, looked him up and down again from head to foot, blushed, and laughed.

'Don't go, dearie,' she said; 'I shall be lonely without you.'

The doctor looked into her eyes, reflected, and kissed her. She did not resist him.

'Come! No more nonsense! Let me get by!'

She said nothing.

'I heard what you said to Merik just now; you love him!' he said.

'That meant nothing; I know whom I love.'

Again she touched the little key with her finger and said softly:

'Give me that!'

The doctor took the key off the chain and gave it to her. She suddenly threw back her head and listened to something; her face became serious, and her eyes seemed to the doctor to grow crafty and cold. He remembered his horse, pushed her aside easily, and ran out into the yard. A sleepy pig was grunting regularly and lazily in the shed, and a cow was knocking her horns against the walls. The doctor struck a match and saw them both as well as the dogs that threw themselves from all sides toward the light, but the horse had vanished. Shouting and waving his arms at the dogs, stumbling over snowdrifts and sinking into the snow, he ran out beyond the gate and stared into the darkness. Strain his eyes as he might he saw only the flying snow that was piling itself into many different shapes; now it was the pale, grinning face of a corpse that glared out of the gloom, now a white horse galloped by ridden by a woman in a muslin dress, now a flock of white swans flew over his head. Trembling with cold and rage and not knowing what to do, the doctor fired a shot at the dogs without hitting one and hurried back into the house.

As he entered the hall he distinctly heard someone dart out of the room and slam the door. He went in. All was dark. He tried a door and found it locked. Then, striking match after match, he ran back into the hall, from there into the kitchen, and from the kitchen into a little room where all the walls were hung with skirts and dresses and the air smelled of herbs and fennel. In a corner near the stove stood a bed with a whole mountain of pillows on it. This was probably where the old woman lived. From here the doctor passed into another little room, and there he found Liubka. She was lying on a chest and was covered with a bright patchwork quilt. She pretended to be asleep. At her head hung an icon with a lamp burning before it.

'Where is my horse?' asked the doctor sternly.

Liubka did not move.

'Where is my horse, I say?' he repeated more sternly still and jerked the quilt off her. 'Answer me, you she-devil!' he shouted.

Liubka jumped up and fell on her knees, shrinking against the wall. With one hand she grasped her chemise, the other clutched at the quilt; she glared at the doctor with horror and fear, and, like an animal in a trap, her eyes craftily followed every movement he made.

'Tell me where my horse is or I'll shake the life out of you!' he yelled.

'Get away, you beast!' she said hoarsely.

The doctor seized the neck of her chemise, it tore; then, unable to contain himself, he caught the girl in his arms. Hissing with rage, she slipped out of his embrace, and, freeing one arm – the other was caught in her torn chemise – she struck him on the head with her fist.

The room swam before his eyes, something roared and thumped in his ears; as he staggered back she dealt him another blow, this time on the temple.

Reeling and clutching at the doors to keep himself from falling, he made his way into the room where his things were and lay down on the bench. After lying still for a while he took a box of matches out of his pocket and struck them one by one in an aimless way, blowing them out and throwing them under the table. This he did till the matches were all gone.

But now the darkness was fading behind the window-panes and the cocks were beginning to crow. Ergunoff's head still ached and he heard a roaring in his ears as if he were sitting under a railway bridge with a train going over his head. He managed somehow to put on his hat and coat, but his saddle and bundle of purchases had vanished and his saddle-bags were empty. It was not for nothing that someone had slipped out of the room as he came in the night before!

He took a poker from the kitchen to keep off the dogs and went out into the yard, leaving the door ajar. The wind had died down; all was quiet. He went out at the gate. The country lay still as death; not a bird could be seen in the morning sky. A forest of little trees lay like a blue mist on either side of the road, as far as the eye could see.

The doctor forced himself to think of the reception that awaited him at the hospital and of what his chief would say. He felt that he absolutely must think of it and decide beforehand how to answer the questions that would be put to him, but these thoughts grew vague and dispersed. He thought only of Liubka as he walked along and of the peasants with whom he had spent the night. He remembered how Liubka, when she struck him the second time, had stooped to pick up the quilt and of how her loosened braid had swept the floor. He grew confused and wondered why doctors and doctors' assistants, merchants, clerks, and peasants existed in the world and not simply free people. Birds were free and wild animals were free, Merik was free – they were afraid of nothing and dependent on no one. Who had decreed that one must get up in the morning, have dinner at noon, and go to bed at night? Or that a doctor was above his assistant; that one must live in a house and love only one's wife? Why not, on the contrary, have dinner at night and sleep all day? Oh, to jump on a horse without asking to whom it belonged and race down the wind, through woods and fields, to the devil! Oh, to make love to the girls and to snap one's fingers at the whole world!

The doctor dropped his poker in the snow, leaned his forehead against the cold, white trunk of a birch tree, and thought; and his grey, monotonous life, his salary, his dependence, his drugs, his everlasting fussing with bottles and flies seemed to him contemptible and sickening.

'Who says it is a sin to lead a wild life?' he asked himself. 'Those who have never known freedom as Merik and Kalashnikoff have! Those who have never loved Liubka! They are beggars all their lives; they love only their wives and live without joy, like frogs in a pond.'

And of himself he thought that if he were not a thief and a ruffian yes – and a highwayman, too – it was only because he did not know how to be one and because the opportunity had never come in his way.

A year and a half passed. One spring night after Easter the doctor, long since dismissed from the hospital and without work, came out of a saloon in Repin and wandered aimlessly down the street and out into the open country.

Here the air smelled of spring and a warm, caressing breeze was blowing. The peaceful stars looked down upon the earth. How deep the sky looked, and how immeasurably vast, stretched across the world! 'The world is well created,' thought the doctor, 'but why and for what purpose do men divide themselves into the drunk and the sober, into workers and those who are out of work, and so forth? Why does the sober, well-fed man sleep quietly at home while the drunken, starving one must wander in the fields without a place to lay his head? Why must the man that doesn't serve others for wages always go unfed, unshod, and in rags? Who decreed this? The birds and beasts of the forest don't work for wages but live according to their own sweet wills.'

A splendid red light flared up over the horizon and spread across the sky. The doctor stood a long time looking at it and thought: 'What if I did take a samovar yesterday that didn't belong to me and throw away the money at the tavern? Was that a sin? Why was it a sin?'

Two wagons went by on the road; in one lay a sleeping woman, in the other sat an old man without a hat.

'Whose house is that burning, daddy?' asked the doctor.

'Andrew Tchirikoff's inn,' answered the old man.

Then the doctor thought of all that had happened to him at that inn one winter's night a year and a half ago and remembered Merik's boast; he saw in imagination Liubka and the old woman burning with their throats cut and envied Merik. As he went back to the tavern and looked at the houses of the wealthy innkeepers, cattle dealers, and blacksmiths he thought: 'How good it would be if I could make my way by night into some house inhabited by people who are still richer!'

Lean and Fat

TWO FRIENDS once met in a railway station; one was fat and the other was lean. The fat man had just finished dinner at the station; his lips were still buttery and as glossy as ripe cherries. A perfume of sherry and *fleurs d'oranger* hung about him. The lean man had just stepped out of the train and was loaded down with hand-bags, bundles, and bandboxes. He smelled of ham and coffee-grounds. The thin little woman with a long chin who peeped out from behind his back was his wife and the tall schoolboy with the half-closed eyes was his son.

'Porfiri!' exclaimed the fat man as he caught sight of the lean one. 'Is that really you? My dear old friend! It is an age since we last met.'

'Good Heavens!' cried the lean man, astounded. 'Misha! The friend of my childhood! Where have you come from?'

The friends embraced thrice and stared at each other with tears in their eyes. Both were agreeably overcome.

'Dear old chap!' began the lean man after the embrace was over. 'I never expected this! What a surprise! Here! Look at me properly! You are the same handsome fellow you always were! The same old darling, the same old dandy! Oh, Lord, Lord! Come, tell me! Are you rich? Are you married? I am married, as you see. Here! This is my wife, Louisa, formerly Vanzenbach – a Lutheran. And this is my son Nathaniel, in the third class at school. Nathaniel, this is a friend of my youth! We were at school together!'

Nathaniel reflected and then took off his cap.

'We were at school together!' the thin man continued. 'Do you remember how they used to tease you and call you Herostratus because you once burned a school-book with a cigarette? And how I used to be teased by being called Ephialtus because I used to tell tales on the others? What boys we were! Don't be afraid, Nathaniel; come up closer! And this is my wife, formerly Vanzenbach – a Lutheran.'

Nathaniel reflected and then hid himself behind his father's back.

'Well, well! And how goes the world with you, old fellow?' inquired the fat man, looking at his friend with delight. 'Are you working now or have you retired?'

'I am working, old man. This is the second year that I have been a collegiate assessor, and I have been awarded the Order of St Stanislas. The salary is small, but never mind! My wife gives music-lessons and I privately make cigarette cases out of wood – first-class cigarette cases! I sell them for one rouble apiece. If you take ten or more I make a reduction, of course. We manage to get along somehow. I used to be employed in one of the departments, you know, but I have been transferred by the administration to this place. And how about you? You are probably state councillor by now, are you not?'

'No, old man; guess higher!' said the fat man. 'I am already privy councillor. I have two decorations.'

The lean man suddenly paled and stood rooted to the spot. His face became distorted by a very broad smile; he shrivelled and shrank and stooped and his bandboxes shrivelled and grew wrinkled. His wife's long chin grew still longer; Nathaniel drew himself up at attention and began doing up all the buttons of his uniform.

'I, your Excellency – I am delighted, I am sure. A friend, one may say, of one's childhood, has all at once become such a great man! Hee! hee! hee!'

'Enough of that!' said the fat man frowning. 'Why affect such a tone? You and I are old friends; what's the need of all this respect for rank?'

'Allow me – oh, really!' tittered the lean man, shrivelling still smaller. 'The gracious attention of your Excellency is something on the order of a life-giving dew. This, your Excellency, is my son Nathaniel. This is my wife, Louisa, a Lutheran – in a way – '

The fat man wanted to retort something, but such obsequiousness, such mawkishness, such deferential acidity were written all over the lean man's face that the privy councillor was nauseated. He turned away from him and gave him his hand in farewell.

The lean man took three fingers of it, bowed with his whole body, and giggled like a Chinaman:

'Hee! hee! hee!'

His wife smiled, Nathaniel scraped his foot and dropped his cap. All three were agreeably overcome.

On the Way

A golden cloud lay for a night
On the breast of a giant crag.

LERMONTOFF

In the room which the Cossack innkeeper, Simon Tchistoplui, himself calls the 'visitors' room', meaning that it is set aside exclusively for travellers, a tall, broad-shouldered man of forty sat at a large, unpainted table. His elbows were resting upon it, his head was propped in his hands, and he was asleep. The stump of a tallow candle, which was stuck in an empty pomade jar, lit his red beard, his broad, thick nose, his sunburned cheeks, and the heavy eyebrows which overhung his closed eyes. Nose, cheeks, and brows – each feature in itself was heavy and coarse, like the furniture and the stove in the 'visitors' room'; but, taken altogether, they made up a harmonious and even a beautiful whole. And this is, generally speaking, the structure of the Russian physiognomy; the larger and more prominent the features, the gentler and kinder the face appears to be. The man was dressed in a gentleman's short coat, worn but bound with new braid, a plush waistcoat, and wide black trousers tucked into high boots.

On one of the benches which formed a continuous row along the wall, on the fur of a fox-skin coat, slept a little girl of eight wearing a brown dress and long black stockings. Her face was pale, her hair was curly and fair, and her shoulders were narrow; her whole body was lithe and thin, but her nose stood out, a thick ugly knob, like the man's. She was sleeping soundly and did not feel that the round little comb which she wore in her hair had slipped down and was pressing into her cheek.

The 'visitors' room' wore a holiday look. The air smelled of its freshly scrubbed floor, the usual array of cloths was missing from the line which was stretched diagonally across the whole room, and a little shrine lamp was burning in a corner over the table, casting a red spot of light on the icon of Gregory the Bringer of Victory. Two rows of bad woodcuts started at the corner where hung the icon and stretched along either wall, observing in their choice of subjects a rigid and careful gradation from the religious to the worldly. By the dim light of the candle and of the little red lamp they looked an unbroken band covered with dark blotches, but when the stove drew in its breath with a howl, as if longing to sing in tune with the wind, and the logs took heart and broke out into bright flames, muttering angrily, then ruddy splashes of light would flicker over the timbered walls and the monk Seraphim or the Shah Nasr-Ed-Din would start out over the head of the sleeping man, or a fat brown child would grow out of the darkness, staring and whispering something into the ear of an uncommonly dull and indifferent Virgin.

Outside a storm was roaring. Something fiendish and evil but profoundly unhappy was prowling about the inn with the fury of a wild beast, trying to force its way into the house. Banging the doors, knocking on the windows and on the roof, tearing at the walls, it would first threaten, then implore, then grow silent awhile, and at last rush down the flue into the stove with a joyous, treacherous shriek. But here the logs would flare up and the flames leap furiously to meet the enemy like watch-dogs on the chain; a battle would ensue, followed by a sob, a whine, and an angry roar. Through it all could be heard the rancorous anguish, the ungratified hatred, and the bitter impotence of one who has once been a victor.

It seemed as if the 'visitors' room' must lie for ever spellbound by this wild, inhuman music; but at last the door creaked and the tavern boy came into the room wearing a new calico shirt. Limping and blinking his sleepy eyes, he snuffed the candle with his fingers, piled more wood on the fire, and went out. The bells of the church, which at Rogatch lies only a hundred steps from the inn, rang out for midnight. The wind sported with the sound as it did with the snowflakes; it pursued the notes and whirled them over a mighty space so that some were broken off short, some were drawn out into long, quavering tones, and some were lost entirely in the general uproar. One peal rang out as clearly in the room as if it had been struck under the very window. The little girl that lay asleep on the fox skins started and raised her head. For a moment she stared blankly at the dark window and at Nasr-Ed-Din, on whom the red light from the stove was playing, and then turned her eyes toward the sleeping man.

'Papa!' she said

But the man did not move. The child frowned crossly and lay down again, drawing up her legs. Someone yawned long and loud in the tap-room on the other side of the door. Soon after this came a faint sound of voices and the squeaking of a door pulley. Someone entered the house, shook off the snow, and stamped his felt boots with a muffled sound.

'Who is it?' asked a lazy female voice.

'The young lady Ilovaiskaya has come,' a bass voice answered.

Again the pulley squeaked. The wind rushed noisily in. Someone, the lame boy most likely, ran to the door of the 'visitors' room', coughed respectfully, and touched the latch.

'Come this way, dear young lady; come in,' said a woman's singsong voice. 'Everything is clean in here, my pretty – '

The door flew open and a bearded peasant appeared on the threshold wearing the long coat of a coachman and bearing a large trunk on his shoulder. He was plastered with snow from his head to his feet. Behind him entered a little female form of scarcely half his height, showing neither face nor arms, muffled and wrapped about like a bundle and also covered with snow.

A dampness as from a cellar blew from the coachman and the bundle toward the little girl and the candle flame wavered.

'How stupid!' cried the bundle crossly. 'We could go on perfectly well! We have only twelve more miles to go, through woods almost all the way, and we shouldn't get lost.'

'Lost or not lost, miss, the horses won't go any farther,' answered the coachman. 'Lord! Lord! One would think I had done it on purpose!'

'Heaven knows where you've brought me to. But hush! There seems to be someone asleep here. Go away.'

The coachman set down the trunk, at which the layers of snow were shaken from his shoulders, emitted a sobbing sound from his nose, and went out. Then the child saw two little hands creep out of the middle of the bundle, rise upward, and begin angrily to unwind a tangle of shawls and kerchiefs and scarfs. First a large shawl fell to the floor and then a hood; this was followed by a white knitted scarf. Having freed her head, the newcomer threw off her cloak and at once appeared half her former width. She now wore a long, grey coat with big buttons and bulging pockets. From one of these she drew a paper parcel and from the other a bunch of large, heavy keys. These she laid down so carelessly that the sleeping man started and opened his eyes. For a minute he looked dully round him as if not realising where he was, then he threw up his head and walked across to a corner where he sat down. The newcomer took off her coat, which again narrowed her by half, pulled off her plush overshoes, and also sat down.

She now no longer resembled a bundle but appeared as a slender brunette of twenty, slim as a little serpent, with a pale, oval face and curly hair. Her nose was long and pointed, her chin, too, was long and pointed, and the corners of her mouth were pointed; in consequence of all this sharpness the expression of her face, too, was piquant. Squeezed into a tight black dress with a quantity of lace at the throat and sleeves, she recalled some portrait of an English lady of the Middle Ages. The grave, concentrated expression of her face enhanced this resemblance.

The little brunette looked round the room, glanced at the man and at the child, shrugged her shoulders, and sat down by the window. The dark panes shook in the raw west wind; large snowflakes, gleaming whitely, fell against the glass and at once vanished, swept away by the blast. The wild music grew ever louder and louder.

After a long period of silence the child suddenly turned over and, crossly rapping out each word, said:

'Lord! Lord! How unhappy I am! Unhappier than anyone else in the world!'

The man got up and tiptoed across to her with apologetic steps that ill suited his great size and his large beard.

'Can't you sleep, darling?' he asked guiltily. 'What do you want?'

'I don't want anything. My shoulder hurts. You are a horrid man, papa, and God will punish you. See if he doesn't!'

'My baby, I know your shoulder hurts, but what can I do, darling?' said the man in the voice of a husband who has been drinking and is excusing himself to his stern spouse. 'Your shoulder aches from travelling, Sasha. Tomorrow we will reach our journey's end, and then you can rest and the pain will all go away.'

'Tomorrow, tomorrow! Everyday you say tomorrow. We're going to travel for twenty days more!'

'But, my child, I promise you we will get there tomorrow. I never tell a story, and it is not my fault that this snow-storm has delayed us.'

'I can't stand it any more! I can't! I can't!'

Sasha rapped her foot sharply and rent the air with shrill, unpleasant wails. Her father made a helpless gesture and glanced in confusion at the little brunette. The girl shrugged her shoulders and went irresolutely toward Sasha.

'Listen, darling,' she said. 'Why do you cry? I know it is horrid to have an aching shoulder, but what can we do?'

'You see, madam,' said the man hastily, 'we have not slept for two nights and have been travelling in a terrible carriage, so of course it is natural that she should feel ill and distressed. And then, too, we have

struck a drunken driver, and our trunk has been stolen, and all the time
we have had this snow-storm. But what's the use of crying? The fact is,
this sleeping in a sitting position has tired me. I feel as if I were drunk.
For Heaven's sake, Sasha, it's sickening enough in this place as it is, and
here you are crying!'

The man shook his head, waved his hand in despair, and sat down.

'Of course, one ought not to cry,' said the little brunette. 'Only little
babies cry. If you are ill, darling, you had best get undressed and go to
sleep. Come, let's get undressed!'

When the child had been undressed and quieted silence once more
reigned. The dark girl sat by the window and looked about the room,
at the icon, and at the stove in perplexity. It was obvious that the place,
the child with its thick nose and boy's shirt, and the child's father all
appeared strange to her. This odd man sat in his corner as if he were
drunk, looked off to one side, and rubbed his face with the palm of his
hand. He sat silent and blinked, and anyone seeing his apologetic
appearance would hardly have expected him to begin talking in a few
minutes. But he was the first to break silence. He stroked his knees,
coughed, and began:

'What a comedy this is, I declare! I look about me and can hardly
believe my eyes. Why, in the name of mischief, should Fate have driven
us into this infernal inn? What was meant by it? Life sometimes makes
such a *salto mortale* that one is fairly staggered with perplexity. Have
you far to go, madam?'

'No, not far,' answered the girl. 'I am on my way from our estate,
which is twenty miles from here, to our farm where my father and
brother are. My name is Ilovaiskaya and our farm is called Ilovaiski,
too. It is twelve miles from here. What terrible weather!'

'It couldn't be worse.'

The lame boy entered the room and stuck a fresh candle-end into
the pomade jar.

'Here, you might bring us a samovar as quick as you can!' the man
said to him.

'Who wants to drink tea now?' the lame boy laughed. 'It's a sin to
drink before the morning service.'

'Never mind, be quick. We shall burn in hell for it, not you.'

Over their tea the new acquaintances fell into conversation. Ilovaiskaya
discovered that her companion was called Gregory Likarieff; that he
was a brother of the Likarieff who was marshal of the nobility in one of
the neighbouring counties; that he himself had once been a landowner,
but had been ruined. Likarieff learned that Ilovaiskaya's name was

Maria, that her father's estate was a very large one, and that she had the entire charge of it herself, as her father and brother were too easy-going and were far too much addicted to coursing.

'My father and brother are all, all alone on the farm,' said Ilovaiskaya, twiddling her fingers. (She had a habit of moving her fingers before her piquant face when she was speaking, and of moistening her lips with her pointed little tongue at the end of each sentence.) 'Men are careless creatures and never will raise a finger to help themselves. I wonder who will give my father and brother their breakfast after this fast. We have no mother, and the servants we have won't even lay the tablecloth straight without me. You can imagine the position my father and brother are in. They will find themselves without food to break their fast with while I have to sit here all night. How strange it all is!'

Ilovaiskaya shrugged her shoulders, sipped her tea, and continued:

'There are some holidays that have a scent of their own. At Easter and Christmas and on Trinity Sunday the air always smells of something unusual. Even unbelievers love these holidays. My brother, for instance, says that there is no God, yet on Easter Sunday he is always the first to run to the vigil service.'

Likarieff raised his eyes to Ilovaiskaya's face and laughed.

'They say there is no God,' the girl continued and laughed, too. 'But tell me, why do all great writers and students and all wise people in general believe in God at the end of their lives?'

'If a man has not been able to believe in his youth, my lady, he will not believe in his old age, were he never so many times a great writer.'

Judging from the sound of his cough, Likarieff possessed a bass voice, but, whether from fear of talking loud or whether from excessive timidity, he now spoke in a high one. After a short silence he sighed and said:

'My idea is this, that faith is a gift of the soul. It is like any other talent: one must be born with it to possess it. Judging from my own case, from the people I have known in my life, and from all I have seen going on about me, I believe this talent to be inherent in Russians in the highest degree. Russian life is made up of a constant succession of beliefs and enthusiasms and Russians have not yet scented unbelief and negation. If a Russian doesn't believe in God then he believes in something else.'

Likarieff accepted a cup of tea from Ilovaiskaya, swallowed half of it at a gulp, and went on:

'I will tell you how it is with me. Nature has placed in my soul an unusual faculty for believing. Between you and me, half of my life has been spent in the ranks of the atheists and nihilists, and yet there has never been an hour when I have not believed. All talents, as a rule, make their appearance in early childhood, and my gift showed itself when I could still walk upright under the table. My mother used to like to have her children eat a great deal, and when she was feeding me she used to say:

' "Eat! Soup is the most important thing in life!" I believed it. I ate soup ten times a day. I ate like a wolf till I swooned with loathing. When my nurse told me fairy-stories I believed in hobgoblins and demons and every kind of deviltry. I used to steal corrosive sublimate from my father and sprinkle it on little cakes and spread them out in the attic to poison the house sprites. But when I learned how to read and could understand the meaning of what I read I kept the whole province in an uproar. I started to run away to America; I turned highwayman; I tried to enter a monastery; I hired little boys to crucify me as if I were Christ. You will notice that my beliefs were all active and never lifeless. If I started for America I did not go alone, but seduced some fool like myself, and I was glad when I froze outside the walls of the town and got a thrashing. If I turned highwayman I invariably came home with a face all beaten up. I had an extremely agitated childhood, I can assure you! And then, when I was sent to school and had such truths instilled into me as that, for instance, the earth revolves round the sun, or that white light is not white but is made up of seven different colours, then how my little brain did hum! Everything was in a whirl in my head now: Joshua arresting the sun in its course, my mother denying the existence of lightning-rods on the authority of the prophet Elijah, my father indifferent to the truths I had discovered. My own insight stifled me. Like one insane, I roved through the house and stables preaching my truths, overcome with horror at the sight of ignorance and burning with indignation toward all those who in white light saw only white – but all that is childish nonsense. My serious enthusiasms began when I was at the university. Have you ever taken a course of learning anywhere, madam?'

'Yes, in Novotcherkass, at the Donski Institute.'

'But you have never followed a course of lectures? Then you probably don't know what a science is. Every science in the world must possess one and the same passport, without which it is senseless; it must aspire to the truth. Every one of them, down to pharmaceutics even, has its object, and this object is not to bring usefulness or comfort into life but to seek the truth. It is wonderful! When you set to work to learn a science it is the beginning which first astounds you. Believe me, there is nothing more splendid, more captivating, nothing that so stuns and grips the human soul as the beginnings of a science. After the first five or six lectures the highest hopes beckon you on. You already fancy yourself the master of truth. And I gave myself up to science, heart and soul, as passionately as I would give myself to a beloved woman. I was its slave, and there was no sun for me but science. Night and day I pored and howled over my books without raising my head, weeping when I saw people exploiting science for their own personal ends. The joke is that every science, like a recurring decimal, has a beginning and no end. Zoology has discovered thirty-five thousand five hundred different species of insects; chemistry can count sixty-five elements; if you were to add ten zeros to the right of each of these figures, zoology and chemistry would be no nearer the end of their labours than they are now; all contemporary scientific work consists in exactly this augmentation of numbers. I saw through that hocus-pocus when I discovered the three thousand five hundred and first species and still did not attain contentment. However, I had no time for disillusionment, for I soon fell a prey to a new passion. I plunged into nihilism with its manifestos, its secret transformations, and all its tricks of the trade. I went among the people; I worked in factories, as a painter, as a boatman on the river Volga. Then, as I roamed across Russia and the scent of Russian life came to my nostrils, I changed into its ardent worshipper. My heart ached with love for the Russian people. I believed in their God, in their language, in their creative power, and so on and so on. I have been a Slavophil and have wearied Aksakoff with letters; I have been an Ukrainophil, and an archaeologist, and a collector of examples of native genius – I have fallen in love with ideas, with people, with events, with places, time upon time without end. Five years ago I was the slave of the denial of the right of ownership. Non-opposition of evil was my latest belief.'

Sasha stirred and heaved a shuddering sigh. Likarieff rose and went to her.

'Do you want some tea, my little one?' he asked tenderly.

'Drink it yourself!' the child answered roughly. Likarieff was embarrassed and returned guiltily to the table.

'So you have had an amusing life,' said Ilovaiskaya. 'You have much to remember.'

'Well, yes, it all seems amusing when one is sitting over one's tea gossiping with a sweet companion, but figure to yourself what that amusement has cost me! What has it led to? You see, I did not believe "zierlich-manierlich" like a German doctor of philosophy; I did not live in a desert; every passion of mine bowed me under its yoke and tore my body limb from limb. Judge for yourself. I used to be as rich as my brothers, and now I am a beggar. On the offspring of my enthusiasms I have squandered my own fortune, that of my wife, and a great deal of the money of others. I am now forty-two, old age is upon me, and I am as homeless as a dog that has strayed at night from a train of wagons. I have never in my life known what peace is. My soul has always been weary and has suffered even from hoping. I have wasted away under this heavy, disorderly labour; I have endured privations; I have been five times to prison; I have trailed all over the provinces of Archangel and Tobolsk. I ache to remember it. I have lived, and in the fumes that enveloped me I have missed life itself. Can you believe it? I cannot recall one single spring; I did not notice that my wife loved me; I did not notice when my children were born. What else can I tell you? To all who have loved me I have brought misfortune. My mother has already worn mourning for me for fifteen years; my proud brothers, for my sake, have endured agonies of soul and blushed for me and hung their heads, and have wasted their money on me till at last they have come to hate me like poison.'

Likarieff rose and then sat down again.

'If I alone were unhappy I would give thanks to God,' he continued without looking at Ilovaiskaya. 'My own personal happiness vanishes into the background when I remember how often in my passions I have been absurd, unjust, cruel, dangerous, far from the truth! How often I have hated and despised with my whole soul those whom I should have loved, and – on the contrary! I have changed a thousand times. Today I believe and prostrate myself, tomorrow I run like a coward from my gods and my friends of today, silently swallowing the charge of dastard that is flung after me. God only knows how often I have wept and gnawed my pillow for shame at my enthusiasms! I have never in my life wittingly told a lie or done an evil deed, but my conscience is not clear; no, I cannot even boast of not having a death on my mind, for my wife died under my very eyes, exhausted by my restlessness. Listen! There now exist in society two ways of regarding women. Some men measure the female skull and prove in that way that woman is the inferior of man; they seek out her defects in order to deride her, in order to appear original in her eyes, in order to justify their own bestiality. Others try with all their might to raise woman to their own level; they oblige her to con the three thousand five hundred species and to speak and write the same folly that they speak and write themselves.'

Likarieff's face darkened.

'But I tell you that woman always has been and always will be the slave of man,' he said in a deep voice, banging on the table with his fist. 'She is a soft and tender wax out of which man has always been able to fashion whatever he had a mind to. Good God! For a man's penny passion she will cut off her hair, desert her family, and die in exile. There is not one feminine principle among all those for which she has sacrificed herself. She is a defenceless, devoted slave. I have measured no skulls, but I say this from grievous, bitter experience. The proudest, the most independent of women, if I can but succeed in communicating my passion to her, will follow me unreasoningly, unquestioningly, doing all I desire. Out of a nun I once made a nihilist who, I heard later, shot a policeman. In all my wanderings my wife never left me for an instant, and, like a weathercock, changed her faith with each of my changing passions.'

Likarieff leaped up and walked about the room.

'It is a noble, an exalted bondage!' he cried, clasping his hands. 'In that bondage lies the loftiest significance of woman's existence. Of all the terrible absurdities that filled my brain during my intercourse with women, my memory has retained, like a filter, not theories nor wise words nor philosophy, but that extraordinary submission, that wonderful compassion, that universal forgiveness – '

Likarieff clinched his hands, fixed his eyes on one spot, and with a sort of passionate tension, as if he were sucking at each word, muttered between set teeth:

'This – this magnanimous toleration, this faithfulness unto death, this poetry of heart – The meaning of life lies in this uncomplaining martyrdom, in this all-pardoning love that brings light and warmth into the chaos of life – '

Ilovaiskaya rose slowly, took a step in the direction of Likarieff, and fixed her eyes on his face. By the tears which shone on his lashes, by his trembling, passionate utterance, she saw clearly that women were not a mere casual topic of conversation; they were the object of a new passion or, as he called it himself, a new belief. For the first time in her life Ilovaiskaya saw before her a man inspired by passionate faith. Gesticulating, with shining eyes, he appeared to her insane, delirious, but in the fire of his glance, in his speech, in the movements of his whole great frame she felt such beauty that, without being conscious of it herself, she stood paralysed before him and looked into his face with rapture.

'Take my mother!' he cried, holding out his arms to her with a face of supplication. 'I have poisoned her existence; I have dishonoured her name; I have harmed her as much as her bitterest enemy could have done – and what is her answer? My brothers give her pennies for holy wafers and Te Deums, and she strangles her religious sentiments and sends them in secret to her worthless Gregory. Those little coins are far stronger to teach and ennoble the soul than all the theories and wise sayings and three thousand five hundred species. I could cite to you a thousand examples. Take, for instance, yourself! Here you are, on your way to your father and brother at midnight, in a blizzard, because you want to cheer their holiday by your tenderness, and all the time, perhaps, they are not thinking of you and have forgotten your existence! Wait until you love a man! Then you will go to the north pole for him. You would, wouldn't you?'

'Yes, if – I loved him.'

'There, you see!' rejoiced Likarieff, and he even stamped his foot. 'Good Lord! How glad I am to have known you! It is my good fortune to keep meeting the most magnificent people. There is not a day that I do not meet someone for whom I would sell my soul. There are far more good people in this world than bad ones. See how freely and open-heartedly you and I have been talking together, as if we had been friends for a century! Sometimes, I tell you, a man will have the courage to hold his tongue for ten years with his wife and friends, and then will suddenly meet a cadet in a railway carriage and blurt out his whole soul to him. This is the first time I have had the pleasure of seeing you, and yet I have confessed to you things I have never confessed to anyone before. Why is that?'

Rubbing his hands and smiling happily, Likarieff walked about the room and once more began to talk of women. The church-bell rang for the vigil service.

'Oh! Oh!' wept Sasha. 'He talks so much he won't let me sleep!'

'Yes, that is true,' said Likarieff, recollecting himself. 'I'm sorry, my little one. Go to sleep; go to sleep – '

'I have two little boys besides her,' he whispered. 'They live with their uncle, but this one couldn't survive for a day without her father. She complains and grumbles, but she clings to me like a fly to honey. But I have been chattering too much, my dear young lady, and have kept you from sleeping. Will you let me prepare a couch for you?'

Without waiting for her permission, he shook out her wet cloak and laid it along the bench with the fur side up, picked up her scattered scarfs and shawls, folded her coat into a roll, and placed it at the head of the couch. He did all this in silence, with an expression of humble reverence on his face, as if he were busied not with feminine rags but with the fragments of some holy vessel.

His whole frame had a guilty and embarrassed look as if he were ashamed of being so large and strong in the presence of a weak being.

When Ilovaiskaya had lain down he blew out the candle and took a seat on a stool beside the stove.

'And so, my little lady,' he whispered, puffing at a thick cigarette and blowing the smoke into the stove, 'nature has given the Russian an extraordinary facility for belief, an investigating mind, and the gift of speculation; but all this is scattered like chaff before his laziness, his indifference, and his dreamy frivolity – Yes – '

Ilovaiskaya stared wonderingly into the shadows and saw only the red spot on the icon and the flickering firelight on the face of Likarieff. The darkness, the ringing of the church-bells, the roar of the storm, the lame boy, the grumbling Sasha, the unhappy Likarieff and his sayings – all these flowed together in the girl's mind and grew into one gigantic impression. The world seemed fantastic to her, full of marvels and forces of magic. All that she had just heard rang in her ears, and the life of man seemed to her to be a lovely and poetical fairy-tale without an ending.

The mighty impression grew and grew, engulfed her consciousness, and changed into a sweet dream. Ilovaiskaya slept, but she still saw the little shrine lamp and the large nose on which the ruddy firelight was playing.

She heard weeping.

'Dear papa!' a tender child's voice besought. 'Do let us go back to uncle! There they have a Christmas tree, and Stephen and Nicolas are there!'

'My darling, what can I do?' entreated the deep, low voice of a man. 'Understand me, do understand!'

And a man's weeping was joined to that of the child. This voice of human woe in the midst of the howling storm seemed to the girl's ears such sweet, human music that she could not endure the delight of it, and also wept. Then she heard a large, dark shadow quietly approach her, pick up her shawl, which had slipped to the floor, and wrap it about her feet.

Ilovaiskaya was awakened by a strange sound of bawling. She jumped up and looked about her in astonishment. The blue light of dawn was already peeping in at the windows which were almost drifted over with snow. A grey half-light lay in the room, and in it the stove, the sleeping child, and Nasr-Ed-Din were distinctly visible. The stove and the shrine lamp had gone out. Through the wide-open door could be seen the large tap-room with its counter and tables. A man with a dull, gypsy face and wondering eyes was standing in the middle of the floor in a pool of melted snow and was holding a large red star on a stick. A throng of little boys surrounded him, motionless as statues, all plastered over with snow. The light of the star shone through the red paper and shed a crimson glow on their wet faces. The little crowd was bawling in a disorderly fashion, and all that Ilovaiskaya could distinguish was the single couplet:

> 'Ho, youngster, you tiny one,
> Take a knife, a shiny one
> We'll kill, we'll kill the Jew,
> The weary son of rue — '

Likarieff was standing near the counter gazing with emotion at the singers and beating time with his foot. At sight of Ilovaiskaya a smile spread over his whole face and he went up to her. She, too, smiled.

'Merry Christmas!' he cried. 'I saw that you were sleeping well.'

Ilovaiskaya looked at him, said nothing, and continued to smile.

After their talk of last night he no longer appeared tall and broad-shouldered to her, but small, as the largest ship appears small when we are told that it has crossed the ocean.

'Well, it is time for me to go,' she said. 'I must put on my things. Tell me, where are you going now?'

'To the station of Klinushka; from there I shall go to Sergyevo, and from Sergyevo I shall drive forty miles to some coal-mines belonging to an old fool of a general named Shashkofski. My brothers have found me a place there as manager. I am going to mine coal.'

'Why, I know those coal-mines! Shashkofski is my uncle. But – why are you going there?' asked Ilovaiskaya, staring at Likarieff in astonishment.

'To be manager. I am going to manage the coal-mines.'

'I don't understand,' said Ilovaiskaya, shrugging her shoulders. 'You are going to the mines. But don't you know that they lie in a barren, uninhabited waste? It's so lonely there you won't be able to stand it a day. The coal is horrible; no one will buy it; and my uncle is a maniac, a despot, a bankrupt – you won't even get a salary!'

'Never mind,' said Likarieff indifferently. 'I'm thankful even for the mine.'

Ilovaiskaya shrugged her shoulders and walked excitedly up and down.

'I don't understand; I don't understand!' she cried, waving her fingers in front of her face. 'It's impossible and – and senseless! Oh, understand that it's – it's worse than exile; it's a living tomb! Oh, Heavens!' she cried hotly, going up to Likarieff and waving her fingers before his smiling face. Her upper lip trembled and her piquant face paled. 'Oh, imagine that barren plain, that solitude! There is not a soul there with whom to speak a word, and you – have an enthusiasm for women! A coal-mine and women!'

Ilovaiskaya suddenly grew ashamed of her ardour and, turning away from Likarieff, walked across to the window.

'No, no, you mustn't go there!' she cried, rapidly fingering the panes.

She felt not only in her soul but even in her back that behind her stood a man who was immeasurably unhappy and neglected and lost, but he stood looking at her, smiling kindly, as if he did not realise his unhappiness, as if he had not wept the night before. It would be better were he still crying! She walked back and forth across the room several times in agitation and then stopped thoughtfully in a corner. Likarieff was saying something but she did not hear him. She turned her back to him and drew a little bill from her purse. This she crushed in her hands for a long time; then she glanced round at Likarieff, blushed, and thrust it into her pocket.

The voice of the coachman was now heard outside the door. Ilovaiskaya began to put on her things with a stern, concentrated expression on her face. Likarieff chatted merrily as he wrapped her up, but each word of his fell like a weight on her heart. It is not gay to hear an unhappy or dying man jest.

When the transformation of a living being into a bundle had been effected, Ilovaiskaya gave one last look at the 'visitors' room,' stood silent for a moment, and went slowly out. Liksrieff followed her to see her off.

Out-of-doors, Heaven knows for what purpose, the winter wind was still raging.

Whole clouds of soft, heavy snow were whirling restlessly along the ground, unable to find peace. Horses, sleighs, trees, and a bull tied to a post – all were white and looked fluffy and soft.

'Well, God bless you – ' muttered Likarieff, seating Ilovaiskaya in her sleigh. 'Don't think ill of me – '

Ilovaiskaya was silent. As the sleigh moved away and made the tour of a huge snowdrift she looked round at Likarieff as if wishing to say something. He ran toward her, but she said not a word and only glanced at him between her long lashes, on which hung the snowflakes.

Either his sensitive soul had really been able to read the meaning of this glance or else his fancy deceived him, but it suddenly seemed to him that, had he but added two or three more good, strong strokes to the picture, this girl would have forgiven him his failure, his age, and his misfortune, and would have followed him unquestioningly and unreasoningly. He stood there for a long time as if in a trance, staring at the track left by the runners of her sleigh. The snowflakes settled eagerly on his hair, on his beard, on his shoulders – the track of the sleigh soon vanished and he himself was covered with snow; he began to resemble a white crag, but his eyes still continued to search for something among the white snow-clouds.

The Head Gardener's Tale

A SALE OF FLOWERS was taking place in the greenhouses of Count N—. There were few purchasers present; only a young timber merchant, a neighbouring landowner of mine, and myself. Whilst the workmen were bearing out our magnificent purchases and packing them into wagons, we sat in the doorway of one of the greenhouses and chatted of this and that. It is extremely pleasant to sit in a garden on an April morning listening to the birds and looking at the flowers which have been carried out into the open air and are basking in the sunshine.

The gardener himself was overseeing the packing of our plants. It was Mikail Karlovitch, a time-honoured old man with a clean-shaven face, wearing a fur waistcoat and no coat. He was not saying a word but was keeping one ear open to our conversation, thinking that we might tell some bit of news. He was an intelligent, very kind-hearted man. For some reason people thought him a German, although his father had been a Swede and his mother a Russian and he went to the Russian church. He knew Russian and German and Swedish and read a great deal in each of these languages, and one could give him no greater pleasure than to let him have a new book to read or to talk with him about Ibsen, for instance.

He had his failings, but they were all harmless ones. For example, he always spoke of himself as the 'head gardener', though no under gardeners existed; the expression of his face was singularly haughty and grave; he could not endure contradiction and liked to be listened to seriously and attentively.

'That young lad over there is a fearful rascal,' said my neighbour, pointing to a dark, gypsy-faced workman driving by on a water barrel. 'He was tried for robbery in town last week and let off. He was pronounced mentally unsound, and yet look at him; he seems healthy enough! A great many scoundrels have been acquitted in Russia lately on the plea of a diseased condition, and the effects of these acquittals and of this obvious weakness and indulgence cannot but be bad. They have demoralised the masses; the sense of justice has been dulled in everyone, for we have now become accustomed to seeing crime go unpunished, and we can say boldly of our times, in the words of Shakespeare:

> For in the fatness of these pursy times
> Virtue itself of vice must pardon beg.

'That is true,' the merchant assented. 'Since all these pardons have been granted we have had far more crimes of murder and arson than formerly. Ask the peasants if that isn't so.'

The gardener Mikail Karlovitch turned to us and said:

'As for me, sirs, I always welcome a verdict of acquittal with delight. I do not tremble for morality and justice when a man is declared to be innocent; on the contrary, I experience a feeling of pleasure. I rejoice to hear it, even when my conscience tells me that the jury have made a mistake in acquitting the prisoner. Don't you think yourselves, sirs, that if judges and juries had more faith in human nature than in speeches and material proofs this faith might, in itself, be more important than any worldly considerations? It is only attainable by the few who know and feel Christ.'

'The idea is a good one,' said I.

'The idea is not a new one. I even remember to have heard a legend long ago on that very theme, a very pretty legend,' the gardener said, smiling. 'It was told me by my grandmother, my father's mother, a shrewd old woman. She told it in Swedish; it would not sound so beautiful, so classical, in Russian.'

But we begged him to tell it and never mind the harshness of the Russian tongue. Delighted, he slowly finished smoking his pipe, glared angrily at the workmen, and began:

'A homely, middle-aged man once came to live in a little town. His name was Thomson or Wilson, it matters not which; that has nothing to do with the story. He practised a noble profession; he was a healer of the sick. He was gruff and uncommunicative always and only spoke when his profession demanded it; he never visited anywhere and never extended his acquaintance with anyone beyond a silent nod and lived as frugally as an ascetic. The thing is, he was a learned man, and in those days learned men were not as common folk. They passed their days and nights in meditation, in reading books, and in healing the sick; everything else they looked upon as trivial and they had no time to waste in words. The citizens of the town knew this very well and tried not to bother him with visits and idle gossip. They were overjoyed that at last God had sent them a man who could cure their sick and were proud to have anyone so wonderful living in their town.

' "He knows everything!" it was said of him.

'But that was not enough; they should also have said: "He loves everyone!" A marvellous, angelic heart beat in the breast of this learned man. After all, the inhabitants of the town were but strangers to him; they were not his kindred, and yet he loved them as though they had been his children and did not even begrudge them his life. He was ill himself of consumption, and yet when he was summoned to a sick-bed he would forget his own illness and, without sparing himself, would climb panting up the mountains, no matter how high they might be. He braved heat and cold and scorned hunger and thirst. He never accepted money, and the strange thing was that when a patient died he would follow the body weeping to the grave with the kith and kin.

'He soon became so indispensable that the citizens marvelled that they had been able to exist without him. Their gratitude knew no bounds. Old and young, good and bad, honest men and rogues – in a word, all – honoured him and recognised his worth. There was not a creature in the town and its vicinity who would have permitted himself to do him an injury or even to entertain the thought of it. When he went away from home he used to leave doors and windows unbolted, in perfect certainty that no thief existed who could make up his mind to do him a wrong. It often happened that his duty as doctor called him out on to the highroads among forests and mountains, where prowled many hungry vagrants, but he felt himself perfectly safe. One night when he was on his way home from the bedside of a sick man, he was attacked by highwaymen in a forest, but when they recognised him these men respectfully took off their caps to him and asked him if he wouldn't have something to eat. When he told them he was not hungry, they lent him a warm cloak and escorted him to the very town, glad that fate had given them an opportunity of repaying in some way the goodness of this great-hearted man.

'Well, my grandmother would go on to say, even the horses and dogs and cows knew him and showed pleasure on seeing him.

'And this man, who seemed to be safeguarded by his saintliness from every evil and who even counted highwaymen and madmen among his friends, one fine morning was found murdered. He lay, all bloodstained, at the bottom of a ravine, and his skull was broken in. His white face expressed surprise. Yes, surprise and not horror had been imprinted on his features when he had seen his murderer before him.

'You can imagine the sorrow that now overwhelmed the town and all the countryside. In despair, scarcely crediting his eyesight, each man asked himself: "Who could have killed this man?" The judges who held the inquest on the body of the doctor said: "We have here every evidence of murder, but, as there is no man in the world who could have killed our doctor, it is clear that murder could not have been committed and that this combination of evidence is simply a coincidence. We must suppose that the doctor fell over the edge of the cliff in the dark and was mortally injured."

'The whole town assented in this opinion. They buried the doctor, and no one any more talked of a death by violence. The existence of a man degraded enough to murder the doctor seemed unthinkable. There is a limit even to baseness, isn't there?

'But – will you believe it, suddenly, by accident, the murderer was discovered! Some scamp who had already been arrested many times and who was well known for his vicious life offered the doctor's snuff-box and watch in exchange for a drink at a tavern. When he was accused of the crime he looked taken aback and *told* some transparent lie. A search was instituted, and a shirt with bloody sleeves and a doctor's gold-mounted lancet were found in his bed. What other proofs were needed? The wretch was thrown into prison. The citizens were indignant, but at the same time they said: "It is unbelievable! It cannot be! Take care that you make no mistake; evidence has been known to lie!"

'At his trial the murderer obstinately denied his guilt. Everything spoke against him, and it was as easy to believe him guilty as it is to believe that earth is black; but his judges seemed to have gone mad. They weighed each bit of evidence a dozen times, kept looking mistrustfully at the witnesses, flushing, and drinking water. The trial began early one morning and lasted until late that night.

' "You have been convicted!" the chief justice said, turning toward the murderer. "The court has found you guilty of the murder of Doctor So-and-So and has, therefore, condemned you to – "

'The judge wanted to say "death", but the paper on which the sentence was written fell from his hands; he wiped the cold sweat from his brow and cried:

' "No! May God punish me if I am giving an unjust verdict! I swear he is innocent. I cannot tolerate the idea that a man should exist who would dare to murder our friend the doctor. Man is not capable of falling so low."

' "No, there is no man capable of it," the other judges agreed.

' "No one!" echoed the crowd. "Release him!"

'The murderer was released, and not one single soul accused the court of giving an unjust verdict. And, my grandmother used to say, for their faith God forgave the sins of all the inhabitants of that town. He rejoices when people believe that mankind is made in his likeness and image, and he is sad when they forget man's worth and judge him more harshly than they would a dog. Even if that acquittal did harm to the inhabitants of the town, think, on the other hand, what a beneficent influence their faith in mankind had on those people – a faith which does not remain inactive but breeds generous thoughts in our hearts and stimulates us to respect every man. Every man!'

Mikail Karlovitch ended. My neighbour wanted to retort something, but the gardener made a gesture, showing that he did not like to be answered and walked away to the wagons, where he once more applied himself to packing our plants with an expression of importance on his face.

Hush!

IVAN KRASNUKIN, a mediocre newspaper reporter, always comes home late at night sombre, solemn, and somehow tremendously concentrated. He looks as if he were expecting to be searched or were contemplating suicide. As he paces up and down his room he stops, ruffles his hair, and says in the tone of Laertes about to avenge his sister:

'I am distracted; I am weary to the bottom of my soul; sorrow lies heavy on my heart; and yet I am expected to sit down and write! And this is called "living"! Why has no writer ever described the tormenting discords which harrow an author's soul when, being sad, he must provoke the crowd to mirth and, being merry, he must shed tears as he is bidden. Yes, I should have to be gay and unconcerned and witty even though I were bowed down with grief, even though I were, let us say, ill, though my child were dying, though my wife were in great pain!'

As he says this he shakes his fist and rolls his eyes. Then he goes into the bedroom and wakes his wife.

'Nadia!' he says, 'I am going to begin writing. Please see that no one disturbs me. I can't write if the kids are bawling or the cook is snoring. And see, too, that I get some tea and – and a beefsteak, possibly. You know I can't write unless I get my tea. It is tea alone that gives me strength for my work.'

Returning to his own room, he takes off his coat, his waistcoat, and his boots. He undresses with deliberation, and then, composing his features in an expression of injured innocence, he takes his seat at his desk.

On that desk is no casual object of everyday life. Everything, every tiniest trifle, seems to be charged with meaning and to be carrying out some stern programme. Here are little busts and pictures of famous authors; here are a pile of manuscript, a volume of Belinski's works with one page turned down, an occipital bone serving as an inkstand, a page from some newspaper carelessly folded but exhibiting a column marked with blue pencil in a large hand, 'Cowardly!' Here, too, lie a dozen newly sharpened pencils and penholders with fresh pens, so that no external cause or accident shall interfere for a moment with the free flight of creative fancy.

Krasnukin throws himself back in his easy-chair and plunges into the consideration of a subject. He hears his wife shuffling about in slippers as she splits kindling for the samovar. She is still half asleep, as he can tell, because every now and then the cover or a leg of the samovar drops out of her hands. The hissing of the samovar and of the frying meat soon reaches his ears. His wife still goes on splitting wood and banging about near the stove, slamming now the oven door, now the damper, and now the door of the fire-box. Suddenly Krasnukin shudders, opens his eyes wide with terror, and begins to sniff the air.

'Good Lord! Charcoal fumes!' he gasps, his face contorted with agony. 'Charcoal fumes! That insufferable woman has made up her mind to suffocate me! Tell me, for Heaven's sake, how can I possibly write under conditions like these?'

He flings into the kitchen and breaks into tragic lamentations. When shortly his wife, walking on tiptoe, brings him a cup of tea he is already sitting in his armchair as he was before, motionless, immersed in his subject. He does not move, drums lightly on his forehead with his fingers, and pretends not to notice his wife's presence. His face again takes on an expression of injured innocence.

Like a girl to whom someone has given a pretty fan, before writing the title he flirts with it for a long time, posing and coquetting for his own benefit. Now he presses his hands to his temples, now he shrinks together and draws up his feet under his chair as if he were in pain, now he languidly half closes his eyes, like a cat on a sofa. At last, hesitatingly, he reaches toward the inkstand, and with the air of signing a death-warrant he writes down the title –

'Mamma, I want some water!' he hears his son's voice cry.

'Hush!' says the mother. 'Papa is writing. Hush!'

Papa is writing quickly, never stopping, never cancelling a word, hardly finding time to turn the pages. The busts and portraits of the famous authors watch his swiftly flying pen and seem to think: 'Aha, brother! Go for it!'

'Hush!' scratches the pen.

'Hush!' rattle the authors, shaken on the table by a push from the writer's knee.

Krasnukin suddenly draws himself up, lays down his pen, and listens. He hears an even, monotonous whispering. It is Foma Nikolaitch, the boarder, saying his prayers in the next room.

'Look here!' calls out Krasnukin. 'Can't you pray more quietly? You keep me from writing.'

'I beg your pardon,' answers Foma Nikolaitch timidly.

'Hush!'

Having written five pages, Krasnukin stretches himself and looks at the clock.

'Heavens! Three o'clock already,' he groans. 'Everyone is asleep; only I, I alone must work!'

Broken down, exhausted, his head hanging to one side, he goes into the bedroom and wakes his wife.

'Nadia, give me some more tea!' he says in a weary voice. 'I'm – I'm feeling weak.'

He writes until four and would like to go on until six, but he has exhausted his subject. His coquetting and showing off before inanimate objects, where he is far from prying, indiscreet eyes, his despotism and tyranny in the little ant's nest over which fate has given him authority, these are for him the spice of life. How little this despot at home resembles the puny, humble, speechless, incapable beings we are in the habit of seeing in the offices of newspapers!

'I am so tired that I don't think I shall be able to sleep,' he says as he goes to bed. 'Our work, this infernal, thankless drudgery of a galley-slave, does not tire the body so much as the mind. I must take some drops of bromide. Ah, Heaven knows, if it weren't for my family I'd throw over the whole thing! Oh, 'tis awful to have to write to order like this.'

He falls into a profound and wholesome slumber and sleeps until one or two o'clock in the afternoon. Ah, how much longer he would have slept, what dreams he would have dreamed, had he been a famous author, or an editor, or even a publisher!

'He was writing all night,' whispers his wife with a frightened face. 'Hush!'

No one dares speak or walk or make a sound. His sleep is sacred, and whoever is guilty of disturbing it will have to pay dearly.

'Hush!' is wafted through all the rooms. 'Hush!'

Without a Title

In the fifteenth century, as now, the sun rose every morning and sank to rest every night. When its first rays kissed the dew the earth awoke and the air was filled with sounds of joy, ecstasy, and hope; at eventide the same earth grew still and sank into darkness. Sometimes a thunder-cloud would roll up and the thunder roar angrily, or a sleepy star drop from heaven, or a pale monk come running in to tell the brothers that he had seen a tiger not far from the monastery – and that was all. Then once again day would resemble day, and night night.

The monks worked and prayed, and their old prior played the organ, composed Latin verses, and wrote out music. This fine old man had a remarkable talent; he played the organ with such skill that even the most ancient of the monks, whose hearing had grown feeble as the end of their lives drew near, could not restrain their tears when the notes of his organ came floating from his cell. When he spoke, even if it were only of the commonest things, such as trees, wild beasts, or the sea, no one could listen to him without either a smile or a tear; the same notes seemed to vibrate in his soul that vibrated in the organ. When he was moved by wrath or great joy, when he spoke of things that were terrible and grand, a passionate inspiration would master him, tears would start from his flashing eyes, his face would flush, his voice peal like thunder, and the listening monks would feel their souls wrung by his exaltation. During these splendid, these marvellous moments his power was unlimited; if he had ordered his elders to throw themselves into the sea they would all have rushed rapturously, with one accord, to fulfil his desire.

His music, his voice, and the verses with which he praised God were a source of never-ending joy to the monks. Sometimes in their monotonous lives the trees, the flowers, the spring and autumn grew tiresome, the noise of the sea wearied them, and the songs of the birds grew unpleasing, but the talents of their old prior, like bread, they needed every day.

A score of years passed. Day resembled day, and night night. Not a living creature showed itself near the monastery except wild beasts and birds. The nearest human habitation was far away, and to reach it from the monastery or to reach the monastery from there one had to cross a desert one hundred miles wide. This only those dared to do who set no value on life, who had renounced it, and journeyed to the monastery as to a tomb.

What, then, was the surprise of the monks when one night a man knocked at their gates who proved to be an inhabitant of the city, the most ordinary of sinners, with a love of life! Before saying a prayer or asking the blessing of the prior this man demanded food and wine. When they asked him how he had got into the desert from the city he answered them by telling a long hunter's tale; he had gone hunting, and had had too much to drink, and had lost his way. To the suggestion that he should become a monk and save his soul he replied with a smile and the words: 'I am no friend of yours.'

Having eaten and drunk his fill, he looked long at the monks who were serving him, reproachfully shook his head, and said:

'You don't do anything, you monks. All you care about is your victuals and drink. Is that the way to save your souls? Think now: while you are living quietly here, eating, drinking, and dreaming of blessedness, your fellow men are being lost and damned to hell. Look what goes on in the city! Some die of starvation, while others, not knowing what to do with their gold, plunge into debauchery and perish like flies in honey. There is no faith nor truth among men. Whose duty is it to save them? Is it mine, who am drunk from morning till night? Did God give you faith and loving and humble hearts that you should sit here between your four walls and do nothing?'

The drunken speech of the townsman was insolent and unseemly, yet it strangely affected the prior. The old man and his monks looked at each other; then he paled and said:

'Brothers, he is right! It is true that, owing to folly and weakness, unfortunate mankind is perishing in unbelief and sin, and we do not move from the spot, as if it were no business of ours. Why should I not go and remind them of the Christ whom they have forgotten?'

The old man was transported by the words of the townsman. On the following day he grasped his staff, bade farewell to the brothers, and set out for the city. So the monks were left without music, without his words and his verses.

They waited first one month and then two, and still the old man did not return. At last, at the end of the third month, they heard the familiar tapping of his staff. The monks flew out to meet him and showered him with questions; but, instead of rejoicing with them, he wept bitterly and did not utter a word. The monks saw that he was thin and had aged greatly and that weariness and profound sorrow were depicted on his face. When he wept he had the look of a man who had been deeply hurt.

Then the monks, too, burst into tears and asked why he was weeping and why his face looked so stern, but he answered not a word and went and locked himself in his cell. For five days he stayed there and neither ate nor drank, neither did he play the organ. When the monks knocked at his door and entreated him to come out and share his sorrow with them his answer was a profound silence.

At last he emerged. Collecting all the monks about him, with a face swollen with weeping and with many expressions of indignation and distress, he began to tell them all that had happened to him during the past three months. His voice was calm and his eyes smiled as he described his journey from the monastery to the city. Birds had sung and brooks babbled to him by the wayside, he said, and sweet, new-born hopes had agitated his breast. He felt that he was a soldier advancing to battle and certain victory, he walked along dreaming, composing hymns and verses as he went, and was surprised when he found that he had reached his journey's end.

But his voice trembled, his eyes flashed, and anger burned hot within him when he began to tell of the city and of mankind. Never before had he seen or dared to imagine what he encountered when he entered the town. Here, in his old age, he saw and understood for the first time in his life the might of Satan, the splendour of iniquity, and the weakness and despicable faint-heartedness of mankind. By an evil chance, the first house he entered was an abode of sin. Here half a hundred men with a great deal of money were feasting and drinking wine without end. Overpowered by its fumes, they were singing songs and boldly saying things so shocking and terrible that no Godfearing man would dare to mention them. They were unboundedly free and happy and bold; they feared neither God nor the devil nor death, did and said whatever they had a mind to, and went wherever they were driven by their desires. The wine, clear as amber, was surely intolerably fragrant and delicious, for everyone who quaffed it smiled rapturously and straightway desired to drink again. It returned smile for smile and sparkled joyfully, as if it knew what fiendish seduction lay hidden in its sweetness.

More than ever weeping and burning with anger, the old man went on describing what he had seen. On the table in the midst of the feasters, he said, stood a half-naked woman. It would be hard to imagine anything more glorious and enchanting than she was. Young, long-haired, with dark eyes and thick lips, insolent and shameless, this vermin smiled, showing her teeth as white as snow, as if saying: 'Behold how beautiful, how insolent I am!' Splendid draperies of silk and brocade fell from her shoulders, but her beauty would not be hidden beneath a garment and eagerly made its way through the folds, as young verdure forces itself through the earth in the springtime. The shameless woman drank wine, sang songs, and surrendered herself to the feasters.

Wrathfully brandishing his arms, the old man went on to describe hippodromes, bull-fights, theatres, and the workshops of artists, where the forms of naked women were painted and modelled in clay. He spoke eloquently, sonorously, with inspiration, as if he were playing on some invisible instrument, and the stupefied monks eagerly hung on his words and panted with ecstasy. Having described all the charms of the devil, the beauty of wickedness, and the enchanting grace of the infamous female form, the old man cursed Satan, turned on his heel, and vanished behind his door.

When he came out of his cell next morning not a monk remained in the monastery. They were all on their way to the city.

In the Ravine

CHAPTER ONE

THE VILLAGE of Ukleyevo lay in a ravine, so that only the church steeple and the chimneys of its cotton-printing mills could be seen from the highroad and from the railway station. If a traveller inquired what village that was, he was told:

'That is the village where the deacon ate all the caviare at the funeral.'

That is to say that, at a wake at the manufacturer Kostiukoff's, a grey-beard deacon had caught sight of some fresh caviare among the other delicacies on the table and had fallen greedily upon it. They had nudged him and pulled his sleeve, but he seemed to have fallen into a trance of delight, for he felt nothing and only went on eating. He ate all the caviare, and there had been four pounds of it in the jar! Long afterward, though the deacon had been dead many years, that episode of the caviare was still remembered. Was life so meagre in the village or were its people unable to notice anything beyond an unimportant event which had happened ten years ago? Who can say? At any rate, no other fact was ever related about Ukleyevo.

Fever was always rampant in the village and the mud was always deep, even in summer, especially near the fences, which were overhung by ancient willow trees that cast broad shadows across the roads. The air always smelled of refuse from the factories and of the vinegar which was used in dyeing the calico. The factories – there were four of them, three cotton-mills and one tannery – lay not in the village itself but at some distance away, on its outskirts. They were small factories; not more than four hundred men worked in all four. The water in the river often stank of the tannery; its refuse infected the meadows, and then the stock of the peasants would suffer from the plague. When this was the case the tannery was ordered to be closed. It was officially closed, but went on working in secret, with the connivance of the commissary of the rural police and of the district doctor, to each of whom the owner paid ten roubles a month. There were only two fair-sized brick houses with tin roofs in the whole village. One was occupied by the district administration, and in the other, which was of two stories and stood directly opposite the church, lived the merchant, Gregory Tsibukin.

Gregory kept a small grocery store, but this was only for the sake of appearances; as a matter of fact, he trafficked in vodka, cattle, hides, grain, hogs, and whatever came handy. For instance, when magpies were wanted abroad to trim ladies' hats he made a profit of thirty copecks a pair on the birds. He bought standing timber, lent money at interest; on the whole, he was a shrewd old man.

He had two sons. The elder, Anasim, was a detective and was seldom at home. The younger son, Stephen, had gone into trade and now worked for his father, but no real assistance was expected from him, as his health was bad and he was deaf. Stephen's wife, Aksinia, was a handsome, shapely woman who went to church on holidays wearing a hat and carrying a parasol; she rose early and went to bed late, and was on the run all day long, with her skirts tucked up and her keys jangling, from the warehouse to the cellar and from the cellar to the store. Old Tsibukin would watch her gaily, with kindling eyes, and at such times he used to wish that his elder son had been married to her instead of his younger one, who was deaf and was obviously no judge of feminine beauty.

The old man had always had a great fondness for domestic life and he loved his family more than anything else in the world, especially his elder son, the detective, and his daughter-in-law. Aksinia had no sooner married the deaf boy than she gave evidence of uncommon executive power. She knew at once to whom she could give credit and to whom she could not; she kept all the keys herself, not even entrusting them to her husband; she rattled away at the counting board; she looked in the horses' mouths like a peasant; and was always laughing and shouting. The old man was touched by whatever she did and said and would mutter when he saw her: 'Go it, little bride! Go it, pretty daughter!'

He was a widower, but, after his son had been married a year, he could endure it no longer and was married himself. A bride was found for him thirty miles from the village, Varvara by name, who, though no longer young, was pretty and striking.

No sooner had she moved into her little room at the top of the house than the whole building seemed to be lighter, as if new panes had been let into the windows. Shrine lamps were lighted, tables were covered with tablecloths white as snow, little red flowers appeared in the windows, and at dinner they no longer all ate out of one dish; each person had a plate of his own. Varvara's smile was gentle and pleasant and everything in the house seemed to smile with her. Beggars, wanderers, and pilgrims began to appear in the courtyard, a thing which had never happened before; the plaintive, singsong voices of the village peasant women were heard under the windows, mingled with the feeble coughing of weak, lean peasants who had been discharged from the factories for intemperance. Varvara helped them with money and bread and old clothes and later, when she grew to feel more at home in the house, began to give them things out of the store. The deaf boy once saw her carrying away two little packets of tea and this confused him.

'Mamma has just taken two packets of tea,' he announced to his father later. 'To whom shall I charge them?'

The old man said not a word, but stood and meditated, working his eyebrows, and then went upstairs to his wife.

'Varvara, child,' he said tenderly, 'if you need anything in the store, help yourself. Take all you want and don't hesitate.'

Next day the deaf boy called up to her as he ran across the courtyard: 'If you need anything, mamma, help yourself!'

There was something new in this almsgiving of hers, something cheerful and free, as there was in the shrine lamps and the red flowers. They felt this influence when they sold out their salt meat to the peasants on the eve of a fast, meat smelling so strong that one couldn't stand near the barrel. They felt it when they took scythes and caps and women's dresses in pawn from drunken men; and when the factory workmen rolled in the mud, stupefied by bad vodka; and when evil seemed to have condensed and to be hanging in the air like a fog, they felt somehow more at ease at the thought that there, in the house, was a neat, gentle woman who had nothing to do with salt meat and vodka. During these painful and gloomy days her charity was for them what a safety-valve is for an engine.

The days in Tsibukin's house were spent in toil. Before the sun was up Aksinia was snorting as she washed her face in an outhouse; the samovar was boiling in the kitchen and droning as if foretelling disaster. Old Gregory, dressed in a long black coat, calico trousers, and shiny high boots, clean and small, was bustling about the rooms tapping on the floor with his heels like the old father-in-law in the song. At daybreak a racing cart was brought to the door and the old man jumped bravely in and pulled his great cap down over his ears, and no one seeing him then would believe that he was already fifty-six. His wife and daughter-in-law came to see him off, and when he had on his long, clean coat and was driving his huge black stallion that had cost three hundred roubles the old man did not like to be approached by peasants with petitions and complaints. He hated and despised peasants and if one of them was waiting for him at the gate would shout angrily:

'What are you standing there for? Move on!'

Or, if it was a beggar, he would cry:

'No; God will help you!'

So he drove away every morning on business, and his wife, in a dark dress with a black kerchief over her hair, put the rooms in order and helped in the kitchen. Aksinia kept the store, and her laughter and shouting and the clashing of bottles and jingling of money could be heard in the courtyard, as well as the angry cries of the customers she had cheated. At the same time it was evident that a stealthy trade in vodka was being carried on in the store. The deaf boy sat in the store or else walked about the streets without a hat, his hands in his pockets, gazing now at the huts, now up at the sky. Tea was drunk six times a day in the house, and they sat down to four meals. In the evening they counted up the day's profits and then went soundly to sleep.

The three factories in Ukleyevo, that of the Elder Hrimins, that of Hrimin's Sons, and that of Kostiukoff, were connected by telephone with the houses of their owners. A telephone had also been installed in the office of the administration, but here it soon fell out of repair, for bedbugs and cockroaches began to breed in it. The head of the district was illiterate and wrote entirely in capital letters, but he said after the telephone had been destroyed:

'Yes, it will be a little hard for us now to manage without a telephone.'

The Elder Hrimins and Hrimin's Sons were in constant litigation, and sometimes the sons quarrelled among themselves and went to law, and then their factory would close down for a month or two, until they had made their peace again. This amused the inhabitants of Ukleyevo, as there was always much gossip and talk about the ground for each quarrel. On holidays Kostiukoff and Hrimin's Sons would go driving and fly galloping about Ukleyevo, running down the calves. Aksinia, decked out in her best and rustling her starched skirts, would stroll up and down the street near her store, and Hrimin's Sons would catch her up and bear her away as if by force. Old Tsibukin, too, would go driving then, to show off his new horse, and would take Varvara with him.

In the evening, after the drive, when the others had gone to bed, the notes of an expensive accordion could be heard coming from the courtyard of Hrimin's Sons; and then, if the moon was shining, a nutter of happiness would stir the heart at the sound and Ukleyevo would no longer seem such a hole.

CHAPTER TWO

The elder son, Anasim, seldom came home, but he often sent back gifts and letters by his fellow villagers. These letters were indited in a very beautiful, unknown hand and were always written on a sheet of writing-paper, like a petition. They were full of expressions which Anasim never used in speaking, such as: 'Kind Mother and Father: I am sending you a pound of the flowers of tea for the satisfaction of your physical requirements.' At the end of each letter was scratched as if with a very bad pen, 'Anasim Tsibukin,' and below this again, in the superb handwriting, 'Agent.'

These letters were always read aloud several times, and the old man would say, agitated and flushed with excitement:

'He wouldn't live at home; he wanted an education. Let him have it! Every Jack to his trade!'

One day just before Shrove Tuesday a heavy rain was falling. The old man and Varvara had gone to the window to watch it, when, behold! there came Anasim driving up in a sleigh from the station. He had arrived quite unexpectedly, and as he entered the room he looked anxious and alarmed, and so he remained for the rest of his visit, with always something reckless in his behaviour. He was in no hurry to take his departure and acted as if he had been discharged from the service. Varvara was glad of his coming; she kept looking at him almost slyly and shaking her head.

'How is this?' she said. 'Here's the lad already twenty-eight, and still playing about as a bachelor. Oh, tut, tut!'

From the adjoining room her quiet, even speech could be heard: 'Oh, tut, tut!' She fell to whispering with the old man and Aksinia, and their faces, too, took on a sly, mysterious expression, as if they had been conspirators.

They decided to get Anasim married.

'Oh, tut, tut! Your younger brother has been married a long time,' said Varvara, 'and you are without a mate still, like a cock at a fair! Why is this? You must marry, and then you can go back to your work, and your wife will stay here and help us. Your life is disorderly, lad; I see you have forgotten the rules. Oh, tut, tut! You city folks are a burden!'

When the Tsibukins married, the prettiest girls were always picked out to be their brides, for they were rich people. And so, for Anasim likewise, a pretty girl was chosen. He himself possessed an unattractive and insignificant exterior. With a weak constitution and a small stature, he had fat, puffy cheeks that looked as if he were blowing them out; his eyes were unwinking, his glance was keen, his beard was sparse and red, and he had a habit of taking it into his mouth and biting it when he was thinking. In addition to this he drank, and this could be seen from his face and his walk. But when they told him that they had found him a bride, and a very pretty one, he said:

'Well, I'm no hunchback myself. I must say, all we Tsibukins are good looking.'

In the shadow of the city lay the village of Torguyevo. Half of it had lately been absorbed by the town, the other half still remained a village. In a little house in the first half lived a widow, and with her lived her sister who was penniless and went out to do charwork by the day. This sister had a daughter named Lipa, a girl who also did charwork. Lipa's beauty was already talked of in the village, but her appalling penury dismayed people; they reasoned that some widower or elderly man would marry her in spite of her poverty, or else would take her to live with him 'so', and in that way her mother would also be provided for. Varvara heard of Lipa from the professional matchmakers and drove to Torguyevo.

After this a visit of the bridegroom to the bride was arranged in the house of the girl's aunt, and at this entertainment wine and delicacies were served, as was proper. Lipa was dressed in a new pink frock made especially for the occasion and a poppy-red ribbon flamed in her hair. She was slight and frail and fair, with delicate, gentle features tanned by labour out-of-doors. There was ever a wistful, timid smile on her lips, and her eyes looked out as trustfully and curiously as a child's.

She was very young, a child still, with a flat little breast, but old enough to be married. There was no doubt of her prettiness, and only one thing about her might not prove pleasing – she had large hands, like a man's, and her arms now hung idly at her sides, like a great pair of tongs.

'She has no dowry, but we will overlook that,' said the old man to the aunt. 'We took a girl out of a poor family for our son Stephen, and we will not be grasping in this case. In a house, as in a business, it is clever hands that count.'

Lipa stood in the doorway and seemed to be saying, 'Do what you want with me, I trust you,' and her mother, the charwoman, hid in the kitchen, swooning with fear. Once, in her youth, a merchant whose floors she was scrubbing had lost his temper and kicked her, and she had been dreadfully frightened and had fainted. Terror had haunted her soul ever since. Her hands and feet were always trembling with fear and also her cheeks. As she sat in the kitchen now, trying to overhear what the guests were saying, she kept crossing herself, pressing her hands to her brow, and glancing at the icon. Anasim, slightly drunk, opened the door into the kitchen and said easily:

'What are you sitting in here for, precious mother? We are lonely without you!'

And the mother, Praskovia, quailed and answered, clasping her hands to her lean breast:

'Oh, don't say that, sir! Oh, indeed, we are delighted with you, sir!'

When the visit of inspection had come to an end a date was fixed for the wedding. After this Anasim spent his days at home walking from one room to another and whistling, or else he would suddenly recollect something, stop, and stand plunged in meditation, motionless, staring fixedly out across the fields, as if he meant to pierce the earth with his gaze. He showed no pleasure at the thought of being married and being married soon, on the Monday after Quasimodo Sunday; he had no desire to see his betrothed and only continued to whistle. It was plain that he was marrying simply because his father and stepmother desired it and because it was the village custom for the son to marry and bring a helper into the house. He was in no haste to leave home and did not behave in anyway as he had on his former visits. There was something unusually free and easy in his manner, and he talked wildly and at random.

CHAPTER THREE

In a neighbouring village lived two dressmakers, sisters, from whom the wedding garments were ordered, and these women came often to the house to try on the clothes and sat for long hours drinking tea. For Varvara they made a brown dress trimmed with black lace and imitation jet and for Aksinia a light green one with a yellow breast and sash. When the dressmakers had finished their work, Tsibukin did not pay them in money but in wares from his store, and they left the house sorrowfully, with their arms full of packages of stearine candles and sardines for which they had no use in the world. When they had left the village behind them and were out in the fields, they sat down on a little heap of earth and began to cry.

Anasim came home three days before the wedding, dressed all in new clothes. He had on shiny new rubber overshoes and, instead of a necktie, wore round his neck a red cord with little balls at the end. From his shoulders hung an overcoat, also new, which he had thrown on without putting his arms into the sleeves.

He said a prayer gravely and then greeted his father and handed him ten silver roubles and ten half-rouble pieces. He gave the same to Varvara, and to Aksinia he presented twenty quarter roubles. The magnificence of this present lay in the fact that all these were picked, new coins, flashing in the sunlight. Anasim tried to appear serious and sedate by composing his features and blowing out his cheeks, and when he did this he smelled of vodka; he had probably run into some station restaurant on the way. There appeared in him, as before, the same lack of restraint; once more there seemed something exaggerated about the man.

'They are all well,' said Anasim. 'Everyone is all right, thank Heaven, but there has been an event in Yegoroff's family; his old woman is dead – of consumption. They ordered a funeral dinner from the pastry-cook's at two-and-a-half roubles a head. And they had grape wine. There were some peasants from our part of the country there, too, and Yegoroff paid two and a half roubles apiece for them as well. The peasants didn't eat a thing – what does a peasant understand about sauces?'

'Two and a half roubles!' exclaimed the old man, shaking his head.

'What of that? The city is not like a village. You go into a restaurant there and order one thing and another, a crowd collects, you all drink, and before you know it it is daylight and you have spent three or four roubles apiece. And if you're with Samorodoff, he likes to finish off with a cup of coffee and cognac, and cognac costs sixty copecks a glass.'

'You don't mean it!' cried the old man, enchanted. 'You don't mean it!'

'I am always with Samorodoff these days. It is he that writes you my letters. He writes beautifully. And if I were to tell you, mother, what Samorodoff is like,' continued Anasim gaily, turning to Varvara, 'you would not believe me. I know all his affairs as well as I know my five fingers. He follows me everywhere; he never leaves me; and we are as thick as thieves. He is a little afraid of me, but he can't live without me. Wherever I go he goes. Do you know, mother, I have a true, straight eye? If I see a peasant at a rag-fair selling a shirt, I cry: "Hold on! That shirt was stolen!" And, sure enough, it turns out that it was stolen.'

'How can you tell that?' asked Varvara.

'I just know it; my eyes are made that way. I know nothing about the shirt, but somehow I am drawn toward it; it is stolen, and that is all. They say among the detectives, "Anasim has gone snipe shooting!" That means hunting for stolen goods. Yes, anyone can steal, but let him have a care! The world is large, but there is no place in it to hide stolen goods!'

'Two rams and two ewes were stolen from Guntorieff last week,' said Varvara, and sighed. 'They ought to be found; oh, tut, tut!'

'Why not? They can be found. That's nothing. That can be done.'

The day of the wedding came round, a cool, clear, joyful April day. Since early morning vehicles drawn by pairs and threes of horses had been trotting about Ukleyevo, their bells ringing, the yokes and manes and tails of the horses adorned with gaudy ribbons. The rooks cawed in the willows, excited by all this traffic, and the starlings chattered incessantly as if they were rejoicing that there was to be a wedding at the Tsibukins'.

In the house the tables were laden with great fish and hams and stuffed birds, with boxes of sardines, with various salt meats and pickles, and with numerous bottles of vodka and different wines. The air smelled of smoked sausages and pickled lobsters. Around the tables wandered the old man, with his heels tapping on the floor, sharpening the knives one against the other.

Everyone was calling to Varvara and asking her for things, and she was running, panting and distraught, in and out of the kitchen, where a man cook from the Kostiukoffs' and a pale woman from Hrimin's Sons had been working since daylight. Aksinia, in curl papers and a corset, with squeaky new boots but without a dress, was flying about the courtyard like a whirlwind, and all that could be seen of her was the flash of her bare shoulders and breast. There was much noise, and scolding and swearing were heard. People passing by paused at the open gate, and it was clear from all signs that something unusual was taking place.

'They have gone for the bride!'

Carriage bells chimed, and the sound of them died away beyond the village. At three o'clock a crowd came running; again bells were heard – the bride was coming! The church was packed; the lustres were burning; the choir was singing from music at the old man's desire. Lipa was blinded by the glare of the candles and the bright dresses; it seemed to her as though the loud voices of the choristers were thumping on her head; her shoes pinched; and the corset, which she now wore for the first time in her life, suffocated her. She looked as if she had just awakened from a swoon, and gazed about her without comprehension. Anasim, in a black coat, with a red cord for a necktie, stood staring absent-mindedly at one spot, crossing himself swiftly at every loud burst of singing. His heart was full of emotion and he wanted to weep. He had known this church since early childhood; his dead mother had brought him here to communion; he had sung in the choir as a boy; he remembered so well every little corner, every icon. And here he was now being married because it was proper to do so; but he no longer thought about this; he had forgotten the wedding. Tears welled up from his heart and strangled him, and he could no longer distinguish the icons. He prayed and besought God that the impending doom which was ready to overwhelm him might somehow pass over, as thunder-clouds pass over a village in time of drought. He had heaped up so many sins in the past, everything seemed so unavoidable and irremediable, that somehow it was absurd to ask for forgiveness, but he did ask it and even sobbed aloud. No one heeded him, for they thought he was drunk.

A child's frightened weeping was heard.

'Dear mummy, take me away from here, dearest!'

'Quiet there!' cried a priest.

The people ran behind the wedding party as it went home from the church, and a crowd collected around the store, at the gate, and in the courtyard under the windows of the house. The peasant women were there to hymn the praises of the young people. As they crossed the threshold the chorus that was standing in the hall with their music in their hands burst into song at the top of their lungs and the band which had been sent for from the city struck up a tune. Foaming drinks were handed about in tall goblets, and Elizaroff the carpenter, a tall, spare old man with eyebrows so thick that his eyes were scarce visible, turned to the young couple and said:

'You, Anasim, and you, little child, love one another, live in the fear of God, my children, and the Queen of Heaven will not forsake you.' He fell on the old father's shoulder and sobbed. 'Gregory, let us weep, let us weep with joy!' he cried in a high voice, and then at once continued in a bass one: 'Ho! ho! ho! and your bride is a beauty! Everything about her is in its right place; everything runs smoothly; nothing rattles; the whole mechanism is in order; there are many springs to it.'

He was a native of the district of Yegorieff, but he had worked since the days of his youth in the factories of Ukleyevo. He had been familiar for many years as always the same tall, thin old man and had long been called Bony. Possibly because he had done repair work at the factory for more than forty years, he judged everything and everybody from a standard of durability and was always asking himself whether they needed repairing. Before sitting down he tried several chairs to make sure they were sound and also touched the fish.

After the foaming drink, everyone began to take seats at the tables. The guests chattered as they pulled out their chairs; the singers shouted in the hall; the band played; the peasant women in the courtyard sang their hymns of praise all on one note – a dreadful, wild babel of sound arose that made the head swim.

Bony twisted about on his chair, nudged his neighbours with his elbows and kept them from talking, and alternately wept and laughed.

'Children, children, children,' he mumbled rapidly. 'My little Aksinia, my little Varvara; let us all live in peace and happiness, my dear little hatchets – '

He seldom drank and a single glass of English bitters had now gone to his head. These foul bitters of unknown manufacture stunned whoever drank them as if he had been hit on the head. People's tongues began to trip.

The clergy were at the party, and the factory clerks with their wives, and the traders and innkeepers from the neighbouring villages. The county clerk, who had never written a word in the fourteen years of his service and who had never let a man leave the county without first having cheated him, now sat beside the head of the district. Both men were bloated and fat and had fed on injustice for so long that their very complexions had taken on a strange, knavish hue. The clerk's wife, a thin woman with a squint, had brought all her children with her and, like a bird of prey, kept one eye on the dishes, grabbing everything that came within reach and concealing it in her pockets and in those of her children.

Lipa sat as if turned to stone, with the same look on her face that she had worn in the church. Anasim had not yet spoken a word to her, so that he did not know the sound of her voice; he now sat silently drinking bitters until he was drunk, and then turned to his bride's aunt sitting opposite and said:

'I have a friend whose name is Samorodoff, a peculiar man. I see through and through him, aunt, and he knows it. Let us drink to the health of Samorodoff, aunt!'

Varvara walked round and round the tables, helping the guests to the viands; she was tired and confused, but was evidently happy at the sight of so much food and magnificence. Nobody could criticise after this! The sun went down, but the dinner still continued. The guests no longer knew what they were eating and drinking, and what they were saying was indistinguishable; only from time to time, when the music died down, some woman in the courtyard could be heard shouting:

'They are drunk on our blood, the oppressors! Down with them!'

In the evening they danced to the music of the band. Hrimin's Sons came and brought their own wine; and one of them held a bottle in each hand and a wine-glass in his mouth while dancing the quadrille, at which everyone laughed. In the midst of the quadrille the dancers suddenly leaped into a headlong peasant dance, and the green Aksinia whirled like a flash, her sash raising a wind behind her. Someone stepped on her flounce and ripped it off, at which Bony shouted:

'Hey! the plinth has been torn off down there, children!'

Aksinia's eyes were candid and steady and grey, and a naïve smile was always on her lips. There was something serpentine in those unwinking grey eyes, in her litheness, and in her little head on its long neck. Dressed all in green with her yellow breast, and a smile on her lips, she looked like one of those little green snakes that raise their heads and stretch their necks and peer out at the passer-by from a field of young rye in springtime. The Hrimins were free in their manner with her, and it was very clear that she and the eldest of them had long been in close relationship. The deaf boy understood nothing of it all and did not even look at her; he sat with his legs crossed, eating nuts and cracking them so loudly with his teeth that it sounded as if he were firing off a revolver.

But now old Tsibukin himself stepped out into the middle of the floor and waved his handkerchief as a signal that he, too, wanted to dance. From the whole house and from the crowd in the courtyard rose a shout of acclamation:

'He's dancing *himself, himself!*'

Varvara danced and the old man only waved his handkerchief and kept time with his heels, but the people in the courtyard, who were clinging to one another and staring in at the windows, were transported with delight and for the moment forgave him everything, both his wealth and the wrongs he had done them.

'Bravo, Gregory Tsibukin!' the crowd shouted. 'That's right! Go on! You can still work! Ha! ha!'

It was late, two o'clock at night, before the festivities came to an end. Anasim, staggering, made the round of the singers and musicians and gave each of them a new silver half-rouble; and the old man, who was not staggering, but who, nevertheless, seemed to be lame in one leg, saw the guests off and said to each one:

'The wedding cost two thousand roubles.'

As the guests were separating someone exchanged an old coat for the innkeeper's new one; Anasim flared up and cried:

'Wait! Let me find it! I know who stole it! Wait!'

He ran out into the street in pursuit, but they caught him, led him home, and thrust him, drunken and damp and flushed with anger, into the room where Lipa's mother had already undressed the girl.

CHAPTER FOUR

Five days went by. Anasim was ready to leave, and went upstairs to bid farewell to Varvara. All her little lamps were burning and there was a smell of incense in the room; she was sitting at the window knitting a red woollen sock.

'You haven't stayed with us long,' she said. 'Is it so tiresome here? Oh, tut, tut! We live well and have everything in plenty, and your wedding was celebrated in decency and decorum; the old man said it cost two thousand roubles. In a word, we live as merchants should, and yet it is sad here. We do the people a great deal of harm. My heart aches, boy, because we do them so much wrong – oh, my Lord! Whether we trade a horse or buy anything or hire a workman, we cheat them in everything. We cheat, cheat, cheat. The sunflower oil in the store is tainted and bitter and more nasty than tar. Tell me, for Heaven's sake, couldn't we sell them good oil?'

'Every Jack to his own trade, mamma.'

'Have you forgotten that someday we shall die? Oh, oh! Talk to your father, do!'

'You should talk to him yourself.'

'I! I tell him what I think and he answers me in a word, as you do: every man to his trade; but God is just.'

'Of course, no one can decide what is right and what is wrong,' said Anasim, sighing. 'There is no God, anyway, so what is there to decide?'

Varvara looked at him in astonishment, laughing and clasping her hands, and he was abashed to see her so honestly surprised at what he had said. She was looking at him as if he were a very comical fellow, indeed.

'Perhaps there may be a God, but people don't believe in him,' said Anasim. 'When I was being married I did not feel like myself. My conscience suddenly began to call as a little chicken calls in an egg that you take out from under a hen. All the time I was being married I kept thinking, "There is a God, there is a God!" but when I came out of the church the feeling went, and how can I tell whether God exists or not? We were not taught it in our childhood. When a baby is still at its mother's breast it is only taught one thing – every man for himself. My father does not believe in God. You told me once that Guntorieff's sheep had been stolen. I found them; they were stolen by a peasant from Shiskaloff, but my father has the hides. There's belief in God for you!'

Anasim blinked and shook his head.

'And the head of the district does not believe in God,' he continued, 'nor the clerk, nor the deacon. The only reason they go to church and keep the fasts is so that people shan't speak ill of them and in case there should really happen to be a last judgement day. People say now that the end of the world has come because we are all growing weak and no longer respect our parents and so on, but that is nonsense. My opinion is, mother, that all misery comes from a lack of conscience. If a man is wearing a shirt that has been stolen, I know it. I can see through everything, mother, and I know. When you see a man in a tavern drinking tea, he appears to you to be drinking tea and nothing more, but I see more than that – I see that he has no conscience. From morning to night I go about and never see a man with a conscience, and the reason of it all is that no one is certain whether there is a God or not. Well, mother, goodbye. Keep well and happy and don't think ill of me.'

Anasim bowed down to Varvara's feet.

'We thank you for everything, mother,' he said. 'You do our family a great deal of good. You are a splendid woman; I like you very much.'

The agitated Anasim went out but soon came back and said:

'Samorodoff has involved me in certain business affairs. I shall either be rich or I shall be undone. If anything should happen, mother, you must console my father.'

'So that's what it is! Oh, tut, tut! God is merciful. You, Anasim, ought to be kinder to your wife; you glare at each other as if you had quarrelled. You might at least smile, really.'

'She is strange somehow,' said Anasim, sighing.

'She doesn't understand anything; she never says anything. She is very young yet; let her grow up.'

A big white stallion was standing at the front door harnessed to a cart. Old Tsibukin ran out of the house, jumped in bravely, and took hold of the reins. Anasim kissed Varvara, Aksinia, and his brother. Lipa was standing on the doorstep motionless, looking off to one side as if she were not there to say goodbye but had come out for no special reason. Anasim went up to her and lightly brushed her cheek with his lips.

'Goodbye,' he said.

She smiled strangely without looking at him; her lips trembled, and for some reason they all felt sorry for her. Anasim also jumped into the cart with a bound and stuck his arms akimbo, as if he thought himself a handsome fellow.

As they drove up out of the ravine Anasim kept looking back at the village. The day was warm and bright. The cattle had been driven out into the fields for the first time that year, and the peasant girls and women were walking about near the herds in their holiday dresses. A brown bull was bellowing with joy at finding himself free and was pawing up the ground with his forefoot. Larks were singing everywhere, above and below. Anasim looked back at the pretty white church – it had been freshly whitewashed – and remembered how he had prayed there five days since; he looked back at the school with its green roof and at the little river in which he had so often bathed and fished. Joy surged up in his breast, and he wished that a wall might suddenly rise up out of the ground and bar his onward way so that he might be left with the past alone.

At the station father and son went into the restaurant and each had a glass of sherry. The old man felt in his pocket for his purse, but Anasim cried:

'My treat!'

The old man patted him on the shoulder with emotion and looked around the little room as much as to say:

'See what a son I have!'

'Stay at home and work at our business, Anasim,' he said. 'I will heap you with riches from head to foot, little son.'

'I can't possibly, daddy.'

The sherry was sour and smelled of sealing-wax, but each finished his glass.

On his return from the station the old man did not at first sight recognise his younger daughter-in-law. Her husband had no sooner driven out of the courtyard than Lipa had suddenly changed and grown merry. She was barefoot now, dressed in an old, worn skirt, with her sleeves rolled up to her shoulders, and was scrubbing down the front steps and singing in a high, silvery voice. As she came out of the house with a big wash-tub in her arms and looked up at the sun with her childlike smile she, too, seemed a little lark.

An old workman who was passing the front door shook his head and grunted:

'Your sons' brides have been sent you by Heaven, master,' he said. 'They are not women but treasures of gold.'

CHAPTER FIVE

On a Friday, the eighth day of July, Elizaroff, or Bony, and Lipa were returning together from a pilgrimage to the village of Kazanski, where they had been celebrating the festival of the Virgin of Kazan. Far in the rear walked Lipa's mother, Praskovia; she was always left behind, for she was infirm and short of breath. It was near evening.

'Ah!' exclaimed Bony, listening to Lipa. 'Ah! And what next?'

'I love jam,' Lipa was telling him. 'I often sit in a corner at home and drink tea with jam in it. Or else Varvara and I drink tea together and she tells me strange stories. They have a great deal of jam there – four jars full! They say to me: "Eat all you want, Lipa! Don't stint yourself!" '

'Ah! So they have four jars?'

'They are rich. They eat white bread with their tea and have as much meat as they want. They are rich, but I am always frightened there. Whew, but I'm frightened!'

'Why are you frightened, child?' asked Bony, looking round to see whether Praskovia had been left far behind.

'At first, during the wedding, I was frightened by Anasim. He was very nice and never did me any harm, but whenever he came near me I felt the shivers running all up and down my back. I did not sleep a single night when he was here, and only lay and shook and prayed. And now I am afraid of Aksinia. She is very nice, but she looks in at the window sometimes, and her eyes are so angry and glow as green as the eyes of a sheep in a stall. Hrimin's Sons say to her: "Your old man has a bit of land at Butekino with sand and water on it. Build a brick-yard there, Aksinia, and we will go shares with you." Bricks are twenty roubles a thousand now; it is a profitable business. Yesterday at dinner

Aksinia said to the old man: "I want to build a brick-yard at Butekino. I'm going into business myself." She laughed as she said that, but the old man's face grew black; one could see he didn't like it. "As long as I am alive," he said, "we can't work apart; we must all hold together!" Her eyes flashed and she gnashed her teeth. When the custard was brought on she wouldn't eat any.'

'Ah!' exclaimed Bony. 'She wouldn't eat any?'

'Then, at night, what do you suppose she does?' Lipa went on. 'She sleeps half an hour and then jumps up and walks and walks, and looks and looks, to make sure that the peasants haven't set fire to anything or haven't stolen anything. She is frightful to live with, daddy! Hrimin's Sons did not go to bed the night after the wedding; they went to town to open a law-suit, and people say it was all because of her. Two of the brothers promised to build her the brick-yard, and the third brother got angry about it, and the factory has been closed for a month, and my uncle Prokor is without work and has to go begging from door to door. "You ought to go and plough or chop wood in the meantime, uncle," I tell him. "Why do you disgrace yourself?" "No," he says, "I've got out of the way of Christian work now; there's nothing I can do, Lipa!" '

They halted near a grove of aspens to rest and wait for Praskovia. Elizaroff did not keep a horse although he had long been a contractor; he went striding all over the country on foot, swinging his arms and carrying a little sack in which he kept onions and bread. It was hard, in walking, to keep pace with him.

At the entrance to the wood stood a boundary post; Elizaroff touched it to see whether it were in need of repairs. Praskovia came up panting. Her wrinkled, perpetually startled face glowed with pleasure. She had been to church today like other folk and had seen the fair and had drunk pear beer there! This had seldom happened to her, and it even seemed to her now as though she had enjoyed herself this day for the first time in her life. When they were rested all three walked on together. The sun was setting and its rays struck through the wood and gleamed on the trunks of the trees. Voices rang out ahead of them. The young girls of Ukleyevo had gone on far ahead, but they had made a halt in the woods, no doubt to pick mushrooms.

'Halloo, girls!' shouted Elizaroff. 'Halloo, my beauties!'

He was answered by laughter.

'Here comes Bony! Bony! The old crow!'

And the echoes laughed, too. And now the wayfarers left the wood behind them. The tops of the factory chimneys were already in sight; the cross flashed on the steeple; there lay the village 'where the deacon had eaten all the caviare at the funeral.' They were nearly home now; there remained but to climb down into that deep ravine. Lipa and Praskovia, who were barefooted, sat down to put on their shoes and the carpenter sat down beside them. Seen from above, Ukleyevo looked pretty and peaceful, with its willows and its white church and its little river, but the view was spoilt by the roofs of the factories, which were painted a sombre grey for economy's sake. On the far slope of the ravine lay fields of rye with the grain in stacks, in scattered sheaves, and in freshly mown rows; the oats, too, were ripe and the fields shimmered like mother-of-pearl in the sunlight. It was harvest-time. The day had been a holiday; the next day would be Saturday, and then they would rake up the rye and haul away the hay. Then Sunday would come, another holiday. Each day was steamy and hot, with thunder growling in the distance; the weather threatened rain. Men wondered, looking at the fields, whether God would give them time to get in their grain and felt both merry and anxious at heart.

'The mowers ask high wages now,' Praskovia remarked. 'One rouble forty copecks a day.'

The villagers were flocking home from the fair at Kazanski: peasant women, factory hands wearing new caps, beggars, and children. Now a wagon drove by, raising a cloud of dust, with a horse trotting behind that seemed to be glad he had not been sold at the fair; now came a man leading a stubborn cow by the horns; now another wagon laden with drunken peasants dangling their feet over the sides. An old woman passed leading by the hand a little boy in a big hat and big boots; the child was exhausted with the heat and by his heavy boots, which prevented him from bending his legs at the knee, but he was incessantly blowing a little toy trumpet with all his might. After the pair had reached the bottom of the ravine and had turned into the street the trumpet could still be heard blowing.

'Our manufacturers are in a bad temper,' said Elizaroff. 'It's a misery! Kostiukoff has been abusing me for putting too many planks into a cornice. "Too many planks, indeed!" said I to him. "No, sir," says I, "as many went into it as belonged to go in and no more. I don't eat planks with my porridge!" I says. "How can you say that," says he, "you block-head? Don't forget yourself! It was I made you a contractor!" he shouts. "And a fine thing you did there!" says I. "Didn't I have tea everyday just the same before I became a contractor?" "You are all cheats!" he cried. I said nothing. "We are all cheats in this world," I thought, "but you will be cheated in the next!" Ho! ho! ho! Next day he felt better. "Don't be angry with me," he said, "about what I said to you yesterday. If I said more than I should, remember that I am a merchant of the first guild. I am your superior and you must hold your tongue." "You are right," I says. "You are a merchant of the first guild and I am a carpenter, but the holy Joseph was a carpenter, too," says I. "Our work is honest and godly work, but you wish to be my superior!' says I. "You are welcome." But after that conversation I began to wonder who was the superior, a carpenter or a merchant of the first guild. Perhaps a carpenter is, children.'

Bony reflected awhile and then added:

'He is the superior, children. He who labours and endures is the superior.'

The sun had gone down and a thick mist as white as milk hung over the river and lay in the churchyard and on the meadows around the factories. Night was swiftly falling, little lights began to shine out in the ravine, and the fog seemed to be concealing a bottomless abyss. Lipa and her mother had been born beggars and had been ready to live as beggars all their lives, ready to surrender everything to others except their meek, timid souls, but now, perhaps, they dreamed for an instant that in this great, mysterious world they, too, had power and were superior to someone. They were happy, sitting there above the village, and smiled joyously and forgot that they must descend to the bottom once more.

They turned homeward at last. A crowd of mowers were sitting on the ground at the gates of the courtyard and around the store. The peasants of Ukleyevo usually refused to work for Tsibukin and he had to hire labourers elsewhere, so they sat there now looking, among the shadows, like men with long, black beards. The store was open and the deaf son could be seen through the door playing checkers with a little boy. The mowers now sang softly, almost inaudibly, now loudly demanded their day's wages, but these no one gave them because the men were wanted for the next day. Tsibukin, in a waistcoat and no coat, was sitting with Aksinia under a birch tree near the front doorsteps drinking tea. A lamp was burning on the table.

'Dad–dy!' called one of the mowers outside the gate in a teasing voice. 'Pay us, if it's only half! Dad–dy!' At this the other mowers laughed and then began to sing again softly. Bony sat down to drink tea.

'We have been to the fair,' he began. 'We have been on a spree, children, a jolly spree, the Lord be praised. But one unfortunate thing happened. Sashka the blacksmith bought some tobacco and gave the merchant he bought it of half a rouble for it. The coin proved to be false,' Bony went on, glancing around. He had meant to whisper, but had spoken, instead, in a hoarse, choking voice and everyone had heard him. 'And the coin proved to be false. Sashka was asked where he had got it. "Anasim Tsibukin gave it to me at his wedding," he said. A policeman was called and he was arrested. Take care, Tsibukin, that something doesn't come of it!'

'Dad–dy!' teased the same voice outside the gate. 'Dad–dy!'

Silence fell.

'Ah, children, children, children!' mumbled Bony rapidly as he rose from his seat. Sleep was overpowering him. 'It's time for bed. I am rotting and my beams are crumbling! Ho! ho! ho!'

As he walked away he said:

'It's time to die, I suppose,' and at that he sobbed.

Old Tsibukin did not finish drinking his tea; he sat thinking, and, from his expression, seemed to be listening to the footfalls of Bony, who was by now far down the street.

'Sashka the blacksmith was lying, perhaps,' said Aksinia, divining his thoughts.

He went into the house and soon came out again carrying a little package. This he opened; it was full of shining new roubles. He took one, tried it between his teeth, rang it on the tray, and then rang another.

'Yes,' he said, looking at Aksinia as if he still doubted it. 'The coins are false. These are the ones that – Anasim brought these home; they are his present. Take them, daughter,' he whispered, slipping the package into her hands. 'Take them and throw them into the well. Away with them! And see that there is no talk about this. Something might happen. Take away the samovar; put out the lights.'

Lipa and Praskovia, sitting in an outhouse, saw the lights go out one by one; up in Varvara's room only the little red and blue shrine lamps were still burning, and from thence breathed peace and contentment and ignorance. Praskovia never could get used to the fact that her daughter had married a rich man, and when she came to his house would hide herself in the hallway with a beseeching smile on her face and her tea and sugar would be sent out to her. Neither could Lipa grow accustomed to this life, and she did not sleep in her bed after her husband's departure, but lay down wherever she happened to be – in the kitchen or in an outhouse. Everyday she washed the clothes or scrubbed the doors and felt that she still was a charwoman. And now, after their return from their pilgrimage, they drank their tea in the kitchen with the cook and then went into an outhouse and lay down on the floor between the sleighs and the wall. It was already dark and the air smelled of harness. The lights went out near the house and they could hear the deaf boy closing the store and the mowers disposing themselves for the night in the courtyard. Far away in the distance Hrimin's Sons were playing on their expensive accordion. Praskovia and Lipa were dropping asleep when they were awakened by the sound of footsteps. The moon was now shining brightly. At the door of the outhouse stood Aksinia with her bedclothes in her arms.

'Perhaps it will be cooler here,' she said and came into the outhouse and lay down near the threshold with the moon shining full upon her.

She could not go to sleep but sighed grievously and lay tossing to and fro in the heat and at last threw off most of what she had over her. What a gorgeous, proud animal she looked in the magic light of the moon! A short time passed and again steps were heard. The old man appeared, all in white, in the doorway.

'Aksinia,' he called, 'are you here?'

'What is it?' she answered crossly.

'I told you yesterday evening to throw the money into the well. Did you do it?'

'The idea of throwing property into the water! I gave it to the mowers.'

'Oh, my God!' groaned the old man in fear and perplexity. 'You insolent woman—oh, my God!'

He wrung his hands and walked away, muttering as he went. Aksinia sat up, sighing heavily with vexation, and then got up and gathered up her bedclothes and went out.

'Why did you marry me into this house, mother?' asked Lipa.

'A girl must marry, my daughter. It is none of our doing.'

A feeling of inconsolable anguish was about to overwhelm them, but it seemed to them as if out of the vault of the dark-blue heaven above them, there where the stars were, someone was watching everything that went on in Ukleyevo and was keeping guard over them. Though evil is mighty, night is peaceful and beautiful, and there exists a justice on God's earth which is as peaceful and as beautiful as the night; everything in the world is waiting to join hands with that justice, as the moonlight joins hands with the night.

Both women were quieted and fell peacefully asleep in each other's arms.

CHAPTER SIX

The news had come long ago that Anasim had been sent to prison for forgery. Months went by, half a year went by. The long winter had passed, spring had come, and in Anasim's home and in the village people had grown used to the thought that he was in prison. If anyone passed his house at night he would remember that Anasim was in prison; if the bells tolled in the cemetery people would recall for some reason that Anasim was in prison, awaiting his trial.

A shadow seemed to hang over the house of the Tsibukins. The rooms were darker, the roof was rusty, and even old Tsibukin himself seemed somehow more sombre in hue. He had long neglected to trim his beard and hair; he climbed into his cart now without a bound and no longer cried to the beggars that 'God would help them!' His strength was failing, and this could be seen in everything. Men feared him less now, and a warrant had been issued against him for selling illicit vodka, although the policeman still received his little bribe as before. Tsibukin was sent to the city to be tried; the case was continually being postponed in default of witnesses and tormented the old man.

He often went to see his son and began doing many little deeds of charity. He took the keeper of Anasim's prison a silver holder for a glass, with a long spoon and an inscription in enamel.

'There is no one to do anything for him,' said Varvara. 'Oh, tut, tut! We might ask someone of the gentry to do something or write to the chief of police. They might at least set him free till his trial. Why should the boy be made to suffer so?'

She, too, was distressed, but nevertheless she grew stouter, and her complexion grew fairer; she still lighted her little lamps and kept the house clean and treated her guests to apple butter and jam. The deaf boy and Aksinia now kept the store. They had started a new business: a brick-yard had been opened at Butekino, and thither Aksinia drove herself everyday in a carriage; when she met an acquaintance on the road she would stretch out her neck, as a little snake does from a field of young rye, and smile naïvely and enigmatically. Lipa spent her days playing with her child, which had been born to her before Lent. He was a wee baby, pitiful and thin, and it seemed strange to think that he could cry and see and was looked upon as a human being and even bore the name of Nikifor. Lipa used to go to the door as he lay in his cradle and bow and say:

'Good-morning, Nikifor Tsibukin!'

And then she would fly back and kiss him and once more go to the door and bow and say:

'Good-morning, Nikifor Tsibukin!'

And the baby would scratch his pink feet, and his laughter and tears would mingle together as they did with Elizaroff the carpenter.

At last a date was set for the trial. The old man left home for five days, and some of the peasants were called from the village to be witnesses; among them was the old carpenter, who had also received a summons.

The trial had been fixed for Thursday, but Sunday went by and still the old man had not returned, and no news had come. On Tuesday evening Varvara was sitting at the open window listening for his return. Lipa was playing with her baby in the next room, tossing him in her arms and crying in ecstasy:

'You'll grow up to be a big, big man! When you're a big peasant, then we'll go out and do charwork together! Yes, we will!'

'Look here!' said Varvara, offended. 'What is that charwork story you have invented, little silly? We are going to make a merchant of him.'

Lipa began to sing softly but soon forgot herself and cried again:

'When you are a big, big peasant we'll go out and do charwork together!'

'What a plan!'

Lipa came and stood in the doorway with Nikifor in her arms and asked:

'Why do I love him so, mother? Why am I so sorry for him?' she went on in a trembling voice, with tears shining in her eyes. 'Who is he? He is as light as a little crumb or a feather, and yet I love him as if he were a real man! He can't speak and yet I read everything he wants to say in his eyes.'

But Varvara was listening to something else. She could hear the evening train as it drew into the station. She now no longer knew nor understood what Lipa was saying nor heeded the flight of time; she was trembling from head to foot, not with fear but with a mighty curiosity. She saw a wagon rattle swiftly by filled with peasants; these were the witnesses returning from the station. As it rolled past the store an old workman jumped out and entered the courtyard. Voices were heard greeting him and asking questions.

'Hard labour in Siberia for six years,' said the old man in a loud voice.

Aksinia came out of the back door of the store: she had been drawing kerosene and was holding a bottle in one hand and a funnel in the other.

'Where is daddy?' she asked thickly, for her mouth was full of silver coins.

'At the station,' answered the workman. 'He said he would come home when it was darker.'

When it became known in the house that Anasim had been condemned to hard labour the cook in the kitchen suddenly set up a wail as if she were at a funeral, thinking, no doubt, that decorum demanded it.

'Oh, why have you forsaken us, Anasim Tsibukin, light of our eyes?'

The excited dogs began howling. Varvara ran to the window, trembling with distress, and called to the cook at the top of her voice:

'Sto–op! Stepanida, sto–op! Don't make us any more miserable, for God's sake!'

The samovar was forgotten; nothing was considered now. Lipa alone could in no wise understand what had happened and went on fondling her baby.

No questions were asked the old man when he came back from the station. He greeted everyone and then walked through all the rooms without saying a word. He did not eat any supper.

'There was no one to do anything,' Varvara began when they were alone together. 'I said the gentleman should have been asked to help, but you wouldn't listen then. A pardon might have been – '

'I did everything,' said the old man with a gesture of impatience. 'When Anasim was sentenced I went to a gentleman who had defended him, but he said that nothing could be done; it was too late. And Anasim himself said the same thing: it was too late. But I did engage a lawyer as soon as I came out of the court and paid him a retaining fee. I shall wait a week, and then I shall go back to town again. God's will be done!'

The old man again walked silently through all the rooms, and when he came back to Varvara he said:

'I must be ill. There is something wrong in my head – things seem confused there – I can't think straight.'

He shut the door, so that Lipa should not hear, and went on in a low voice:

'I'm not right about money. Do you remember that Anasim brought me a lot of new roubles and half-rouble pieces before his wedding? I put away one packet of them at the time, and the rest I mixed with my other money. I used to have an uncle named Dimitri, who, when he was still living – God rest his soul! – used to travel all over the country buying merchandise, from Moscow to the Crimea. He was married, and while he was away travelling his wife used to amuse herself with other men.

My uncle had six children. Well, when he had been drinking he used to laugh and say: "I can't for the life of me make out which of these are my children and which belong to the others." He was a light character, you see. Well, and so it is with me; I can't for the life of me tell which of my money is real and which is false. It all seems false to me.'

'God bless you! What a notion!'

'If I buy a ticket at the station and give three roubles for it I think the coins are false. I am frightened. I must be ill.'

'We are all in the hands of God. Oh, tut, tut!' said Varvara, shaking her head. 'We must think about this, Gregory. Some misfortune might happen; you are not a young man. If you were to die the others might do some harm to your grandson. Oh, I am afraid for Nikifor! They will wrong him! In a way he has no father, and his mother is foolish and young. You ought to secure something to the boy, if it's only your land, Butekino, for example. Yes, Gregory, really! Think of it!' Varvara entreated. 'He is such a pretty boy; it's a pity! Do go tomorrow and make a will! Why wait?'

'I had forgotten my grandson,' said Tsibukin. 'I must say good-evening to him. So you say he's a pretty boy? Well, I hope he'll live to grow up. God grant it!'

He opened the door and beckoned Lipa to him with his forefinger. She came toward him with her baby in her arms.

'If you need anything you must ask for it, little Lipa,' he said. 'Eat all you can; we don't begrudge you anything, so long as you keep well.' He made the sign of the cross over the baby. 'Take good care of my little grandson. My son is gone, but my grandson is left.'

The tears were coursing down his cheeks now; he sobbed and turned away. In a little while he lay down and slept heavily after his seven sleepless nights.

CHAPTER SEVEN

The old man made only a short visit to the city. Someone informed Aksinia that he had been to the notary to make a will and had left Butekino to his grandson, Nikifor. She was told this one morning when the old man and Varvara were sitting under the birch tree at the front doorsteps drinking tea. She shut the door of the store that led into the street and the door that led into the courtyard, collected all her keys, and flung them down at the feet of the old man.

'I won't work in your house any longer!' she shouted vehemently and suddenly burst into tears. 'It seems I am not your daughter-in-law, but a servant. Everybody is laughing at me: they say, "Look at that servant the Tsibukins have found!" I did not hire myself out to you! I am not a beggar or a penniless wench – I have a mother and father.'

She fixed her angry, tear-filled eyes on the old man without troubling to wipe them; her face and neck were flushed and tense as if she had been yelling with all her might.

'I won't be a servant any longer!' she continued. 'I am run off my feet! When it comes to work, then I have to sit day in and day out in the store and sneak out at night after vodka, but when it comes to receiving land, the convict's wife gets it with her devil's spawn! She is the mistress here and a fine lady, and I am her servant. Give the prisoner's wife everything, and let her choke on it! I am going home. Find another fool for yourselves, you damned scoundrels!'

The old man had never in his life scolded or punished his children, and had not imagined that a member of his family could speak rudely to him or treat him disrespectfully. He was terribly frightened now and ran into the house, where he hid behind a cupboard. Varvara was so appalled that she could not rise from her seat and only kept brandishing both arms as if she were defending herself from a swarm of bees.

'Oh, oh, what is the matter?' she murmured in horror. 'What is she shrieking so for? Oh, tut, tut! People will hear you! Oh, be quiet, be quiet!'

'You have given Butekino to the convict's wife!' Aksinia shouted on. 'Now give her everything; I don't want a thing from you! Bad luck to you! You are nothing but a gang of thieves. I've had enough of it. I've done with you all. You rob all who come near you, old and young, you pickpockets! Who sells vodka without a licence? Who commits forgery? You have stuffed your coffers full of false coins, and now you no longer need me!'

By this time a crowd had gathered around the open gates, and the villagers were staring into the courtyard.

'Let the people see!' shrieked Aksinia. 'I will heap shame on your heads! You shall burn with it! I will make you grovel at my feet! Hi! Stephen!' she called to the deaf boy. 'We are going home this minute to my father and mother; I won't live with convicts! Get ready!'

The washing was hanging out on a line that was stretched across the courtyard. She snatched down her blouses and skirts and flung them to the deaf boy and then flew about the courtyard in a frenzy among the clothes, tearing everything down, throwing everything that was not hers on the ground and trampling on it.

'Oh, the Lord have mercy! Take her away!' groaned Varvara. 'Give her back Butekino! Give it back to her for Christ's sake!'

'Ah-ha, what a woman!' exclaimed the neighbours at the gate. 'How furious she is! She's a terror!'

Aksinia ran into the kitchen where the clothes were being washed. Lipa was working there alone, the cook had gone down to the river to rinse the clothes. Steam was rising from the wash-tub and from the boiler near the stove, and the air of the kitchen was stifling and dense with vapour. A pile of soiled clothes lay on the floor, and near them on a bench sprawled Nikifor playing with his rosy feet, laid down there so that he could not hurt himself if he fell off the bench. Lipa was picking a chemise of Aksinia's out of the pile of clothes as the other came into the kitchen; she put it into the tub and stretched out her hand for the big scoop of boiling water that lay on the table.

'Give it to me!' shouted Aksinia looking at her with hatred and dragging her chemise out of the tub. 'You have no business to touch my clothes! You are a convict's wife: you ought to know your place and who you are!'

Lipa looked at her mildly without comprehension, but all at once, as she caught the glance which the woman threw at her baby, she suddenly understood and turned pale as death.

'You have taken my land, take this!'

Saying these words, Aksinia seized the ladle of boiling water and dashed it over Nikifor.

At this a shriek went up the like of which had never been heard in Ukleyevo, and no one could have believed that a weak little creature like Lipa could have uttered such a cry.

Silence suddenly fell over the courtyard. Aksinia went into the house without saying a word, with the same naïve smile on her face. The deaf boy was strolling about the courtyard with his arms full of clothes. He silently and without haste proceeded to hang them out once more. And until the cook came back from the river no one dared go into the kitchen to see what had happened there.

CHAPTER EIGHT

Nikifor was taken to the county hospital and died there that evening. Lipa did not wait for anyone to come for her but wrapped the little body in a blanket and started to carry it home.

The hospital was new, with large windows, and stood high on a hill. It was gleaming now in the rays of the setting sun and seemed to be ablaze on the inside. A little village lay at the foot of the hill. Lipa walked down the road and before she came to the village sat down on the edge of a pond. A woman came leading a horse to the water, but the horse refused to drink.

'What more do you want?' asked the woman softly and wonderingly. 'What do you want?'

A boy in a red shirt sat at the water's edge washing his father's boots. Not another soul was in sight either in the village or on the hill.

'He isn't drinking,' Lipa said to herself, watching the horse.

The woman and the boy departed, and now no one was to be seen. The sun sank to rest and folded himself in a tissue of gold and purple, and long crimson and lilac clouds lay stretched across the sky, guarding his sleep. A bittern was booming in the far distance dully and lugubriously, like a cow in a shed. The cry of that mysterious bird resounded every spring, but no one knew what sort of a creature it was nor where it had its abode. The nightingales were pouring forth their songs on the hilltop, in the bushes around the pond, beyond the village, and in the fields on either hand. A cuckoo was counting and counting and always losing count and commencing again. The frogs in the pond were splitting their throats in a frantic chorus, and one could even distinguish the words they were shouting: 'Ee tee takova! Ee tee takova!' What a din there was! Every living being seemed to be shouting and singing on purpose to keep any creature from sleeping this evening of spring, so that all, even the angry frogs, might enjoy every minute of it – after all, one can live but one life!

A silver crescent moon was gleaming, and stars without number were shining in the sky. Lipa did not remember how long she had been sitting by the pond, but when she arose and walked on, the village was already asleep and no lights were burning.

She was probably about nine miles from home, but her strength was exhausted, and she had no idea in which direction to go. The moon hung now on her right and now before her, and the same cuckoo was crying, though hoarsely by now: 'Oho! Look out, you're off the road!' Lipa hurried on, and the kerchief slipped from her head. She looked up at the sky and wondered where the soul of her boy now was. Was he walking behind her or was he floating up there overhead near the stars, already forgetful of his mother? Oh, how lonely it was at night in the fields, in the midst of all this singing, for one who could not sing! How lonely among these incessant shouts of gladness for one who could not rejoice! The moon looked down from heaven and was lonely, too; it did not care whether the season were winter or spring or whether people were dead or alive. It is sad to be alone when the heart is full of misery. If only her mother were with her, thought Lipa, or Bony, or the cook, or some peasant!

'Boo-oo! Boo-oo!' cried the bittern.

Suddenly a man's voice became clearly audible, saying:

'Harness the horses, Vavila!'

A camp-fire burned before Lipa on the side of the road. The flames had already died down, and only the red embers were still glowing. She could hear horses munching. Two men and two carts were visible in the darkness; one cart carried a barrel, and the other, smaller one was laden with sacks. One man was leading a horse to be harnessed, the other was standing by the fire with his hands behind his back. A dog growled near the carts. The man who was leading the horse stopped and said:

'I think someone is coming along the road.'

'Sharik, be still!' the other man called to the dog, and from his voice it could be heard that he was old. Lipa stopped and cried:

'Help, in God's name!'

The old man approached her and said after a pause:

'Good-evening!'

'Will your dog bite?'

'No, come on! He won't touch you.'

'I have been to the hospital,' said Lipa after a silence. 'My little boy died there. I am carrying him home.'

This must have been unpleasant for the old man to hear, for he drew back and said hastily:

'That is nothing, my dear. It is God's will. You are dawdling, boy!' he cried, turning to his companion. 'Be quick!'

'Your yoke isn't here,' cried the lad. 'I can't find it.'

'Your wagon is on the right-hand side, Vavila.'

The old man picked up a brand and blew on it, and a light glowed on his eyes and nose. When the yoke had been found he went back to Lipa, carrying the brand, and looked into her face. His glance was compassionate and tender.

'You are a mother,' he said. 'A mother is always sad at the loss of her child.'

He sighed as he said this and shook his head. Vavila threw something on the fire and stamped it out. The night suddenly grew very black, the vision vanished, and nothing remained but the fields, the sky with its stars, and the noisy birds keeping each other awake. A rail began calling on the very spot, it seemed, where the camp-fire had been burning.

But before a minute had elapsed the old man and the tall Vavila became visible once more. The wagons creaked as they hauled out into the road.

'Are you holy men?' Lipa inquired of the old man.

'No, we are peasants from Firsanoff.'

'My heart melted when you looked at me a little while ago. And that is a quiet lad. So I thought you were holy men.'

'Have you far to go?'

'To Ukleyevo.'

'Get in! We'll take you as far as Kuzmenok. Your road branches off to the right there and ours to the left.'

Vavila mounted the wagon with the barrel, and the old man and Lipa got into the other. They travelled at a foot-pace, with Vavila ahead.

'My little son suffered all day,' said Lipa. 'He looked at me so with his little eyes and could not utter a sound. He wanted to say something and couldn't. Holy Mother of God! I fell to the floor with grief. I was standing by the bedside and fell down. Tell me, daddy, why should a baby suffer before he dies? When a grown person, a man or a woman, suffers his sins are forgiven him, but why should a little one suffer that has no sins? Why?'

'Who can say?' answered the old man.

They travelled on for half an hour in silence.

'One cannot know the reason for everything,' said the old man. 'A bird is not given four wings but two, because two are all that he needs to fly with, and so people are not allowed to know everything but only a half or a quarter. Everybody knows as much as he needs to know in order to live.'

'Daddy! It is easier for me to walk! My heart beats so!'

'Never mind! Sit still.'

The old man yawned and made the sign of the cross over his mouth.

'Never mind,' he repeated. 'Your grief is only half a grief. Life is long. You will yet have good times and bad times. You will have a little of everything. Russia is a mighty mother!' he said, looking around him. 'And I have travelled over all Russia and have seen everything. You can believe my words, child, you will have good times yet and bad times. I have been to Siberia on foot. I have been on the Amur River and in the Altai Mountains; I emigrated to Siberia and tilled the soil there, but my heart was heavy for mother Russia, and I went back to my native village. I went back on foot. I remember I was crossing a river once on a ferry-boat, all thin and ragged and shivering, gnawing a crust of bread, and a gentleman who was on the same boat – God rest his soul if he is dead! – looked at me with compassion and with the tears streaming down his cheeks. "Alas!" he cried. "Your bread is black, and black are your days." When I got back I had neither hut nor home. I had had a wife before, but I had left her behind me in Siberia; we buried her there. So now I hire myself out as a day-labourer. And what of it? I tell you I have had good times and bad times since then. I don't want to die, child. I could live twenty years more, so that means there has been more good than bad in my life. Russia is a mighty mother!' he said and once more looked from side to side.

'Daddy,' asked Lipa, 'when a man dies, how many days does his soul stay on earth?'

'Who can say? Let us ask Vavila. He has been to school, and they teach everything now. Vavila!' the old man called.

'Yes?'

'Vavila, when a man dies, how many days does his soul stay on earth?'

Vavila first stopped his horse and then answered:

'Nine days. When my Uncle Kiril died his soul went on living in our hut for thirteen days.'

'How do you know that?'

'Because we heard a thumping in the stove for thirteen days.'

'Very well. Go ahead!' said the old man. He evidently did not believe any of this.

The carts turned into the highroad near Kuzmenok, and Lipa proceeded on foot. Day was breaking. The huts and the church of Ukleyevo were hidden in mist as she climbed down into the ravine. The air was chill, and she seemed to hear the same cuckoo calling.

The cattle had not yet been driven out when Lipa got home. Everyone was asleep. She sat down on the doorstep to wait. The first to come out was the old man and he saw at a glance what had happened. For a long time he could not utter a sound and only stood mumbling with his lips.

'Ah, Lipa!' he cried at last. 'You did not take care of my grandson!'

Varvara was waked. She wrung her hands and burst into tears and at once began to care for the little body.

'He was a pretty boy,' she said. 'Oh, tut, tut! you had only one boy, and you did not take care of him, little stupid!'

A requiem mass was sung for the baby both morning and evening. He was buried next day, and after the funeral the guests and the clergy ate a great deal, as greedily as if they had not tasted food for an age. Lipa waited on the table, and the old man raised his fork on which he had impaled a salt mushroom and said to her:

'Don't grieve for the baby. The kingdom of heaven is for such as he.'

Only after the guests had departed did Lipa fully realise that Nikifor was gone for ever, and as she realised it she burst into tears. She did not know into which room to go to cry, for since the boy's death she felt that there was no place for her in this house, that she was superfluous here now; and the others felt the same thing.

'Here, what are you bawling for?' suddenly shouted Aksinia, appearing in the doorway; she was wearing a new dress for the funeral and had powdered her face. 'Be still!'

Lipa tried to stop but could not and sobbed louder than ever.

'Do you hear me?' cried Aksinia, stamping her foot in great wrath. 'Whom am I speaking to? Quit this house and never set foot here again, you convict! Begone!'

'Come, come, come!' said the old man anxiously. 'Aksinia, calm yourself, my daughter. Of course, she is crying, her baby is dead.'

'Of course, she is crying!' mocked Aksinia. 'Let her spend the night here, but after tomorrow let her not dare to show her face here again! Of course, she is crying!' she mocked once more and laughed and went into the store.

Early next morning Lipa walked back to Torguyevo to her mother.

CHAPTER NINE

The roof and doors of the store are painted now and shine like new; gay geraniums blossom in the windows as before, and the happenings of three years ago are almost forgotten in the house of the Tsibukins.

Now, as before, the old man is still called master, but, as a matter of fact, the business has all passed into Aksinia's hands. She buys and sells, and nothing can be done without her sanction. The brick-yard is working well; bricks are needed for the railway, so that their price has gone up to twenty-four roubles a thousand. The women and children haul them to the station and load them into the cars, and for this they get a quarter of a rouble a day.

Aksinia has gone into partnership with the Hrimins and their brick-yard is now called 'Hrimin's Sons and Co.' A tavern has been opened near the station and the expensive accordion is played there now instead of at the factory. Thither the postmaster, who has opened a business of some sort himself, often goes, and thither goes also the station-master.

Hrimin's Sons have given the deaf boy a gold watch, and this he pulls out of his pocket from time to time and holds to his ear.

It is said of Aksinia in the village that she has acquired great power, and in truth one is conscious of this as she drives to the brick-yard every morning and gives her orders there, handsome and gay, with a naïve smile on her lips. Everyone fears her at home, in the village, and at the brick-yard. When she goes to the post-office the postmaster jumps up from his seat and says:

'Kindly sit down, Madam Aksinia!'

A certain landowner, a dandy in a coat of light cloth and high patent-leather boots, who was selling her a horse one day, was so enchanted by his conversation with her that he came down in his price to her figure. He held her hand for a long time, looked into her gay, wily, naïve eyes, and said:

'I would do anything in the world to please a woman like you. Only tell me when we can meet without being interrupted.'

'Whenever you like.'

This elderly dandy now comes every day to drink beer in the store, horribly bad beer, as bitter as wormwood, but he shudders and drinks it all the same.

Old Tsibukin no longer has a share in the business. He does not keep the money himself because he cannot tell true coins from false, but he says nothing of this and never mentions his weakness to anyone. He has become forgetful of late, and if food is not offered him does not ask for it. The household has grown used to dining without him, and Varvara often remarks:

'Our old man went to bed again last night without eating anything.' She says this with equanimity because she is used to it. For some reason he always wears his fur coat both winter and summer, and only stays at home on very hot days. As a rule, he puts on his coat, turns up his collar, wraps himself up, and walks about the village and up the road to the station, or else he sits motionless from morning till night on a bench at the church door.

The passers-by bow to him, but he does not return their salute because he still does not like peasants. If anyone asks him a question he answers sensibly and politely but shortly.

There is a rumour in the village that his daughter-in-law has driven him out of the house and won't give him anything to eat, and that he lives entirely on alms; some rejoice at this, and some pity him.

Varvara has grown still stouter and fairer; she still does her little deeds of charity and Aksinia does not interfere with her. There is so much jam now that they cannot finish it all before the new berries come in; it turns to sugar and Varvara almost weeps, not knowing what to do with it.

They are growing forgetful of Anasim. There came a letter from him once, written in verse on a sheet of paper like a petition; it was in the same familiar, beautiful handwriting; evidently his friend Samorodoff was serving his sentence with him. At the end of the verses a single line was scrawled in a rough, almost illegible hand: 'I am ill here all the time; it is very hard; help me, for Christ's sake.'

One bright autumn evening Tsibukin was sitting at the church door with the collar of his fur coat turned up so that all that could be seen over it was his nose and the peak of his cap. On the other end of the long bench sat Elizaroff the carpenter, and beside him was Jacob the watchman, a toothless old greybeard of seventy. Bony and the watchman were gossiping together.

'Children should provide food and drink for the aged – honour your father and your mother,' Jacob was saying with irritation. 'But his son's wife has driven her father-in-law out of his own house. The old man has nothing to eat or drink – where can he go for it? This is the third day that he has been without food.'

'The third day!' marvelled Bony.

'There he sits and never says a word. He is growing weak. Why keep silence? She ought to be arrested!'

'Who has been arrested?' asked Bony, not hearing aright. 'What's that?'

'The woman isn't bad; she's a hard worker. A business like theirs cannot be run without that – without sin, I mean.'

'Out of his own house!' Jacob continued irritably. 'She first gets a home, and then chases everyone out of it! She's a terrible woman, I declare! A pest!'

Tsibukin listened without stirring.

'What difference does it make whether one lives in one's own house or in somebody else's, as long as it is warm and the women don't scold?' chuckled Bony. 'I used to grieve terribly for my Anastasia in my young days. She was a gentle woman. She used to say continually: "Buy a horse, husband, buy a horse! Buy a horse, husband!" When she was dying she was still saying: "Buy yourself a racing cart, husband, so that you won't have to walk!" And I never bought her anything but gingerbread.'

'Her husband is deaf and stupid,' Jacob went on without heeding Bony, 'the same as a goose. How can he understand what's going on? If you hit a goose on the head it still won't understand.'

Bony rose to go back to his home at the factory and Jacob rose with him. They strolled away together, still talking. When they had gone about fifty paces Tsibukin rose and crawled after them with uncertain footsteps, as if he were walking on slippery ice.

The village was already sunk in the shades of evening, and the sunlight fell only on the summit of the cliff and shone on the upper end of the road that wound snakelike down the steep incline. Some old women and children were returning from the woods carrying baskets of mushrooms. A crowd of women and young girls were returning from the station, where they had been loading the cars with bricks, and their cheeks and noses were powdered with red brick-dust. They were singing. At the head of the procession walked Lipa singing in a high voice, warbling her song as she looked up to heaven as if she were exulting that the day was done and the time for rest had come. Her mother, Praskovia, walked in the throng carrying a little package in her hand, breathing heavily as she always did.

'Good-evening, Elizaroff!' cried Lipa as she caught sight of Bony. 'Good-evening, daddy dear!'

'Good-evening, little Lipa!' rejoiced Bony. 'Little women, little girls, won't you fall in love with a rich old carpenter? Ho! ho! Oh, my children, my children!' (Bony sobbed.) 'My dear little hatchets!'

Bony and Jacob continued on their way and the girls could hear them gossiping together. After passing them the crowd met Tsibukin, and suddenly all were hushed. Lipa and Praskovia slackened their pace, and when the old man came up beside them Lipa bowed low and said:

'Good-evening, sir!'

The mother bowed also. The old man stopped and looked at them in silence; his lips trembled, his eyes filled with tears. Lipa took a slice of pie with porridge from the package her mother held and gave it to the old man. He took it and began to eat.

The sun had gone down; its light had faded from the road; the evening was dark and chill. Lipa and Praskovia continued on their way and kept crossing themselves for a long time after the encounter.

WORDSWORTH CLASSICS
General Editors: Marcus Clapham & Clive Reynard

JANE AUSTEN
Emma
Mansfield Park
Northanger Abbey
Persuasion
Pride and Prejudice
Sense and Sensibility

ARNOLD BENNETT
Anna of the Five Towns

R. D. BLACKMORE
Lorna Doone

ANNE BRONTË
Agnes Grey
*The Tenant of
Wildfell Hall*

CHARLOTTE BRONTË
Jane Eyre
The Professor
Shirley
Villette

EMILY BRONTË
Wuthering Heights

JOHN BUCHAN
Greenmantle
Mr Standfast
The Thirty-Nine Steps

SAMUEL BUTLER
The Way of All Flesh

LEWIS CARROLL
Alice in Wonderland

CERVANTES
Don Quixote

G. K. CHESTERTON
*Father Brown:
Selected Stories*
*The Man who was
Thursday*

ERSKINE CHILDERS
The Riddle of the Sands

JOHN CLELAND
*Memoirs of a Woman of
Pleasure: Fanny Hill*

WILKIE COLLINS
The Moonstone
The Woman in White

JOSEPH CONRAD
Heart of Darkness
Lord Jim
The Secret Agent

J. FENIMORE COOPER
*The Last of the
Mohicans*

STEPHEN CRANE
*The Red Badge of
Courage*

THOMAS DE QUINCEY
*Confessions of an English
Opium Eater*

DANIEL DEFOE
Moll Flanders
Robinson Crusoe

CHARLES DICKENS
Bleak House
David Copperfield
Great Expectations
Hard Times
Little Dorrit
Martin Chuzzlewit
Oliver Twist
Pickwick Papers
A Tale of Two Cities

BENJAMIN DISRAELI
Sybil

THEODOR DOSTOEVSKY
Crime and Punishment

**SIR ARTHUR CONAN
DOYLE**
*The Adventures of
Sherlock Holmes*
*The Case-Book of
Sherlock Holmes*
*The Lost World &
Other Stories*
*The Return of
Sherlock Holmes*
Sir Nigel

GEORGE DU MAURIER
Trilby

ALEXANDRE DUMAS
The Three Musketeers

MARIA EDGEWORTH
Castle Rackrent

GEORGE ELIOT
The Mill on the Floss
Middlemarch
Silas Marner

HENRY FIELDING
Tom Jones

F. SCOTT FITZGERALD
*A Diamond as Big as the
Ritz & Other Stories*
The Great Gatsby
Tender is the Night

GUSTAVE FLAUBERT
Madame Bovary

JOHN GALSWORTHY
In Chancery
The Man of Property
To Let

ELIZABETH GASKELL
Cranford
North and South

KENNETH GRAHAME
*The Wind in the
Willows*

**GEORGE & WEEDON
GROSSMITH**
Diary of a Nobody

RIDER HAGGARD
She

THOMAS HARDY
*Far from the
Madding Crowd*
The Mayor of Casterbridge
*The Return of the
Native*
Tess of the d'Urbervilles
The Trumpet Major
*Under the Greenwood
Tree*

DISTRIBUTION

**AUSTRALIA
& PAPUA NEW GUINEA
Peribo Pty Ltd**
58 Beaumont Road, Mount Kuring-Gai
NSW 2080, Australia
Tel: (02) 457 0011 Fax: (02) 457 0022

**CYPRUS
Huckleberry Trading**
3 Othos Avvey, Tala Paphos
Tel: 06 653585

**CZECH REPUBLIC
Bohemian Ventures spol s r o**
Delnicka 13, 170 00 Prague 7
Tel: 02 877837 Fax: 02 801498

**FRANCE
Copernicus Diffusion**
23 Rue Saint Dominique, Paris 75007
Tel: 1 44 11 33 20 Fax: 1 44 11 33 21

**GERMANY
GLBmbH (Bargain, Promotional
& Remainder Shops)**
Schönhauser Strasse 25
D-50968 Köln
Tel: 0221 34 20 92 Fax: 0221 38 40 40

**Tradis Verlag und Vertrieb GmbH
(Bookshops)**
Postfach 90 03 69
D-51113 Köln
Tel: 0 22 03 3 93 40

**GREAT BRITAIN & IRELAND
Wordsworth Editions Ltd**
Cumberland House, Crib Street
Ware, Hertfordshire 3G12 9ET

**INDIA
OM Book Service**
1690 First Floor
Nai Sarak, Delhi – 110006
Tel: 3279823-3265303 Fax: 3278091

**ISRAEL
Timmy Marketing Limited**
Israel Ben Zeev 12
Ramont Gimmel, Jerusalem
Tel: 02-865266 Fax: 02-880035

**ITALY
Magis Books SRL**
Via Raffaello 31/C
Zona Ind Mancasale
42100 Reggio Emilia
Tel: 1522 920999 Fax: 0522 920666

**NEW ZEALAND & FIJI
Allphy Book Distributors Ltd**
4-6 Charles Street, Eden Terrace
Auckland,
Tel: (09) 3773096 Fax: (09) 3022770

**PHILIPPINES
I J Sagun Enterprises**
P O Box 4322 CPO Manila
2 Topaz Road, Greenheights Village
Taytay, Rizal
Tel: 631 80 61 TO 66

**PORTUGAL
International Publishing Services Ltd**
Rua da Cruz da Carreira, 4B,
1100 Lisbon
Tel: 01 570051 Fax: 01 3522066

**SCOTLAND
Lomond Books**
36 West Shore Road, Granton
Edinburgh EH5 1QD

**SINGAPORE,
MALASIA & BRUNEI
Paul & Elizabeth Book Services Pte Ltd**
163 Tanglin Road No 03-15/16
Tanglin Mall, Singapore 1024
Tel: (65) 735 7308 Fax: (65) 735 9747

**SLOVAK REPUBLIC
Slovak Ventures spol s r o**
Stefanikova 128, 94901 Nitra
Tel/Fax: 087 25105

**SPAIN
Ribera Libros, S.L.**
Poligono Martiartu, Calle 1 - no 6
48480 Arrigorriaga, Vizcaya
Tel: 34 4 6713607 (Almacen)
     34 4 4418787 (Libreria)
Fax: 34 4 6713608 (Almacen)
     34 4 4418029 (Libreria)